They say I fear neither god nor devil, reverence neither king nor bishop, love no man and all women under fifty. They also say my verse is vile, my morals worse, and that I never miss my man at thirty paces.

All these things are untrue. But they point in the right direction.

My name—as I told the damsel in distress that night—is Lord Christopher Arundel. And ill-disposed people have in fact been known to call me Lord Libertine.

Another vile slander, of course. Well, more or less.

Fawcett Crest Books
by Anthony Esler:

THE BLADE OF CASTLEMAYNE

LORD LIBERTINE

LORD LIBERTINE

by
Anthony Esler

A FAWCETT CREST BOOK

Fawcett Publications, Inc., Greenwich, Connecticut

LORD LIBERTINE

THIS BOOK CONTAINS THE COMPLETE TEXT OF THE
ORIGINAL HARDCOVER EDITION.

A Fawcett Crest Book reprinted by arrangement with William
Morrow and Company, Inc.

Out upon it, I have lov'd
     Three whole days together—
And am like to love three more,
     If it prove fair weather!
         —*Sir John Suckling*

Contents

BOOK 3: *PLACE DE LA GUILLOTINE*

BOOK 4: *AFTERWARD*

Preface

*In the form of a letter to the
Reverend James Throgmorton,
D.D., F.R.S., ETC., ETC.*

Reverend Sir,

I deliver the following manuscript into your grace's
hands, as per my master's last instructions to me. As his
lordship himself states herein, you are respectfully requested to make whatever use of it your honor feels will be
most efficacious to counter certain *totally unjust rumors*
current in the capital.

These rumors have largely to do with some alleged ac-
tions of my master, Lord Christopher Arundel, both here
in London and in foreign parts. They have also to do with
the alleged behavior of a certain *lady*—indeed of several
ladies, and of other young women of lesser degree some
of them, I must in all honesty confess, no better than they
should be. And finally, these slanderous assertions
concern—as your honor cannot but be aware—certain
particular *matters of state* of the highest import, relating
to the present government of England and to that *revolutionary* regime which still, alas, prevails in France. The
truth of all these matters and affairs, both private and
public, is contained herein.

Whatever use your honorable grace may see fit to make
of this document, there is, if I may make bold to say so, a
lesson contained in it for all of us.

Not only, as my master himself suggests, a *moral* lesson, a most solemn warning to all those of the *libertine persuasion* whose gaming, tosspotting, and rakehelling so dishonor our age. But also, if I may venture to suggest it, a *political* lesson to those poor innocents who may be tempted, in these troubled times, to espouse the evil doctrines, the *democratical and leveling principles,* preached by certain foreigners from beyond the seas.

With this pious hope, then, and with the humble reminder that I am presently, and through no fault of my own but Fate, *at liberty* and unemployed, and will be duly grateful for any help your grace might give in finding a post suitable to my needs and avocations, I remain,

> Your honor's obedient
> servant to command,
>
> Jeremy Twill

1 October 1792

BOOK I

Hanover Square

1

In Which I Introduce Myself

"Oh God, sir," the lady murmured as she neared her point of points, "but you are marvelous kind!"

Her pert young head rolled from side to side on the cushions. The bed shook, the hangings swayed with the vigor of our exertions. I recall her face exactly—the tight chestnut curls atangle, lips parted, nostrils dilating with each quick breath. Her cheeks were deeply flushed, her lids fluttering as her head rolled on the pillow. There was a gleam of perspiration on her brow.

"Oh God, sir—yes—dear Lord—"

Her hands clutched at my buttocks to speed my thrusts, and her own ripostes grew even more passionate. I felt myself approaching the precipice and labored mightily to pull her over with me.

"Ah, sweet Betsy—Queen of Love," I whispered into the dark curls that tented one small ear. "Come give me all your sweetness now—"

Uninspired, certainly. Yet I murmured the fondest endearments I could muster under the circumstances, which were in fact those of a very casual encounter. For I have found that words will bring a woman sooner to her final rapture than the most ardent physical stimulation. Applied as that rapture draws nigh, a poetic phrase or two will almost always hasten her over the edge into the infinite moment that is, for some choice spirits at least, the fairest thing in life.

"My nymph, my goddess," I whispered more urgently

still, timing my thrusts to the meter as best I might, "my joy, my only pleasure-trove—"

"My lord—oh, Lord Christopher—"

Her trembling throat arched back, her belly contorted wildly against mine, and I felt my own seed start. I bore down upon her, burying my face in her bosom, and for long moments knew no more.

"Dear Lord—dear Lord Christopher," I dimly heard her gasp, "but you're a cock and a *half,* my lord!"

The evening thus commenced as evenings, alas, too often do for me—in bed with a beautiful woman.

It is a canard, and the mark of the amateur in *amours,* to imagine that the *end* of the evening is the proper time for making love. Some drama there is in it, to be sure. Scented sheets and clinging arms to make a fitting climax to a night's entertainments. Practically speaking, however, it is the sheerest folly to postpone to the end of a long and frequently bibulous evening, often replete with vigorous dancing, wearying rounds of cards, or dreary conversation, an enterprise that should find us at the height of our powers.

How goes the old tavern ditty?

> *She gave me this, I gave her that,*
> *And tell me, had she not tit for tat?*

If we are indeed to give as good as we get, and to savor properly the rites of Eros ourselves, we are far better advised to steer well clear of the midnight hour. All romantical tradition to the contrary.

The ideal time of day for an amorous encounter—if I may venture a generalization on the subject—is four o'clock in the afternoon.

No hour fits more comfortably into a gentleman's schedule: up betimes—around noon—for breakfast, a ride in the Park or a turn on the Mall, a mild half-hour at my Lady So-and So's genteel Tuesday afternoons at home—and *then* to your dalliance, for an hour or two. Thence to dinner and the club, a fête, a play, the opera, or what have you, marvelously refreshed and relaxed for the evening. A pleasant round for a gentleman of pleasure, with the shrine of Venus centrally located, as it ought to be.

So it was that day, Tuesday, the seventh of August in this year of doubtful grace 1792, when my difficulties all began.

It had all commenced casually enough with a bit of troublesome business to mar the day's schedule of pleasure pure and unalloyed—a visit to my solicitor. The lady who was currently expiring in my arms was in fact that staid barrister's lady wife.

His name was Murrain, and he was precisely that—a plague upon the landscape. A dour bespectacled Scot, with all the dull virtues and cold nature of the soberer strains of that race. None of your Highland dash and recklessness about Murrain. He was a Lowland drudge from Glasgow, impeccable at his lawbooks and accounts, and unbearable otherwise. I came to see him punctually once a quarter, to pick up another installment of my dwindling fortunes.

His wife now, Mrs. Betsy, was a different thing entirely. A trim ankle, a languishing eye, a fine figure, and a wonderful enthusiasm for the joys of the bedchamber—that was Betsy Murrain. I could never believe he did not know anything of her ways. Sometimes, indeed, I rather suspected him of exploiting her passionate nature to his own business advantage. I'm sure he never lost a client by her roving eye and eager hands.

And so, to make the story short, my impeccable solicitor was out, out for the day; and his wife was in. We proceeded then, from a cold collation in her little drawing room (cakes and wine) to intimate confessions (of her husband's many failings) to gentle caresses (of commiseration) to chaste kisses and more ardent ones, the hand inside the bodice, the sighs the moans the protests *et cetera,* ending unclothed and sweatily coupling in the connubial bed upstairs.

An unedifying picture, you may say. Scarcely the way to commence so moral a tale as this will in fact turn out to be.

Why do so then, you ask? Why begin with such a scene of carnal intercourse? Except of course to titillate the reader and hold him for another chapter, in hopes of still more outrageous matter to come? (A hope—allow me to relieve your anxiety at once—which shall most assuredly be fulfilled.)

But there is more exalted motive here as well. Let me get it out at once, lest the reader grow vexed with my philosophizing-in-the-bedroom and demand a return to more prosy business—such as the couple last seen expiring on that shaking bed in Fleet Street. The prime moral cause, then, of beginning my narrative with such a degraded passage at arms as this is simply that the reader may the better appreciate the regeneration of a fallen character of which this is the record.

For this is the story of a vicious nature come back to grace, of virtue triumphant over vice. So at least it seems to me, the central figure in my own composition. Though the reader may perhaps dispute the moral when the piece is done.

In any case—behold me in my degradation. Grunting like an animal, rutting like a stag in my panting lady's arms. Behold me thus, and hiss your shocked disgust— that you may cheer the final scene, when you see me in my newfound state of grace. Or not, as pleases you. I lay no obligations on the reader, except that he may enjoy himself in the reading of what follows.

It ended then, as alas it always must, and we lay all asprawl, cooling our overheated bodies, letting our breathing and our hearts settle back to a steadier pace. Sounds of carriage wheels and hawkers' cries reached us from the narrow street below. Through the low dormer window across the room, I calculated the sun's angle and the lateness of the hour, debating a second engagement before dinner.

We lay side by side on a bed so small that my ankles hung over one end and my head was jammed against the headboard at the other. I stand six feet and an inch or two in height; Murrain cannot be much more than five.

"You are so *big,* my lord," Betsy sighed, reaching. But it was not my six feet from heel to square-headed, pigtailed poll she spoke of so admiringly. The tall gentleman to whom she had reference measures in truth not a tenth part of that—though he grew momently beneath her fingers' casual caress.

I laughed and fondled one round pink-centered breast, as one might a melon in a stall. "You too, my dear Mrs. Betsy, are blessed with charms enough to raise a gentleman's passion to transports beyond containing."

"My lord, indeed, was most importunate." She blushed. She blushed very easily, as I remember, did Betsy Murrain. But she did not take her hand from my instrument, already stiffening once more for the fray.

"Truly, I would regret my passion most heartily if I could," I assured her. "But it would be the rankest hypocrisy to do so. Such delight comes too seldom in this life to be *regretted.*"

"But not in your life, surely, my lord? If a tithe of what rumor says be true—"

"Rumor is a notorious liar, my dear. As a solicitor's

wife should know well enough. Why, if every man that was *rumored* for a robber were hanged for it, what tradesman from Westminster to the Tower would escape the noose?"

"It is not for a robber I've heard *you* spoken of, my lord."

"Ah, and if every fifth son of a four-quartered peer that is *well-known* for a lecher and a profligate—"

"My lord is far too hard upon himself," she whispered more quickly now, her importunate hand moving still more ardently belowstairs. "Oh, yes, too hard by half. It were a marvel—"

At which unpropitious moment, my stomach—damn its unromantic soul—chose to growl like an empty keg rolling down a staircase. A whole series of staircases, really, bounding from landing to landing, and rolling on and on. And I realized abruptly that I was hungry as the very devil.

"Alas, mistress—you see the inner man makes his demands, and will brook no denial."

I rose up on one elbow, kissed her small uptilted nose, gave her breast one final friendly squeeze. My mind—which tends not to distinguish as clearly as it might between the baser appetites—was already filling with fragrant visions of steaming golden-brown sole in butter sauce, high-seasoned, from Mr. Hayward's table at the Black Lion in Water Lane. Just around the corner, in fact, from Mr. Murrain's.

"Ah, my lord," Mrs. Betsy murmured, reaching up with one white arm to draw me down to her, "but the *inner woman* must make her demands as well!"

Not bad, I thought, for a Glasgow solicitor's wife!

"Ah, well—if my lady will—" The golden-brown fillet of sole evaporated before another sort of lust resurgent. *Later, Master Belly—Master Cock must have his turn before you!* I rolled upon her once again, and we went to it.

So it was late when I set out at last for Mr. Hayward's in Water Lane. And later still when I went on from there—Mr. Belly now as satisfied as his compeer—for White's Club in St. James's.

Being in some haste to join the company I had promised to meet at the gaming tables some two hours earlier, I looked about for a hackney coach or a sedan chair. But the weather was wet that night, and I could find none. I therefore pulled my cloak close about me and set off through the ill-lit streets on foot, choosing a shorter if less savory route than I would normally take.

And thus blundered full-tilt into the thoroughly unlikely incident with which this strange narrative more properly begins.

2

In Which I Meet the Most Beautiful
Woman in the World

It was, as I said, early in August—a summer evening, no doubt, in many more favored lands. In this our England it was another dank, dark, drizzly night, season indeterminate.

I was proceeding through the darkest, dankest streets along the river, alone and in pitchy blackness. My boots were an unholy mess. My heavy cloak soon bore twice its own weight in accumulated moisture. I advanced slowly, peering beneath the dripping brim of my French tricorne, stumbling into open drains, kicking aside a screaming cat, barking my shins against an abandoned barrow. Now and again another late-goer, cloaked and dripping like myself, shoved past me in the narrow, irregularly cobbled street.

Then, about the corner of Hog Lane and the Strand, I heard the first shriek. A woman's scream, high-pitched and desperate, out of the dead-black cul-de-sac upon my left.

My first thought, of course, was for footpads and banditti. The gentlemen of the road press into the very heart of town in these disordered times. And I had heard of unwary victims lured to disaster by more devious gambits than this. God knows there are dissolute women enough about for such purposes! I hesitated momently, therefore, straining my eyes into the darkness, swinging my tasseled cane under the rain-wet cloak. I had no mind to be made a fool of. On the other hand, a cut at some latter-day Turpin or Colonel Jack might be worth a short detour from White's.

The girl screamed again.

Up the lane, a dark lantern flashed briefly, flooding the scene with a pale glow.

There were half-a-dozen of them—a parcel of ugly rogues indeed. Battered hats and threadbare coats, armed with cudgels and ancient horse pistols. I saw a knife gleam in one gristly hand.

Two green-liveried footmen confronted this motley crew. Or rather, cowered before them, making little effort to defend the abandoned sedan chair that lay, *sans* bearers, slaunchwise across the far end of the lane. The top of the sedan chair was up, the door swinging loose and broken on its hinges. Two of the villains were rummaging eagerly inside. Beside the ravaged vehicle sprawled a dumpy lace-capped servingwoman apparently in a swoon. And just this side of the main melee, lit by the bolt of illumination from the dark lantern, a young girl struggled in the arms of a huge, blue-jawed man with a patch over one eye.

It was as mannered and *opera buffa* a scene as ever I saw.

And yet, such things do happen. Girls are kidnapped by importunate lovers, or by fortune-hunting would-be husbands, every day. The gazettes are full of them, and the rumor mills are fuller still.

And this was surely far too elaborate a stage setting for a gang of surly footpads to conceive.

Time, in short, for action.

In three strides I was upon the ill-shaven, patch-eyed rascal with the rain-spattered girl struggling against his chest. I swung him round from his sweet prey and delt him a jolting buffet that sent him floundering. I came upon two more of the ruffians unawares, laid my cane alongside one shaggy head, and dropped the other with a left that would have done honor to any pugilist in the land.

Had the wretched footmen in their fine green liveries only stuck to their guns, the odds would have been about even then, and the fight all but over. But the two of them—country louts by the cut of their hair and clothes—seized the chance to bolt. They were gone in an instant, the clack of their flying heels echoing up the pitch-black alley. I was left alone with three armed villains still before me, the big blue-jawed fellow rising angrily behind.

"Hoot—there's nae but ane o' 'em, lads!" called a lean rat-faced man with a thick Scottish burr. "Aye and quality too by the look of 'em. There'll be watches and a snuffbox and muckle siller too!"

"Circle round behind wi' Patch, then, Figgis," called a chunky, smallpox-scarred rogue in a scarlet coat, clutching a horse pistol in one hand. "Then we'll 'ave 'im sure!"

"Can we 'ave 'im, then, Patch, can we 'ave 'im?"

squealed the third, a hideous hunchbacked little wretch, laboriously cocking a pistol almost as long as his arm.

"Aye, Trip!" grunted Patch, as the leader was apparently called. "The lady's for 'is lordship as pays our wages in this business. But the gennelman'll be ours for the stripping!"

He laughed a nasty, grating laugh. I heard the unmistakable sound of steel sliding out of a leather sheath. So I had a sword behind me as well as a knife and two horse pistols in front.

"Beware, sir—oh, beware your back!" the young lady's voice cried out. It was the first time she had spoken. A crisp, clear voice, I noticed even then.

I spun in a crouch and saw the big man with the eyepatch almost on me, swinging a seaman's short sword above his head.

I lunged out of my crouch straight at him, head down, and butted him like a charging ram just below the breastbone. Patch went down a second time, his head slamming resoundingly against the cobbles.

"Well done, sir!" gasped the lady. She was still only a blur of white gown, pale skin, and dark, lustrous hair in the glimmering light of the fallen lantern. But I flashed a reassuring smile at her as I wheeled back to confront my three surviving antagonists.

The pocky-cheeked villain's horse pistol was leveled straight into my eyeball at a range of perhaps six inches.

"Blow 'is brains to the devil, Fag!" screeched crookbacked little Trip delightedly. "Oh, do!"

The shot took my hat clean off, and singed my hair into the bargain.

But Master Fag paid for my hat before the crashing echo of his shot had died away down the scuttering alleyway. An admittedly abominable dockfighter's blow—this one with the knee of my right leg—left him rolling in agony on the stones.

"O sir!" I heard the lady's voice again behind me, a bit less totally approving now.

There was still Figgis with his knife and the little hunchback with the pistol. I could have routed them with my cane, of course. But I felt an urge, somehow, to finish the affair without recourse to arms. A misdirected sense of honor—a dash of bravado—a childish urge to impress the lady? And then, of course, this scruffy pair did look rather like small beer.

Pride goeth, as they say, before a fall.

I judged the hunchback to be the more immediate danger. With a perfectly executed kick, I sent his unwieldy weapon flying, caroming off the wall of the nearest close-pressing housefront, exploding as it did so. *Exquisite!* I thought fleetingly amid the din and the flash of powder.

With the same exquisite motion, unfortunately, I slipped on the rain-wet cobblestones. I landed jarringly flat on my back, a yard from the plump unconscious serving woman, my head ringing and all the breath knocked out of me.

The rat-faced Scotsman was on me in an instant, his foot-long dirk across my throat. The little hunchback fastened on my left leg like a terrier. And at almost the same instant, with a mighty roar, the indestructible Patch threw himself once more upon me.

"Dear Lord!" the lady in the shadows gasped. "I fear I've brought the poor gentleman to a desperate pass!"

"Aye, *lord* indeed, by God!" boomed Captain Patch suddenly, crouching close above me. His wide mouth, still bleeding, cracked open in a grin. "It's the one they call Lord Libertine! As foul a flaming Macaroni as walks in Lunnon town! There's many an honest maid will cheer this night's work, lads, I'll lay to that!"

The dirk pricked the skin. Just above the jugular, as I subsequently ascertained.

"Slit 'is pipe for 'im then, Figgis," gloated Patch, bending close beside the Scotsman, breathing a gust of garlic and rotten fish into my face, "and you shall 'ave a round arf 'is purse!"

Figgis grinned wolfishly and set his blade against my throat once more. I prepared to risk all in a desperate lunge for freedom, fully expecting to see my own blood spurt skyward in a geyser of expiring life.

When suddenly his weaselly Scottish face disappeared behind a lump of flying rock and a gush of blood.

He rolled off me, howling, both hands pressed to his broken nose, his knife lost somewhere beneath us. I twisted about for one quick look behind me. There was the damsel I had come to rescue, kneeling determinedly in her muddied gown, efficiently working loose another five-pound cobblestone.

I made short work of little Trip the hunchback then, plucking him off my leg and hurling him at the nearest wall. He slid down it, looking stupefied. Captain Patch had turned with a curse upon my mysterious lady, but I got him by the scruff of the neck before he could lay more than than a single horny hand upon her. I whirled the surly brute around and dealt him a blow that vibrated down my whole six feet and more of moderately well-muscled frame. It was a buffet intended to lay him out for good. But the fellow had remarkable recuperative powers. He had scarcely struck the cobbles before he was up again.

Up and running. For now my cane was free, and in an instant I had thumbed the catch and slid out the glittering three-foot blade.

The rest of the ruffians quickly followed their captain. Even bloody-faced Figgis and battered Fag with his aching groin floundered off up the lane. In a matter of seconds the lady and I and her still unconscious servitor were alone in the drizzling alley.

"Madame," I said, panting and muddy but as courtly

as might be under circumstances, "I believe I owe you my life."

"And I owe you more than that, sir," she answered serenely. "I owe you my honor!"

"You know these villains, then?"

"I do not. But their purpose"—she shuddered slightly and tossed her head—"their purpose must be all too clear."

A cool and forthright answer, I thought, as I scooped up the lantern and shone it full upon her.

She was beautiful.

Thick waves of lustrous auburn hair framed her face and throat. Her eyes were seagreen flecked with hazel, her lips full and strong and—so I dared hope—dark with slumbering passion. The white column of her throat, the slender shoulders, the firm breasts thrusting against her rain-soaked gown all added to the stunning impact of her loveliness. I caught my breath and stared. She was, quite simply, the most beautiful woman I had ever seen.

"My name," I blurted then, "is Arundel. Lord Christopher Arundel. At your service always, madame."

"The one they call Lord Libertine?" she asked, in that cool, crisp voice of hers. "Was that not how yonder ruffian called you?"

What could I say? I bowed again, as ruefully as I might. "And may I know your name as well?" I added quickly, lest the conversation follow this unpropitious direction further.

"My name—" She seemed to hesitate. Then she tossed her lovely head again and looked me squarely in the eye. "My name is Lady Barbara MacFarlane, of Holyrood House, in Berkshire." There was a strange air of truculence, almost of defiance, in that straight look, that uptilted chin. Almost as though I should know the name, and respond to it in some way.

I looked at that firm chin, that exquisitely sculptured

mouth, and I felt a sudden, well-nigh overpowering urge to kiss her on the spot.

But at that moment the dumpy servingwoman sprawling by the sedan chair groaned loudly and opened her eyes. "Mary and Joseph and all the saints," she whispered, "preserve us from Satan's wiles!" Then she caught sight of her young mistress and scrabbled to her feet, blithering with terror, "O my lady, are we all ravished?"

"No, Bridget." The lady smiled. "Thanks to this gentleman, we are all well."

"Thanks to Mary mother of God!" Bridget corrected stoutly, rolling up her· eyes. She smoothed down her voluminous skirts and turned away, calmed and clucking like a mother hen, to reestablish some order in the ravaged sedan chair.

"And now, sir," said Lady Barbara MacFarlane, "as I see my people are returning, I must be on my way again." Her footmen were indeed in view once more, clamoring up the alley with what looked like half the watch and all the Bow Street runners in London, lanterns blazing in the night. "With all thanks to you once again for your help in my—trouble."

She curtseyed to me regally, her clear eyes still looking coolly, almost challengingly into mine. Then she turned swiftly, flushed with sudden anger, on the returning servants who had abandoned her in her danger.

Spirit, by God! I thought. *And what a body! What shoulders, what a throat. And hair—such lustrous locks! I have not seen—*

I stood marveling still like some country lout as Lady Barbara MacFarlane's sedan chair swayed off into the darkness. I stood a long time alone in the rain before, shaking my head and sighing, I took up once more my solitary road to White's.

3

The Perfidious Durward

They say I fear neither god nor devil, reverence neither king nor bishop, love no man and all women under fifty. They also say my verse is vile, my morals worse, and that I never miss my man at thirty paces.

All these things are untrue. But they point in the right direction.

My name—as I told the damsel in distress that night—is Lord Christopher Arundel. And ill-disposed people have in fact been known to call me Lord Libertine.

Another vile slander, of course. Well, more or less.

We were discussing my villainous reputation at White's Club later that same night—the night this whole miserable, glorious, unbelievable affair began.

There were five of us seated around the oval table, in an alcove off the main room. There had been wagering and scandal earlier, and several rounds of port. Now the evening had settled down to loo and faro and the sort of desultory banter that flourishes over cards.

Candle flames in crystal chandeliers gleamed palely on the scarlet draperies, the huge Turkey carpet, the dusky green tabletops. Servants in immaculate white periwigs and silver-buckled shoes moved silently about their tasks. There was a murmur of laughter, a rumble of voices. A strong odor of wine, tobacco, and snuff drifted toward the dim gold ceiling far above.

It was a typical night at White's.

"Our dear Lord Libertine," the Reverend Dr. Throgmorton was just remarking, "has no sense of *discretion*, that is all. He does not know how to be *discreet*. There are sinners as great as he in London, I have no doubt—or almost as great." His plump pink cheeks shook, his eyes radiated good humor. "But others are simply not so *blatant,* my dear Arundel. They see no need to conduct their affairs on the stage at Covent Garden, as it were. Hence all their peccadilloes remain obscure and unremarked. While *yours*—"

He let a gesture of silent horror suffice.

"Prudence, sir, prudence!" he ended finally, with the obligatory apothegm: "The highest point of virtue, sir, is prudence in our vices!"

He beamed rosily, our ale-swilling, fox-hunting parson, as the men around the table nodded, grunted, and reached for their wine or their snuffboxes. The Reverend Dr. Throgmorton was a type of preacher far from uncommon in these degenerate days—a red-faced, soft-bellied, worldly, witty man without a shred of religious sensitivity in his bones. He was the life and soul of every assembly, and he knew it.

"The parson's right, damme if he isn't!" expostulated Colonel Tolliver, juggling his cards in thick, speckled hands. "Pitt can be most vilely drunk in Parliament every day in the year—what?—and none speak of it outside St. Stephen's! And why, sir? Do you know why, eh what?" He leaned portentously forward, glaring around the table. "I'll tell you why! Because the King's Chief Minister of State has at least the sense to withdraw quietly to the back alley before he pukes it up, that's why! Discretion, what? Discretion is all!"

Colonel Tolliver, like our good King George, has the habit of punctuating every other sentence with a *what*? or two.

"Truly," young Lord Danforth burst in, "truly the reverend doctor has a point, my lord. This sailor Nelson fellow can pollute Lady Hamilton's bed with complete impunity, sir—while your mere presence at one of Lady Arbuthnot's balls provokes no end of the foulest calumnies. And for one reason only, sir—*prudence*. The simple discretion not to be seen kissing the lady in question in an open carriage in St. James's Park!"

Lord Danforth was a chinless young peer, much flushed with drink, and I forgave him in my heart. Besides, I knew that he himself, for all his bluster to the contrary, had long had his own bloodshot young eyes on Caroline, Lady Arbuthnot.

"Face it, my lord," said Throgmorton with a twinkle, sweeping in the cards from all quarters and beginning to shuffle. "You are become a veritable synonym for low vice and moral impropriety. Lord Libertine—a byword in our day!" He shook his head and sighed, his jowls wobbling, and sent the printed pasteboards skimming across the green-baize tabletop with practiced fingers.

"Indeed!" a cold, unpleasant voice relentlessly took up the refrain. "Arundel's behavior brings no credit to the aristocracy. And that is in itself no service to any of us. Nor to the nation, gentlemen! Nor to the nation!"

It was Lord Mortimer Durward.

Suave, cold debonair, Durward was every inch the born aristocrat, from polished pointed shoes to slimly tapered fingertips. His periwig was always powdered to perfection, his waistcoat snowy white. His long face, thin peaked lips, and pointed nose were the epitome of noble breeding. The short upper lip and the slightly protuberant eyes only added to his air of patrician elegance. An impropriety had scarcely been known to pass his lips.

At a glance he seemed the absolute antithesis of myself.

I wear no wig, but my own hair, and that unpowdered. My waistcoat is seldom snowy. My hands are blunt and square, my face rectangular, with a jaw that would crush granite. My lips, I have been told, are unduly sensuous; my nose—a simple nose.

Rather an Irish look, actually. I have in fact had to live down a distant maternal connection with Wolfe Tone, the Irish rebel.

Durward's remarks that night at White's were altogether typical of him. The *honor of the aristocracy* was a phrase as common on his thin aristocratic lips as on my Irish cousin, Edmund Burke's. Durward was forever lamenting the decay of the squirarchy, or warning darkly of the threat posed by "radical democracy" to the "natural order of society"—meaning the caste system into which he had been born. If the good Lord had meant us to be ruled by rabble, He would have made every man a gentleman from the beginning—such was Lord Mortimer's frequently expressed philosophy.

Personally, I have no politics. But I must admit that there are times when I wonder if the *demos* could do a worse job of ruling this world of ours than King George III and Louis XVI and their fellow hereditary lords of the universe have done. The Americans, after all, seem to have made some sort of democracy work for a dozen years or so at least. And now, so we are told, the French are trying it.

Which is precisely what sets Lord Mortimer raving. There is, he insists, an "international conspiracy" to put the "democratic rabble" in charge in every land. And so on and so on, his long genteel fingers reaching agitatedly for his silver snuffbox.

My prime objection to Lord Mortimer, however, is not political. Nor is it social, since my own blood, however bastardized down the centuries, is as blue as his own. My main objection to Durward is actually a moral one.

The man is an insufferable prig.

By which I do not mean that Durward's moral conduct

is impeccably ascetic and abstemious. Indeed, he is far from a paragon of virtue—as any number of housemaids, tenants' daughters, and others helplessly dependent on his lordship can attest. He is also, as my man Jeremy informs me, a notorious opium-eater.

But you would never know it to hear him talk. He talks like the English Prayer Book come to life. Psalms and sermons, parables and moral maxims flow from him like Thames water over a milldam. Noble principles and mealymouthed adulation of King and Country hover about him like a fog. Whatever his conduct, as they say of the Wesleyans, he has a fine line of cant. A Roman satirist or a French comedian might call it what it is: rank hypocrisy.

The result is all the same, however, whatever the label. Elderly ladies fawn upon him. Statesmen ponder his opinions. Country squires send their sons up to London with stern instructions to emulate his example. Aristocratic mothers trot out their prettiest and most marriageable daughters for his inspection.

None of which, needless to say, has ever happened to me.

In the highest circles of British society, Lord Mortimer is considered a man of sound principle and character. "A bit too Continental," some will say, "too European—too much on vintages and the latest cut of coat and breeches, if you take my meaning." But generally solid, even the crustiest old retired colonel of the Life Guards will agree. "A credit to his class."

And so I looked up with some interest but no surprise at all when Lord Mortimer Durward announced that my behavior reflected no credit on the noble orders of society.

"Lord Mortimer," suggested Throgmorton, who never missed a chance for a quip on every side of any question, "fears that Lord Libertine's scandalous conduct may yet bring Jacobins and Revolutionaries into England. He can see it now, I've no doubt. The mob storming up the Strand, the Guillotine set up on the Mall, King George a prisoner at Windsor, and the Cult of Reason worshiped at St. Paul's." He chuckled, setting the rosy Throgmorton jowls into motion. "A horrifying vision, truly. And all for Lord Christopher's pinching one barmaid's bottom too many."

"I refer to nothing so innocuous as a barmaid's bottom my dear doctor," responded Durward, with his usual unruffled calm. "I refer, as young Danforth here has done already, to the shocking business of Lady Arbuthnot.

"Lord Arbuthnot, as I am sure we must all agree, is a pillar of Tory principle. A perfect exemplar of all the noble virtues—of privilege *with* responsibility. In publicly humiliating poor Arbuthnot, our friend Arundel has dragged the whole nobility of England through the mire. I call that dangerous and uncalled for, gentlemen." His lips pursed in that prissy look that told the world that *this was a serious matter*.

"Now, my lord," I said softly, at the conclusion of his harangue, "would you be making a matter of honor of it then?"

I had been itching for a good number of years to get Durward at the other end of a dueling pistol. But he was a cagey villain and had always proved too slippery for me. As he did again that night.

"Arundel," he answered firmly, "I seek no quarrel with you personally, as you know well enough. It is a matter of principle, sir. There is—" he paused, "such a thing as innocence."

Innocence! From him!

It was too much. Durward has always brought out the tiger in me, ravenous for prey. And so on this occasion. To my everlasting disarray.

"Durward," I said, "I here and now defy you openly,

before all this distinguished company"—the worldly cler-
gyman, the would-be rakehell, and the bloody-minded
colonel all looked at me—"to point to one single person,
known to all of us, whose heart might by the wildest
stretch of the imagination be described as —innocent!"

"Preposterous!" snapped Durward, glowering. "There
are any number—"

"A name, Lord Mortimer, pray," said I. "A name both
uncorrupted and uncorruptible. A name, male or female,
that I cannot drag through the public mire within a
month!"

Durward tried to speak again. But the table, intrigued
at the prospect of so unorthodox a wager, cut him off
with a single cry:

"A name! A name!"

Durward's face went livid, pale as the salt sea-foam, or
somewhat dingy snow.

"Lady Barbara MacFarlane," he said distinctly, "of
Holyrood House, in Berkshire."

4

The Fatal Wager

"I beg your pardon?" I said.

"My dear sir—surely you jest!" the Reverend Dr.
Throgmorton expostulated, raising his hands in theatrical
astonishment. "Everyone in London has heard of Lady
Barbara MacFarlane!"

"The woman's a byword, sir!" grunted Colonel Tolliver. "A veritable byword, what? The incarnation of the
most shocking Foxite principles—all that rascally crew.

Shocking—shocking—" His big freckled hands actually shook upon the cards. He chewed his cud ferociously.

"I've heard it said," Lord Danforth murmured delicately, "that the lady positively dotes on Thomas Paine. That she hails every new atrocity in France as another step toward the Millennium."

"French principles!" snorted Tolliver again. "Source of all our misfortunes, what? Doctrinaires—theoreticians! Pah!"

"The lady in question," said Lord Mortimer stiffly, "has indeed been one of the shriller advocates of the cause of the French Revolutionaries. But it is not these political follies that render Lady Barbara MacFarlane of Holyrood House so perfect a test for the—ah—moral theories of our friend Arundel. Not these at all."

I was relieved to hear it. I am by nature a totally unpolitical person. "French principles" meant nothing to me, and French politics—even the more colorful revolutionary ones—even less.

"Would anyone care to enlighten me, then," I inquired of the table at large, "as to what precisely *does* qualify the celebrated Lady Barbara aforesaid as a proper challenge to my own commonsense view of life?"

"My dear Arundel," said Parson Throgmorton with a jovial chuckle, "it is not only *political* principles to which the lady clings with such uncalled-for enthusiasm."

"Woman's a perfect little puritan, sir" snorted Tolliver. "A prude to end all prudes—some sort of female monk or other!"

"The lady pretends at least to believe," said Durward icily, "in pristine virtue for its own sake. In the empire of virtue over all the more—ah—earthy passions."

"In fine," Throgmorton magisterially summed up, "Lady Barbara MacFarlane believes in honor its own reward. In purity, decency, and plain moral conduct. In all the things you have been morally color-blind to from the day you were weaned, my dear Lord Libertine." He beamed and chuckled and reached for the cards.

"*Formidable!*" I murmured. "She must be the most horrendous bore in London." I said it, but remembering those seagreen eyes, that level gaze, I could not really believe it.

"On the contrary!" Danforth broke in with more spirit than he had managed all the evening. "Far from it, I assure you."

"Lord Danforth," said Throgmorton archly, "is one of the lady's unhappy rejectees. London is quite littered with them, these last months."

Danforth bit his lip and said no more.

"A hopeless iceberg, then," I offered, "frigid as a northern winter—damp as a London drizzle."

"Not at all!" said Lord Mortimer Durward testily. "Those who know her better say she has no lack of *impulses*. She simply has the moral character—to master them!"

"Tight-reined filly," muttered Tolliver, emerging with glistening jowls from his port. "Whalebone—starchy, what?"

"All the impulses," said Throgmorton judicially, "in which *you* have any interest, Lord Christopher." I remember Lady Barbara's full, strong lips, the perfect body beneath the rainwet gown—entirely unbuttressed by whalebone, Tolliver to the contrary. And I agreed for once with both Lord Mortimer and the parson. Surely the lady of Holyrood House must have all the impulses.

"It sounds a fair challenge to me," I said after a moment's pretended meditation. "What shall the wager be? That I'll bed her within one month from date, and bring some intimate evidence thereof—a garter or—"

"Really, sir," murmured the reverend doctor with a twinkle. "Some respect—"

Young Lord Danforth looked unhappily away, but said nothing.

Durward smiled broadly, a painful spectacle on so thin and arrogant a face. " 'Drag her through the public mire' was, I believe, the phrase," he said slowly. His elegant fingers played idly with the cards on the smooth green surface before him. But his cold eyes bored into mine, and I suddenly detected depths there, layers of motivation, abysses of intrigue, that made me acutely uneasy.

There was, however, no help for it now. I shrugged and nodded. The table, I noticed, was abruptly still.

"And the stakes?" I asked then. "Five hundred guineas, shall we say? To make it interesting?"

"Not five hundred—not five thousand!" hissed Lord Mortimer Durward, leaning forward in his chair. "A far more precious thing than that!"

"Name it!" My own eyes were hardening, I knew, and my Irish temper rising. Sooner or later, I thought, I must, I really must reduce that supercilious face to a proper mush.

"A stake worth wagering," said my living, breathing antithesis with slow venom. "Your total and complete *absence,* sir—or mine!"

I must have blinked my incomprehension.

"The absence," he amplified with relish, "of your face, sir, from my own immediate milieu. From London! From the country! From anywhere and everywhere that I might ever come across it again!"

"A noble prospect," I answered, "from my point of view as well. But how exactly to be achieved?"

"Exile!" he snapped exultantly. "Emigration! Banishment! The loser to exile himself from the City, from the country, from all Europe. To take ship at once for Australia—America—any other hemisphere but this! Exile to the most barbarous wilderness—for life!"

There was a stillness so palpable now that conversations stopped at other tables, and questioning faces turned our way. Servants passing near us found some excuse to pause, immaculate periwigs tilted sharp to listen. Ardent gamblers left off their own haggling over horseflesh and turned toward the velvet alcove where we sat.

White's is famous for wild wagers. The prune-faced old steward remembers the time Lord Bolingbroke laid a thousand guineas to one that the national debt would never pass a hundred millions. Or the night Mr. Henry Holland wagered his finest racehorse he would have the Earl of Sandwich's daughter in marriage—and won. They are all there still, duly registered in the records of the club.

But this was something else again.

Exile. Banishment from Europe. From the elegant country houses and the continental tours—from the gondolas of Venice, the music of Vienna, the glories of Paris and Versailles. And worst of all, from London! From Vauxhall and the Rotunda, from the theaters at Covent Garden, from White's and Brooks's and Child's Coffee House, from the Cheshire Cheese and the Blue Periwig and the steaming golden fillet of sole in butter sauce at the Black Lion in Water Lane. From—God help me—my sweet whore Mrs. Betsy Murrain, and Sally Love at the Rose, and Lady Arbuthnot, and all the other lovely scented doxies past and present and to come!

Exile from civilization itself—for a life of labor in some rude forest or savage desert on the other side of the world!

"Well, sir?" Lord Mortimer Durward was leaning toward me, his cold protuberant eyes glistening, his face pale and taut.

"Done!" I said, and smiled, wondering how long poor Durward would survive in the sweltering plantations of Jamaica or the snowgirt logging camps of Canada.

And that's how my troubles all began.

5

In Which My Man Jeremy Reprimands Me Sharply

My rooms in Hanover Square are few but snug. The furniture is old and dark, heavier than is the fashion now. The fireplace in the principal parlor is a large, roaring affair with a comfortable old-fashioned settle and a cushioned stool in front of it. There, when the world is too much with me, I am inclined to retire to brood upon the blaze.

Here I sat the morning after my first meeting with Lady Barbara MacFarlane and the unlikely wager with Lord Mortimer, sipping my chocolate and discussing the matter with my man Jeremy.

"A piece of utmost folly, sir!" was Jeremy's succinct opinion. "A record, sir. Even for you."

I sighed and let the insinuation pass.

Jeremy Twill is nobody's idea of the perfect gentleman's gentleman. He is a thin, sallow, sharp-featured Cockney who went into service, as he cheerfully confessed the day I hired him, "because it beats 'eaving casks and bales down at the East Inja Docks"—to which manual profession his father, a gin-soaked stevedore himself, had apparently destined him. "Especially for an 'usky brute like mesself, sir, there really don't seem to be much future in 'eaving cargo, but only aches and ruptures." He grinned and stared me down, bold as brass for all his scrawny insignificant frame. I engaged him on the spot.

Jeremy is a slow hand for service, though quick-fingered enough when it comes to a gratuity. He tyrannizes over the two maids and the French cook who complete my slender Hanover Square establishment. And he is insufferably insolent, as Lord Mortimer would no doubt say. But he has a way with a head left throbbing after too much madeira. He is better company than nine-tenths of his betters. And he never burns my toast.

He also knows every rumor, scandal, untoward occurrence, and odd character in London. Hence the tenor of that morning's conversation. For I really knew very little about Lady Barbara MacFarlane. If anyone could enlighten me, it would be Jeremy.

"I may well win *this* wager, you know," I told Jeremy presently, sucking meditatively on my chocolate. "She's only a woman, after all."

"Only a woman, sir!" he snorted. "She's a rutting prodigy!"

"Come come, Jeremy. This isn't a Charing Cross mermaid we're talking about! The lady's a bit of a bluestocking, I understand. A bit much for Prayer Book principles, perhaps—"

"Prayer Book principles I couldn't speak for, sir. But Jacobinical preachments and levelers' doctrines I'll dare swear to!" Next to Durward, or perhaps Colonel Tolliver, I know no one so down on the "leveling tendencies" of the "democratic spirit" as Jeremy.

"Not so bad as that, surely."

"Worse, sir, worse! A very Judith of the Revolutionaries, sir! She'd be the one for 'eads on poles, and marching on Versailles!"

He bent to his duties as he spoke, and eggs and ham succeeded toast before me. I am one of those odd individuals who require more than thin tea and dry bread for breakfast.

"Tush, man," I mumbled through a mouthful of gammon. "You exaggerate."

"Not a bit of it, sir. The chop'ouses and the coffee'ouses talk of no one else this winter. 'Er face 'as quite driven the Prince and Mrs. Fitz out of the printshop windows, sir. They show 'er got up as a Amazon, with a red-white-and-blue French cockade on 'er 'elmet!"

"Oh, I've no doubt the printmakers have a holiday with so charming a face and figure! But come now, what has the lady actually said—or written, does she write?—to merit such obloquy?"

"She's spoke in public, sir, and written too, on more weighty matters nor the Parlyment 'as passed upon this term! Meddled in every poor wretch's lot in Christendom—and some beyond as well, sir."

"Come—be specific, man!"

"Well, there's the beatin' of animals, sir. She's against that."

"Animals?"

"Yes, sir. Dogcart whips to oxgoads, she's against 'em! Crooly to poor dumb creatures, so she calls it."

"Indeed. Well . . ."

I brushed crumbs off my dressing gown and gazed bemused out the wide bow window on my right, overlooking Hanover Square. Half-a-dozen carriages and gigs were in plain view, trotting around the white-fenced, grassed-in central area. Matched pairs, four-in-hands. How many countless thousands of horses in London alone? How many millions, pulling the carts and wagons and plows of every farm in England? And then, all the oxen, asses, and what have you that felt an exasperated driver's crop, goad, whip every day of the year?

Put an end to cruelty to *animals*? Say rather, tell the wind to blow no more, or put an end to rain, because the bad weather offends her ladyship's sensibilities!

"Worse yet, sir," Jeremy pursued with some asperity. "She declares there shall be no more 'anging of 'ighwaymen, no more flogging of prisoners . . ."

It was at this point that I seriously began to doubt my Jeremy's candor in the matter. I gave him a sharp look, to see if there was a glint of mirth in those beady little eyes. But he was busy collecting my plate and silverware, and there was something in the outraged set of his narrow shoulders that made me believe he was in earnest after all.

"Next she'll be telling me I'm not to pinch our Jane's bottom!" he muttered, clattering the dishes onto the side-board with unnecessary violence. "Nor cuff that rutting Frenchy's ear when he uses a pound of London butter and 'alf the spices in the cabinet to fry a dozen eggs! Croolty to scullery maids, she'll call it. And the rutting rights of *emigrays!*"

"Surely not the most radical root-and-branch man, Jeremy," I hastened to demur, "would deprive you of Jane's pretty bottom!"

"Why, 'er ladyship's for blackamoors, and chimney sweeps, and God only knows what other wretches, sir! A rank leveling *democrat,* sir, and I don't care who 'ears me say it."

I wondered how sizable a gratuity it would take to muffle all this righteous indignation the first time the lady in question visited me in my chambers.

"Why, sir—" He paused at the door for a parting shot. "Lately she's even clamoring in the public prints for what she's pleased to call the Rights of Women!"

"The Rights of Women?" I answered blankly. My staunchly apolitical mind groped vaguely back, fumbling for some tirade of Tolliver's. "Surely you mean *The Rights of Man.* This fellow Paine—"

"Nothing of the sort, sir! As if such firebrand stuff were not bad enough It's the Rights of Women, sir!"

My mouth hung open like a fish with a gaff through its gills as Jeremy, sallow cheeks pale with outrage, little eyes agleam at having moved me to some response at last, marched off up the stairs to lay out my suit and linen for the day.

The Rights of Women, my God!

6

Lady Barbara at the Political Club

My next glimpse of Lady Barbara MacFarlane—for it was little more than that—came only two nights later. I saw her in a most unlikely place for me—at a political meeting. And if I came away uninspired politically, my passion for Lady Barbara herself was clearly cranked up another notch or two.

It began in much more congenial surroundings for a gentleman of pleasure—at Vauxhall.

A silly, festive place full of silly, festive people is Vauxhall Gardens down the Thames. The acme of frivolity, with its aimless paths and foolish pavilions and myriad multicolored lights. I have always enjoyed it hugely.

"A perfect evening," young Lord Danforth murmured, stretching exaggeratedly and surveying the cheerful crowds with the mock indolence of the perfect Macaroni. "Would you not say so, sir?"

"Indeed," responded the Reverend Dr. Throgmorton, fanning the soft evening air with a pudgy hand. "Though I am surprised you noticed, sir," he added with a twinkle. "It was my impression that you had eyes for no one but Lady Hamilton yonder."

I glanced over at the Lady in question, large eyes and pouting mouth under a wide hat, seated with old Hamil-

ton himself in a booth just under the orchestra. Like everything else at Vauxhall that evening, she was a pleasure to
look at.

Danforth flushed and pulled out his elaborately engraved snuffbox to distract attention from his confusion.
"They say she sings beautifully, and can pantomime all
the antique statues in an Indian shawl. I *should* like to see
it, upon my soul I should. But as for more than that . . ."
He elevated his brows and lowered his lids in his most
worldly manner, and took a pinch of snuff.

Lady Hamilton was his latest passion—all London
knew it. And as hopeless as most of his passions, alas.

"She's lovely, she is!" exclaimed Annie, the fruit girl
from St. James's Street, speaking from the other end of
our table. "Though I am surprised a lady of 'er sort
should be doing postures in a shawl!"

"Not *pos*tures, miss—*panto*mimes!" Jeremy corrected
her sharply. "It's a different thing entirely!"

"I'm afraid he's right, Annie," I tossed in with a heart-
felt sigh. "And of course Lady Hamilton performs with
*som*e clothing at least under the Indian shawl."

"Indeed, sir?" wondered Annie, obviously unable to
grasp the point of the performance if the lady was to be
completely clothed. I rather wondered too, now that I
thought about it.

"Indeed, Annie. And pass me a strawberry, there's a
good girl."

I settled back and gazed about me at the pageantry of
Vauxhall at twilight. Colored lanterns glittered in the
trees and under the arches. A sentimental German tune
floated across the grass from the Grand Pavilion. At our
own table under an oak tree, Jeremy and Annie chopped
up a couple of chickens into a large bowl, pausing only
occasionally to pour wine for the three gentlefolk. I
popped another strawberry in my mouth and smiled
benignly on the world.

"Well, Arundel!" A chipper, brittle voice intruded upon my serenity. "Exploiting the wretched of the earth as usual, I see!"

It was Charles James Fox himself, sardonic and sartorially impeccable as usual, from his blue-powdered hair to his bright-red shoes. The most radical of Whigs, the most brilliant defender of the French Revolution, was also the most fashionable gentleman in England!

"Not at all, Fox," I cheerfully demurred. "Not so at all. You know Jeremy robs me blind. Not a strawberry in three, not half of any bottle of wine ever reaches my lips. And as for Annie here, why, she's free enough to hie her back to her post in St. James's. Only we've bought all her fruit for the evening, and laid out two shillings and a boatman's fee to get her here as well. Isn't it so, Annie?"

She grinned and nodded.

"I think even you would have some trouble finding much oppression here, Fox."

"Won't you join us, Mr. Fox?" Parson Throgmorton urged upon him in his turn. "It is a cold collation, but quite in keeping with the picnic atmosphere."

"You are too kind, sir. But alas, I must decline." Fox fished out a gold watch and squinted at it in the gloaming as he spoke. "I have an urgent appointment—with the enemies of oppression, as it happens." And then, looking at me directly: "Would you care to join me, sir?"

"What, for a revolutionary march on Whitehall? Or will you be putting the West End to the torch tonight?"

"We are organizing, sir," Fox explained quite seriously, "to express our ardent sympathies. This very night at the Freemasons Tavern. Will you not come, and lend your support to the good work?"

"What—another Friends of the French Revolution society, Fox?" Throgmorton chuckled, sipping his wine. "Are there not enough already to make your voice heard from one end of the land to the other?"

"This is to be a thoroughly respectable group, I assure you," Fox replied. "Subscription of ten pounds sterling required of each. No firebrands, no *hoi polloi*. It is called," he added, "The Friends of the People."

"Friends of the People indeed," I heard Jeremy mutter, dismembering a chicken with particular ferocity. "Friends of the rutting *mob,* 'e means."

"It does not sound nearly so pleasant, Fox," I said, "as a quiet evening at Vauxhall, with strawberries and *Lieder* and all the comedy of mankind for entertainment. I at least prefer such simple pleasures to beer and tobacco smoke and speeches full of doctrinaire enthusiasm."

"Really. Ah, well then." He turned to go. "I must in any case be off. I've promised to speak briefly, in company with Mr. Priestly and Lady Barbara MacFarlane. I fear they will both be finished before I come."

"Lady Barbara?" asked Throgmorton, with some interest. "Is she to speak, then? Do you know, I've never heard her?"

"Lady Barbara MacFarlane?" Danforth echoed. "Why, neither have I, now you mention it. They say she's an orator worth hearing. For one of her sex, of course." But his voice was all quivering eagerness, his debonair casualness evaporating on the instant. *What,* I could not help but grin to myself, *Lady Hamilton's pantomimes quite forgot already?*

"Come along then, Arundel," said the Reverend Throgmorton. "Let's do go and hear the paragon." And then, in a lower tone, as I shrugged and rose with the rest: " 'Know your enemy' is a prime maxim for any sort of campaign, eh, my lord?"

His logic, of course, was impeccable. Even if it did mean an evening of sweaty political effusions. And so I went.

The low-raftered main taproom of the Freemasons Tavern was full of red-faced men in elegant clothing, swilling ale and porter and puffing on their pipes, periodically slapping their thighs, nodding agreement, shouting *huzzah* or *hear, hear* or *dead right, by God!* The room reeked of malt and wine and tobacco and something rancid and indefinable that I finally identified as the odor of political passion itself. The acrid scent of the true believer, rather like the odor of a dog in heat.

I shoved into the rear of the room and stopped, giddy with this barrage of unhealthy sights and sounds and smells. My first thought on entering was to turn around and leave at once.

Then I heard her voice.

"Our first concern as lovers of our country"—the words rose crisp and clear above the muted hubbub— "must be to *enlighten* it." There were nods, and a periwigged gentleman at my elbow said, "Hear, hear!"

"Why are the nations of the world so patient under despotism? Why do they crouch to tyrants and submit to be treated as if they were a herd of cattle? Is it not because they are kept in darkness? Is it not because they lack knowledge?"

"Quite so!" and "It is, damme!" from two or three down front.

"Enlighten them"—the girl's crisp voice rose slightly— "and you will elevate them! Show them they are human, and they will *act* like human beings! Give them a just idea of civil government—show them that government exists but to defend *their* rights—and it will be impossible for them to submit any longer to the unjust governments which now exist in the world!"

There were huzzahs and much nodding and clapping. New clouds of smoke rose to the rafters, and glasses rang upon the table. I moved slightly to my left, in order that I might see as well as hear the Judith of the Jacobins.

She stood behind a table, leaning forward slightly, slender and poised. Her fingers just touched the tabletop, and she emphasized her points by almost invisible taps with her fingertips upon the wooden surface. She seemed calm and cool, totally in command. Very far from the ranting image I had formed of the enthusiast in politics.

"In short," she said, drawing toward her conclusion, "we may in this instance learn our duty from the oppressors of the world themselves. *They* know that light is hostile to them, and therefore they labor to keep men in the dark. Remove that darkness, in which they envelop the world, and their usurpations will be exposed—their power will be subverted—and the world emancipated!"

She sat down to a storm of applause, bending her head to acknowledge a compliment from old Priestly, the chemist, seated on her left behind the table. These meetings were never complete, I remembered hearing somewhere, without old Priestly peering piously through his spectacles and adding an air of scientific support for any and all enlightened political causes.

Just behind Lady Barbara, I detected the faithful *duenna* Bridget. Her doughy face was set in an expression of mingled disapproval and apprehension as she looked unhappily about her. This, in her judgment, was clearly no place for a lady.

On Lady Barbara's other side I noticed a man I had never seen before. He was short and dark-complexioned, in a green, distinctly foreign military uniform with a tricolor cockade in his tricorne hat. His cheeks were thin, gleaming with perspiration, and he had an impatient glitter in his eye.

"And who might the French gentleman be, sir?" I queried Fox.

"That is Citizen Machaud," responded Fox in a whisper. "He is a Jacobin and a leader in the Assembly at Paris. He came with M. Talleyrand's friendship mission in the spring, and has stayed on among us as an honored guest." He smiled reprovingly. "If you spent more time in the company of good Whigs, Arundel, you would long since have made his acquaintance. He is a man passionately dedicated to his principles."

Looking up, I saw Citizen Machaud's glittering eyes fixed upon me down the jabbering, smoke-clogged room. Looking into those hot, impatient eyes, I did not doubt the passion of his dedication. But somehow I felt quite willing to forgo the pleasure of his acquaintance.

But the glittering eyes of the Jacobin Machaud could scarce spoil the savor of an otherwise eminently enjoyable evening. I stepped back out into the street with a familiar gingery tingle stirring once more in my vitals. It was the purely visceral excitement that comes with the taste of ancient wine, the thunder of a great horse pounding to victory—or the sight and scent and feel of a perfectly beautiful piece of womanflesh!

7

The Jacobin Machaud

I spoke to Lady Barbara MacFarlane for the second time the following Friday, at a ball at Lord and Lady Arbuthnot's great house on Berkeley Square. The circumstances were ideal, the opportunity to press my suit unexcelled. Alas, I must admit that I did not improve the shining hour.

It was a glittering affair, done up in splendor, as is Lady Arbuthnot's way. The high arched windows that stretched the length of the vast facade glowed with yellow light. Ladies with bare shoulders and trailing ball gowns swept up the broad marble stairs on the arms of gentlemen wearing elegant cloaks and swinging twinkling canes. In the outer darkness of the square itself, beyond the wrought-iron railings, the common folk stared and murmured, exclaiming at my Lord So-and-So's equipage, or at Lady Such-a-One's towering coiffure.

Up the stairs and through the wide double doors one passed, into the ephemeral fairyland which few could stage manage as brilliantly as Caroline, Lady Arbuthnot.

Everyone, as they say, was there.

Edmund Burke and Charles James Fox stood cheek by jowl, Burke as simply clad, Fox as resplendent as usual. The greatest orator and the most brilliant man in England, respectively, as alike as two peas in a pod underneath, despite their celebrated clashes on the floor of Commons.

William Pitt himself was present, the King's Prime Minister of State almost a decade now. A tall, ungainly man, stiffish in company. He had port-wine blotches on his cheeks, and a good deal of Lord Arbuthnot's excellent port under his belt already, though the evening was just begun.

My nemesis Lord Mortimer Durward passed by, saturnine and aristocratic to his fingertips, his thin lips peaked and pursed as though he had just bitten into a lemon. I divined that he was in search of someone to impress, a guess which proved to be more than accurate.

The beautiful Gunning sisters were there, and Lady Hamilton, and no end of other *belles* drifting through the high-ceilinged marble salons, chattering, laughing, preparing for the next cotillion. Jewelry flashed, ostrich plumes nodded in high-piled hair. The high waist *à la grecque* was much in evidence, with plenty of *décolletage* as usual. Here and there the new diaphanous gowns swirled past, ostentatiously simple, clinging seductively to uncorseted young bodies. Music and unmuted laughter, banal pleasantries, unconvincing coquetry, and endless whispered scandal filled the great gilded ballrooms.

I should no doubt pause at this point for an epigram or two on the artificiality and falseness of the world of fashion. The fact is that I enjoyed it all immensely. And when Lady Arbuthnot herself knifed through the scintillating throng to my side, my cup was full to overflowing.

"Lord Christopher!" she exclaimed in that rich, throaty voice of hers. "How good of you!" Her gray appraising eyes crinkled as they did at all her guests. But her small mouth formed a soft round O to me that spoke volumes more.

"Lady Arbuthnot." I bowed. "How good of *you*."

Her little figure was exquisite in green silks and satins. Her throat and shoulders were perfect, and her bodice was cut breathtakingly low. Even her ridiculous green-satin turban with its two extravagant ostrich plumes was a delight that night. The soft mouth and the crinkling eyes brought back glowing memories of other, more private interviews than this.

I grinned and cocked an eyebrow. Lady Arbuthnot was well-known as one of the most perfect hostesses in London. Her servants were always drilled to perfection, her cooks' confections always done to a turn. The helpless-hostess-swept-away-by-it-all was simply a conventional ploy which she chose to adopt on occasion. It was something to say. And what *do* you say, after all, when you have two hundred people to greet in the hour before dinner?

To me, she made her little O again. I remembered the passion that mouth contained, the groans and gasps and clutching hands on a sun-spangled summer afternoon not long past. While I was remembering, she swept away to greet the Prince of Wales.

"Our hostess is charming, is she not, Lord Libertine?" The voice was musical and mocking and only half familiar yet. I turned politely and beheld Lady Barbara MacFarlane at my side.

She stood at the foot of the grand staircase, one hand resting easily on a monstrous sculptured urn. Her auburn hair was unpowdered, falling massively from a simple chignon at the back of her slender neck. She wore a white gown, bound high under the breasts, clinging lightly to her uncorseted figure. A single touch of color glowed in all that virginal white: a small red-white-and-blue cockade—the symbol of the French Revolution—nestled in the white tulle that shielded her bosom above the low-cut gown.

The tricolor cockade, the sheen of her auburn hair, and the emerald gleam of her eyes stood out brilliantly in that sweep of snowy satin and alabaster skin. She was a living statue, an Athena after Phidias, heart-stoppingly beautiful.

"Our hostess is charming indeed, my lady," I replied at last. "A nymph—to your ladyship's divinity." The phrase, I will confess it, was one that I had used before. But it came from the heart that night.

Lady Barbara looked amused but not, I thought, entirely displeased.

"You have had no further encounters with Captain Patch and his scurvy crew, I hope, madame?" I added, consciously lightening the tone. It is always well to keep the tone light in the early stages.

"None"—she smiled—"nor ever expect to. It is not the sort of experience one would care to repeat."

I began to formulate an elaborate compliment, something to the effect that I would cheerfully offer my poor carcass to the pummeling of Fag, Trip, Figgis, and their comrados any evening in return for so charming a new acquaintance as her ladyship. Then I saw that she was not alone. For there, shadowed by the gigantic urn, stood a half-remembered figure.

"Christopher Arundel"—I noticed how carefully she avoided the title—"may I present Citizen Jacques Machaud, of the French National Assembly?"

Machaud did not smile, did not in fact acknowledge Lady Barbara's introduction at all, beyond the slightest brusque inclination of the head. My first thought was to dismiss him as an even more boorish character than myself. My second was to recognize that there was something nastily impressive about the short, olive-skinned man with the look of smoldering impatience about the eyes.

I decided to try something nonpolitical by way of conversation, though I had a feeling it was not going to work.

"I see, sir," I began, "that you wear the uniform of the King of France. May I inquire which regiment?"

Citizen Machaud drew himself up to his full five feet four or five. "I wear the uniform of *France*, sir," he rasped, "not of Citoyen Louis Capet."

"I beg your pardon?"

"Citizen Louis Capet, whom some misguided individuals still refer to as King Louis the Sixteenth."

"*Citizen* Louis Capet?" A new voice intruded sharply upon the conversation. "I had no idea that the Jacobins had abolished the blood royal, along with so much else that many of us have valued in your country."

It was Lord Mortimer Durward. Posturing as usual.

A small group was gatering round—our host Lord Arbuthnot for one—and the Prime Minister himself was strolling over. Durward saw his audience collecting and played to it shamelessly. But he had met his match in Machaud. The swarthy little Frenchman looked down his nose, as though he was preparing to make a speech. Which he was.

"The *people* are the new France, sir!" he intoned, his voice taut with all the fervor of the true believer. "And we who have the honor to serve France serve them! We

are the embodiment of the general will of the nation—
the incarnate will of the people of France!"

"The people of England," said Durward, extracting a
pinch of snuff from a silver monogrammed case, "are that
riffraff outside in the park. An improvident, unindustrious,
immoral lot, much addicted, I understand, to the use of
gin." He took his snuff.

"Has it ever occured to you gentlemen," said Lady
Barbara MacFarlane sharply, "that the people take too
much gin because they are compelled to dwell in the Gin
Lanes of this city? That strong spirits are the only escape
left to the poor of the realm from the degrading squalor
in which they are condemned to live?" Her eyes flashed,
and a high color suffused her cheeks.

A judicious silence followed this bold sally. Then
Machaud's voice crackled forth, harsh and triumphant.

"The people of England," he informed us on a rising
note, "will sooner or later find their voices as well!
Indeed—" He paused for a long significant moment. "I
think they have found one vastly eloquent voice to speak
for them already!"

He inclined his head in a stiff Jacobinic substitute for a
bow, turned on his heel, and strode away—with Lady
Barbara MacFarlane on his arm.

8

An Assignation: or, All Cats
Are Gray in the Dark

I saw Machaud twice more that evening, brooding in
corners like a prophet in Babylon. But of Lady Barbara I
saw almost nothing.

Supper came. Lady Arbuthnot seated her guests in the daring modern way—"promiscuous" they call it, gentlemen and ladies alternately. I had Lady Arbuthnot herself on one side of me, and a recently defunct rear admiral's widow on the other. Far up the endless table, beyond countless tall white candles, vistas of crystal and silver, range on range of steaming meats and fish and fowl, I could barely glimpse the pale shoulders and shining copper-colored hair of Lady Barbara MacFarlane.

So I flirted alternately and outrageously with the widow and with Caroline in her awesomely low-cut gown, and exchanged a *mot* or two with the Reverend Dr. Throgmorton, seated just across from me. I only half heard Durward's fulminations against the "Hydra of Revolution," as he so eloquently termed it. But I bridled properly at Colonel Tolliver's latest stentorian call to arms: "If it's war the Frenchies want, I say give 'em war! The Austrians and the Prooshians are already massing on their borders, what? Shall we allow the *Prooshians* into the field before us?" And I tried to look intelligent while Pitt droned on about fiscal responsibility and the sad state of the revenues, which made all talk of war "imprudent—most imprudent" at this time. Pitt, they say, is never too drunk to talk about the sad state of the revenues.

It was the most unconscionably political evening I could remember. I clung like a drowning man to Throgmorton's flow of apothegms, to Caroline's scented cleavage —and to the occasional brief glimpse of Lady Barbara's smooth white shoulders.

Meanwhile, we ate our way through quarters of veal, sides of mutton, joints of good old English beef. Through plovers and partridge and quail and woodcock. Through onions and asparagus and cucumbers and peas and no end of other side dishes, soups, sauces, and ragouts.

Then the table was cleared, the ladies left us, and the serious drinking began.

We drank toasts to our own good King George III. To poor Louis XVI and his unhappy Queen Marie Antoinette, languishing beyond the seas. To the British Army (ever victorious). To the British Navy (hearts of oak). To our noble host (sterling fellow!). To stouthearted Britons everywhere (they never would be slaves). By which time the veined yellow marble over the huge fireplace was bginning to run into the magenta brocaded hangings left and right, and I was finding it difficult to distinguish Burke's ponderous patriotic pronouncements from Arbuthnot's scabrous anecdotes about his last trip to Paris "before the late unpleasantness."

And still all I could think of was Lady Barbara's milk-white shoulders.

It was in the midst of one of Arbuthnot's most risqué tales that a liveried servingman bent obsequiously over my left shoulder and handed me a scented note.

My dear Lord Christopher,

If you should find the gentlemen's conversation languishing, I should be glad of an opportunity to continue our own all-too-brief talk of earlier this evening.

If you should care to join me, a lady's maid will await you on the first-floor landing.

There was no signature, but the forthright manner of it was unmistakable, even to one with so little acquaintance of the Lady Barbara as I yet had.

Overjoyed at this unlooked-for opportunity to press my suit, I rose at once. Muttering something about the necessary house (though chamber pots had already been hauled out of the sideboard), I lurched out of the room.

The halls were empty but for bustling servants. I heard the murmur and laughter of the ladies from the cardrooms. Mounting the wide curved staircase, I found the maid waiting as promised on the first-floor landing. She bobbed me a silent curtsey and led me off through a maze of corridors to a dim secluded door. There she curtseyed once again, still without a word, and retreated quickly down the hallway, leaving me alone.

What sort of conversation can the lady have in mind? I wondered, astonished at this extraordinary procedure. Cocking an eyebrow and assuming my most debonair mien, however, I boldly lifted the latch and stepped inside.

"My lady," I began, "I am gratified indeed—"

I stopped. The room was pitch dark. And it was clearly not a drawing room. Judging by the hint of fragrance in the air, the half-heard rustle of silken curtains, it was in fact a lady's boudoir.

"Here, my lord," a woman's voice whispered from the pulsing darkness somewhere on my left. "And do close the door."

So this, I exulted in joyful disbelief, is the secret Lady Barbara! The lady of Holyrood House that nobody knows but I! *The lady has all the impulses*, the Reverend Dr. Throgmorton's voice echoed in my brain, *all the impulses in which* you *have any interest, my dear Lord Libertine*. All the impulses indeed, my God! And I had guessed it that first night in the rain.

I closed the door as I was bade, and groped eagerly through the blackness toward the voice and the unmistakable rustle of bedclothes that accompanied it.

In a moment I blundered into perfumed damask hangings, and my hand touched a brocaded pillow. I heard a subdued laugh, a sudden movement in the high four-poster bed. Then naked arms slid around my neck and pulled me down among the coverlets.

"Lord Christopher!" whispered Caroline, Lady Arbuthnot. "How good of you to come!"

And her mouth made the familiar little O against my own.

There is a saying—attributed, I believe, to the French —that all cats are gray in the dark. This is not strictly speaking so, as any experienced amorist will surely agree. But there are certain fundamental similarities between one lovely young female body and another. Suffice it to say, then, that the tall man belowstairs adjusted rapidly enough to the situation. A different nest was offered than Master Cock had been expecting—but a soft nest nonetheless.

In a moment I was naked. In two we were at it, shaking the elegant canopied bed with the violence of our passion.

"Caroline," I murmured, "my Queen of Love—"

"O Lord Christopher—"

She was a woman of fervid appetite, was Lady Arbuthnot. I had scarce driven my lusty truncheon into her before an excess of pleasure seemed to stir her to her very vitals. Her faltering accents, her broken breathing, as well as the frantic agitation of her body against mine, were proof enough of the wanton delight that filled her.

"O my lord—it is too much—" her voice panted beneath me in the darkness.

"Nay, madame—it is scarce enough," I responded, slowing my exertions to savor the tide of pleasure that rose within me. "Scarce sufficient for your sweet desserts, I mean, my lady. Let us be in no haste, but taste each delight at leisure, like the epicures of old . . ."

But Caroline's passion brooked no restraint. Her reservoir of joy all too quickly reached its floodmark. With a final cry of "O my lord!" she expired, gasping and shuddering under me.

A charming testimony, I have no doubt. Yet I felt some disgruntlement as, with a final twist and thrust, I followed my charming bedmate over the precipice of pleasure. So happily begun an encounter, I thought, might well have gone on to further refinements, building more subtly to that final spasm of delight.

But we lay snugly enough together in the blackness then, our breaths mingling, so close that I felt her eyelids flutter against my cheek. His lordship's wine warmed my belly as his lordship's wife my bed, and all conducted to a most pleasant frame of mind. I began to think about a second passage at arms. It was after all not her ladyship's fault if she could not contain her passion under my expert ministrations.

"Pray, what o'clock is it, sir?" her rich contralto voice said suddenly, and indeed rather brusquely, against my ear.

"What o'clock? Why, madame, I do not know—eleven perhaps. What does time matter," I added gallantly, "when we two are together thus, body to body—"

"What does it *matter*? Why, sir, how long do you think I can be absent from my own drawing room on the excuse of a 'temporary indisposition'?"

She rose with remarkable alacrity for one who had a moment since been helplessly awash with passion. I heard her bare feet pad across the floor, and then a candle sprang to life on the chintz-covered dressing table on the other side of the room. She raised the taper, looking unutterably charming in her sleek, round-bottomed nudity, and gazed at the porcelain clock upon the wall beside her mirror.

"The ladies must rejoin the gentlemen in a quarter of an hour from now!" Her tone was clearly alarmed as she set down the candle and reached for her petticoats and stays. "Do you think," she added pettishly, "I can be absent then?"

She was indeed the perfect hostess, Caroline, Lady Arbuthnot.

Within a quarter of an hour we were both miraculously clothed, coiffured, and off on our separate ways. She to join the ladies, and thereafter the gentlemen. I in search of the necessary house—which, after so much port, madeira, and other selected vintages, I now discovered that I did in fact most desperately need.

9

The Gothic Ruin: or, My First Assault on Lady Barbara's Virtue

The Arbuthnots' Berkeley Square mansion was a sizable affair. Its massive facade stretched the length of one whole side of the square. Nevertheless, it was a town house, not one of his lordship's country seats, and there was room for no more than a couple of dozen acres of gardens in the rear. Hence I had only a hundred feet or so to traverse to reach the necessary, which was situated at the back of the garden.

A hundred feet as the proverbial crow flies, that is. But the gardens of Arbuthnot House were not laid out as the crow—or any other sane bird—flies. For these were English gardens, designed according to the latest "natural style," and they were devilish places to find your way through in the dark. A cock still swollen with half-satisfied lust and a painfully distended bladder did nothing to sharpen a mind which was—I must confess it—somewhat addled with drink.

So I wandered for a painfully long time along meandering paths and serpentine brooks, among painstakingly patternless groves and through tangles of exotic imported flora that only a trained botanical eye could distinguish from plain English weeds. The same imitation antique statuary, the same quaint garden buildings drifted by me again and yet again—Aphrodite and Bacchus, the Chinese Pagoda and the Grotto, all gleaming in the misty moonlight.

I had given up in despair and had just plunged into a cluster of phlox to answer nature's now undeniable call when my goal loomed up before me at last. I was standing in the very shadow of Lady Arbuthnot's pride and joy, the Gothic Ruin. And there beside it, cunningly concealed in the shrubbery between the Ruin and the back wall of the property, was the necessary house at last.

I emerged, closing my breeches and feeling immeasurably relieved, just in time to hear footsteps on the path.

I rounded the corner of the Gothic chapel and saw a slender white ghost gliding through the blue shadow of a Virginia snow tree. It was a meditative specter, eyes cast down as it drifted along the pathway. But I recognized the slim white silhouette at once.

"Lady Barbara!"

"Why—Lord Christopher, is it not?" She looked up, startled, and the shadow of a smile touched her cheek. "What, still seeking hapless souls to rescue from the Mohocks? The gardens of Arbuthnot House are a less propitious hunting ground than Hog Lane, I think."

"Indeed, madame, I wonder more at your ladyship's risking the night airs so late, and missing the society within."

She made a wry face. "I walk to settle my digestion, sir. And to speak the truth, I was not vastly entertained by that weary round of chatter and scandal that you call society. I am country-bred, you know, in the wilds of Berkshire, and I find your town houses—and your city gossip—a bit steamy and cloying for my taste."

"My sentiments precisely, madame!" I assured her as gravely as I could manage. Considering the mix of wine and passion that still seethed in my belly, and my high excitement at this amazing piece of good fortune, I think I did rather well. "But may I not share your nocturnal promenade, my lady, and discuss the matter further?"

"I should be glad of your company, sir." She smiled. "I hear you are a famous satirist. A touch of wit would be welcome after all that nonsense and Toryism within doors."

And so we fell in step and strolled off beneath the Italian cypresses. I was close enough to hear the rustle of her petticoats, to inhale the freshness of her flesh, and every inch of me responded.

"I have in fact heard much about you since last we met, Lord Christopher," said Lady Barbara as we walked.

"Have you, my lady?"

"Not all of it, I am afraid, has been entirely to your credit."

"Every man has his faults, my lady," I replied uneasily.

"Is it true, for instance, that you have gambled away all but a pittance of the solid legacy your father left you?"

"Alas, my lady—"

"That you are widely known as a 'two-bottle man,' mentioned in the same breath with the lamentable Mr. Pitt and his port-swilling comrados?"

"Alas again—though madeira and not port—"

"And that your name has repeatedly and scandalously been linked, not only with the gayest gay ladies in the town, but with some of the noblest as well?"

"Madame," I said, making an attempt at least to stand upon my dignity, "surely not my worst enemy would aver—"

"I have it on impeccable authority, my lord," she answered serenely. "That of your own card-playing crony, Lord Mortimer Durward."

"Ah," I said.

"I fear, sir, that you are not a man of principle," her ladyship said presently. Her tone was the oddest combination of cheerful frankness and cool disapproval I had ever heard.

"I have no objection to principles, my lady," said I. "Nor any great interest in them either. I am a plain blunt man, madame, with little of the metaphysician in my makeup."

"It is not metaphysics, sir, but plain morality," she began. Then she stopped and laughed and shook her head. "There would seem to be some justification for the unfortunate appellation the patch-eyed gentleman of the road laid upon you that night when we first met. Lord Libertine indeed!"

"Madame," I acknowledged huskily, "you are right. I am a most weak vessel. And yet I flatter myself that I have my virtues too. I am, for instance, a most sentimental man at heart."

"Really, sir?" she responded skeptically.

"Really, madame. Take for example that crumbling medieval structure yonder. Would you believe that I feel a sentimental inspiration in its presence that borders on idolatry?"

Our aimless peregrinations had in fact brought us once more in sight of Lady Arbuthnot's masterwork, the Gothic Ruin. It loomed above us now, a shattered roofless cloister artistically draped with vines. It had been built by the most fashionable architect in England to her ladyship's own specifications. And it did in very fact stir a sudden inspiration in my lecherous heart.

"I must confess, my lord," said Lady Barbara skeptically, gazing up at the naked vine-tangled arch rising against the stars, "that I find it difficult to imagine the heart of Lord Libertine melting at the sight of an artificial Gothic Ruin."

"Ah, but you must look within for the true glories of that vanished age, my lady," I continued eagerly. "If you will but step this way—" With feverish hands I plucked aside the tangle of vegetation which impeded our entrance.

"It is much too dark to see anything of the interior in any case," she objected reasonably enough. But I was not to be put off.

"There is no roof, my lady," I urged. "The moonlight will be bright as day inside." And I slipped my arm about her waist and drew her across the cracked and broken threshold.

"My lord, this is preposterous!"

Her tone was sharp now. I let her go at once—not to frighten, not to disturb the delicate balance of her self-confidence against the obvious perils of her situation. But not to let her go—dear God, no! For my hand and arm still tingled from that first touch of her, my fingers trembled for that warm smoothness beneath her gown.

"You will notice, madame, how perfectly the artisans have captured the medieval charm of that shattered pillar yonder. See how exquisitely they have duplicated the pitting of the centuries in the carving of the altar." I was babbling and I knew it. But as I talked I took her hand and drew her with me across the littered stone floor, deeper into the nave. "Notice the perfection of the simulated decay—"

"Lord Christopher!" She stopped, pulled her hand free of mine. "I have no interest at all in Gothic matters, sir. And less in architectural tours by moonlight at the back of the garden!"

I stopped, crestfallen in my turn, only two steps from my goal.

"Lady Barbara, you are right." My voice was crisp and clear as her own. Indeed, if I may say so, a capacity for instant adjustment to time and tone and circumstance is indispensable for success in affairs of the heart. "It is ridiculous, of course. I must apologize." I raised one blunt-fingered hand to my forehead. "It is Lord Arbuthnot's port, no doubt. Or that French ensign's pistol ball."

"You were in the war, my lord? You scarce look old enough."

"Ah—no. An affair of honor. Half-a-dozen years ago it was. A lady's good name was at stake, you understand. Grazed my temple, no more. It seemed the merest scratch. Yet still it comes upon me from time to time—a foolish giddiness—I must apologize most profoundly—" I swayed, stumbled forward two steps into the shadow of the ruined choir, and collapsed—quite convincingly, I thought—upon the long, low bench that had been my goal since I had glimpsed the Gothic Ruin once again.

She followed me into the darkness. What else could she do? Leave an injured man half swooning, alone in the vast acres of the deserted gardens?

There was, incidentally, a real French ensign. But it was his head, not mine, that was grazed by the pistol ball. Whether he comes over giddy from it now and again I have no knowledge. If so, I wish him well of it. There is something about an old wound, nicely clean and healed over, which the sex can never resist.

Lady Barbara, as I say, stepped into the shadow after me, half knelt upon the bench. She was there beside me at last in the breathing darkness, close enough to touch. I inhaled the fragrance of her, the smell of clean linen and country-fresh skin and of her hair. I saw her slender body bending toward me, silhouetted against the moon-blanched nave behind her. But I had sense enough to restrain myself still.

"You are ill, sir?" she said. "Shall I seek help from the

house?" Her voice was rather unduly calm, I thought, considering my putative condition.

"No, no, my lady. 'Tis nothing. It will pass." I stroked my temple, shook my head groggily.

"Are you feverish, sir?"

She stretched out her hand and pressed it to my forehead. A largish hand, I noticed, with strong competent fingers. Rather less delicate and dainty than the ideal lady of romance should have. But to my inflamed desires, that brief cool pressure was a goad beyond bearing.

"There is some heat there," she said dryly, withdrawing her hand. "But not much, I think."

I groaned and reached up and caught her retreating fingers in my own.

"My lord?"

"My lady—Lady Barbara!" I pressed her hand to my lips and covered it with kisses.

"Lord Christopher!" She rose to her feet, strove to free her hand. But this time I did not let it go. I rose instead in my turn and put one arm around her and pressed her to my bosom.

Well, more or less to my bosom. I still held her right hand prisoner, but she brought the left one up to push vigorously against my chest, twisting from me as she did so.

"O my lady," I whispered, kissing her throat. "Forgive me. I can no longer smother the fires your beauty had kindled in my heart." I pressed her closer, nibbled at her ear. "Surely you must have seen it, my lady. Surely you will have some mercy, give me some reason to hope—"

"Surely you must be mad, sir! Mad or—" My lips advanced too close to hers, and she turned her face away with a grimace of distaste. "Mad or most foully drunk! Release me at once! At once, sir!"

"Oh madame! Feel my fires, my transports! Oh, see what you can do for me!"

"In*deed*, sir!" She gave me a sudden violent shove that sent me staggering back a step. The back of my knees came up against the low stone bench. I lost my balance and sat down suddenly. And she broke free.

"The best thing I could do for you, my lord, is to dispatch you straight to the nearest hackney coach and home. I bid you good night, sir!" She swirled away and strode briskly across the dusty nave toward the entry arch.

I was up and after her in an instant.

"Lady Barbara—have pity!"

"Lord Christopher—have some sense!"

But I knew every inch of the Gothic Ruin intimately, and she did not. I knew how deceptive the place could be. How difficult it was to tell the arched entrance from the blind, vine-laced arches on either side of it. With a step and a gentle pressure of the hand, I now guided Lady Barbara MacFarlane into one of these latter.

Gnarled spines and tendrils caught at her hair, her dress. She reached an impatient hand to sweep them aside and touched cold stone.

"Where the devil have you got me now," she snapped crossly, "with your Gothic nonsense?"

"My lady!" I croaked, pawing after her through the vines. "My Isolde, my Guinevere—"

"*Sir!*"

My groping hand had touched one breast in the darkness. One perfect cone, the faintest suggestion of a nipple through the bunched tulle . . .

Then the butt of her hand came slamming against my chin, her palm hard across my face. It was as much a blow as a push, and delivered with astonishing force for so slim a girl. The thrust of it propelled me backward once again, out of the niche. Reeling back, I slipped on something—an acorn, a pebble, the merest nothing. But I was genuinely dizzy now, dazed with wine and my own passion. I flailed at the air and fell, this time at full length, my head banging painfully against the stone floor.

Stars flashed above me, and two moons oscillated in the sky, blending and parting and blending again into one. I muttered a curse and sat up jerkily, gathering myself for yet another assault. Lady Barbara stood looking down at me, cool and perfect and inviolate still.

"The devil take it!" I said querulously. "My head *does* hurt now!"

In spite of herself, she laughed and stretched out her hand to help me up. "But you *are* such a fool, Lord Christopher!" she said.

"Is he not, my dear?"

The voice was colder than Lady Barbara's, and frosted with contempt. Wincing with pain, I turned my head and saw Caroline, Lady Arbuthnot, standing in the ruined arch.

"Is he not a perfect fool, with his clumsy, brutal attempts at lovemaking? I could never comprehend how any woman of taste and sensibility could surrender to such a bumbling lout myself." But Caroline's eyes were bright with anger, and her voice dripped with a venom that spoke volumes. Volumes in which Lady Barbara, I could see, read easily enough.

"Bumbling indeed, my lady," another all too familiar voice intruded. "He can scarce keep his feet, it seems, so overpowering are his giddy passions. Well, well—I always thought Lord Libertine's prowess was somewhat exaggerated in the telling."

Through the Gothic arch behind Lady Arbuthnot stepped the lean, arrogant, impeccably elegant figure of Lord Mortimer Durward. Even in the shadow of the pitted stone, I could see his thin lips curl in an icy smile.

10

In Which I Begin to Fathom the Depths of Lord Mortimer's Duplicity

Morning in Hanover Square. A more irascible morning than most, full of snarls and disgruntlement. It seemed to me somehow that my mornings had been considerably more irascible than usual since I had undertaken the pursuit of Lady Barbara MacFarlane.

"He did it deliberately, Jeremy!" I complained bitterly, glowering at him over my chocolate. "Brought Lady Arbuthnot there of set purpose, to compromise me before Lady Barbara! Just as he's passed on to her every unsavory tale about me he could cull from coffeehouse gossip, tavern talk, the babble of the bagnios. He's made me out an atheist, a profligate, a sot, a lecher—"

"Quite so," said Jeremy.

"The fellow has no sense of honor," I grumbled, gazing morosely into the fire. "To besmirch a gentleman's reputation thus, before a lady! It is not honorable. It is not gentlemanly. I've half a mind to call him out for it!"

Jeremy, hovering over my toast browning on the grate, made no comment.

"The fellow would do anything to win the damned wager, Jeremy," I insisted. "The man's absolutely obsessed with it. Had you but seen the smile—nay, the leer, the sneer—that suffused that prissy, priggish countenance as he burst in upon us, just as I moved to effect my conquest—"

"I can quite believe it, sir. Considering 'is own lack of success as 'er ladyship's lover."

It took a moment for the words to register. Then I spilled the chocolate down my shirt as I jerked round to confront the little villain.

"*Lord Mortimer?*"

"Lord Mortimer Durward, yes, sir."

"Pray be more circumstantial, Jeremy! Do you say that *Lord Mortimer* was Lady Barbara MacFarlane's lover?"

"*Would 'ave been* 'er lover, sir. And 'er 'usband too, 'ad 'is suit prospered. But your ludship was well enough aware of that, sir?" He looked genuinely startled.

"I was not aware of that, no, Jeremy."

"It was quite the talk of St. Paul's, sir, and White'all as well, I understand. 'E was quite desperate for 'er ladyship's 'and, they say. 'Is ludship's creditors—and 'e 'ad a many of 'em—counted their debts as good as paid, if 'er ladyship could but be brought to the altar. 'Er father the Earl 'as fifty thousand the year from 'is land in Kent and Berks alone. And the lady 'as no brothers."

"So Lord Mortimer sought her hand."

"Most ardently, by 'ook or by crook or by any means. They say 'is ludship's rents will scarce support 'is carriage and six, sir."

"He sought her hand." I sorted it out through the slowly dissolving fumes of the night's dissipations. "And she rejected his suit."

"Most publicly, sir, as I understand it. Spurned him at the Opera, snubbed him in the Park—"

"Yet she speaks quite civilly to him now."

"Yes, sir. They say she cannot abide 'im personally— 'is character, if you take my meaning. But she considers 'is ludship a rare thing in these times, sir—a *man of principle*. She does not share 'is Tory views, of course. But she's been 'eard to say that 'In an age of trimmers and Marcaronis, a man of principles—any principles—is not lightly to be put by.' Besides which, she thinks 'im a poor spirit who, now as 'e knows there can be no match be-

tween them, 'as given over 'is—ah—passion, sir. I 'ave it
from Mr. Walpole's man that she would go with 'im into
any bagnio in the city, and feel quite safe."

Quite safe. Given over his passion.

Suddenly I saw once more the blue-jowled face of Captain Patch in that drizzly alleyway, and heard his words:
'The lady's for 'is lordship 'as pays our wages in this
business. . . .' And how many brides were kidnapped and
brought to the altar *by hook or by crook,* last year alone?

"You were not aware of that, sir, when you accepted 'is
ludship's wager? If I may say so, sir, I felt that that was
the cream of the jest!"

The cream of the jest, my God! *I* was the cream of it!
If Lord Mortimer's bullyboys failed him, I—I should be
the one to execute his vengeance for him! If she would
not have the peerless Durward, then the nefarious Arundel would drag her reputation through the public mire as
no one else in London could! The notorious Lord Libertine could always be depended on to do the dirty work, to
humiliate the proud woman who had dared to spurn Lord
Mortimer Durward!

"Why, the villain!" I said aloud. "The unutterable villain!"

"Yes, sir," said Jeremy. "I'll just fetch the post, sir."
He passed quietly out of the room on his routine chore.
But I could have sworn I heard a dry Cockney chuckle
as he vanished down the hall.

A cat's-paw! I swore silently. A tool in his thin aristocratic hands! For a wager was a wager, and a gentleman's
bond. And I had wagered Lord Mortimer Durward that I
would do his will, accomplish his purposes, and that
within a month. It was insufferable—it was intolerable—
and there was absolutely nothing to be done!

But you are *such a fool, Lord Christopher!* The voice
of Lady Barbara MacFarlane echoed suddenly across my
seething brain. *Gambled away your legacy . . . a two-*

bottle man . . . linked to the gayest gay ladies in the town. . . . The galling phrases tumbled through my mind. And I saw those vivid mocking eyes look down at me once more, as Lady Barbara's strong young hands helped me to my feet, there in the moon-gilded Gothic Ruin.

I could not get them out of my mind, the eyes of this strange, infuriating, totally unprecedented young woman. Gray-green irises flecked with amber. Lashes dark but not particularly long. Straight, frank brows, unplucked and unpainted. A look neither coquettish nor calculating, but steady, honest, unabashed.

A truly terrifying look!

And it was through her that my nemesis had reached me at last! Through this devilish high-principled lady who rejected my advances, passed lofty judgments on my moral character, humiliated me before my hostess. This celebrated lady of Holyrood House, reeking of health and good sense and moral dedication!

Durward and Lady Barbara—Lady Barbara and Durward. Trapped between a devil and a saint, what hope had an honest sensualist?

11

A Message from Mr. Pitt

But there were more strands yet to be woven in the net that was slowly but inexorably enveloping me. Perhaps the most critical of them will be made clear in this, the shortest chapter in this narrative, and in the chapter following, one of the longest. If the reader finds the contents somewhat baffling, he may be assured that he is not alone. I did not believe a word of it myself, even while it was happening to me.

I was glowering over Jeremy's latest bit of evidence concerning my infuriating quarry when he returned with the tray full of envelopes. The evidence in question was a slim political tract from Lady Barbara's own hand. I will call it political, at any rate. I had actually never seen anything like it before in my life.

"*A Declaration of the Rights of Women.*" I read the title page aloud in a petulant tone as Jeremy reentered the room. " 'By a Lady of Quality.' For all her talk of principles, I see she hasn't put her name to it."

" 'Er ladyship's initials are at the conclusion of the Preface, sir," my man responded grudgingly. "She's made no secret of it. Fair proud of it, she is."

I shrugged with undue vehemence and flicked the page. It was the Table. " 'Observations on the State of Degradation to Which Woman Is Reduced.' What the devil is she talking about?"

"I'm sure I don't know, your ludship," Jeremy replied, standing with an air of elaborate and somehow quite unconvincing respect before me, the tray still balanced in one hand.

"And this: 'Reflections on the Moral Improvement That a Revolution in Female Manners Might Naturally Be Expected to Produce.' I am no enemy of the sex, Jeremy, as the world can testify. But I'm damned if I can see what Moral Improvement the world might expect from a Revolution in Female Manners."

"I understand 'er ladyship's logic 'as escaped many, sir."

Indeed, I thought distastefully. Men like Colonel Tolliver and Lord Arbuthnot. Men like Lord Mortimer Durward. I snapped the book shut irritably. Decidedly, I did not like to be forced into such company as Tolliver and Durward!

It was all becoming too unconscionably complicated!

"Cards and the post, your ludship," Jeremy said then,

having waited a discreet few seconds to see if I had any further observations to offer. He placed the silver tray on the small round table at my side. Glad of any distraction, I reached for my usually unutterably dull correspondence with some alacrity.

There were the engraved cards of half-a-dozen visitors whom I had slept through that morning. There was the usual array of duns from impatient tradesmen. And there was an unfamiliar envelope, sealed with red wax and a coat of arms all England knew.

I opened it and stared at the scribbled lines:

Downing Street, August 11th 1792

My dear Arundel,

I should very much like to see you on a matter of considerable urgency. I shall leave instructions to have you admitted *at any time* today or tonight.

Yours,
W. Pitt

The charm, as the Bard has it, was now wound up. My doom, though I did not know it, was firmly and irrevocably sealed.

12

The Nation Imperiled!

Even so apolitical an animal as I am does not ignore a summons from the Prime Minister of England.

I took my time. I spent the afternoon at Lady

Traherne's, supped at the Blue Periwig, idled away an hour at White's. But by ten-thirty that night I was strolling across the deserted Horse-Guards drill ground toward the north side of Downing Street, where Number 10 was located. Before the clock tolled eleven I was admitted to the book-lined, candle-lit study of Mr. William Pitt, First Lord of the Treasury and His Majesty's Prime Minister of State.

"Ah, Arundel!" said Pitt, with as much affability as that unaffable man could ever muster. "Good of you to come. Please do be seated."

I sat.

It was a stiff and formal room, like the man behind the big mahogany desk before me. Latin classics crowded the shelves and lay about on tables. Historians. Plutarch's *Parallel Lives of the Eminent Greeks and Romans*. Pitt had been a notable scholar at Cambridge, it was said.

The years had marked him, I thought, as I watched him clean his quill, cap his ink bottle, and straighten the stack of papers before him. They had called him "the boy statesman" when he took office, almost a decade ago, at the unlikely age of twenty-four. He was in his middle thirties now, my own age. But he was a boy no longer, however much he might seem "the Younger Pitt" to aging Tories who remembered his famous father, the great War Minister Pitt.

"An agreeable night out, is it? I hope I haven't inconvenienced you." He cared not a jot what sort of night it was, and infinitely less whether I had been inconvenienced or not.

William Pitt had been tallish and almost slender once. He was an awkward, ungainly figure now, beginning to put on weight about the middle, going puffy in the face. He wore his hair powdered and was a bit blotchy in the cheeks. He had no mistresses and did not gamble. His besetting vice, all men agreed, was port wine. His besetting passion was fiscal responsibility and economy in government. His greatest terror was that archdevourer of government revenues—war.

"It is an indifferent pleasant evening, sir," I told him. Somehow I always addressed him as one would a considerably older man. "And the stroll has done my digestion more good than another bottle of madeira would, I'm sure."

"Excellent. Excellent. But will you—ah—will you have some port, then?"

"No, thank you, sir." I felt acutely out of place, sitting here at the center of the web of power in England. I thought I had best keep my wits about me.

Pitt nodded briskly. He squared his papers one final time and thrust them primly into a back corner of his desk. Then he swiveled round in his chair, fumbled in a pile of tracts, broadsides, and other ephemera on a long table behind him, and finally swung back to me with a tinted print in one hand—a political caricature by the look of it.

"A Gillray," he said, sliding it across the desk toward me. "Have you seen it?"

"No, sir, I haven't," I confessed, examining it politely.

It was entitled "John Bull's Uninvited Guests, or, Feeding the Kitty," and was done in Gillray's blowsiest, most raffish style.

The center of the print depicted a roly-poly gaggle of little children playing with a couple of scruffy-looking stray kittens. To the right loomed the angular, florid figure of Prime Minister Pitt and the orotund shape of His Majesty King George III, every inch the disapproving elders, looking sternly down at the antics of their offspring. The latter, for all their childish smocks and ribbons, bore the familiar adult faces of Mr. Charles James Fox, the radical Whig; Mr. Wilberforce, the antislavery agitator; the Reverend Dr. Richard Price, whose notorious sermon on the French Revolution had stung Edmund Burke to his even more famous *Reflections* on the subject; and of Lady Barbara MacFarlane, with a tricolor mobcap and a copy of *The Rights of Women* in the pocket of her apron.

The children clustered gleefully about the two kittens, whose collars were inscribed, respectively, "Democratical Clap-Trap" and "The Spirit of Reform." "They're such sweet little Tabbies, Dad!" Fox was explaining to Pitt as he thrust a saucer of milk under one feline nose. "And they'll make such Marvelous Ratters," Lady Barbara chimed in cheerfully, stroking the bristling fur of little Clap-Trap. "You'll see!"

But the kittens were clearly not kittens at all, but lion cubs. And up the path outside the open door on the left their father came padding—a gigantic yellow lion, labeled with a tricolor sash and the single word REVOLUTION.

The message could not have been clearer. Gillray had outdone himself.

"Ah, I said. "I see."

"Yes," Pitt grimaced. "It might better be called 'The Friends of the Revolution, or, Feeding the Fires of Sedition,' I should say."

I grinned and said nothing more. My ignorance of politics is so well-known that I am never put to the trouble of inventing clever things to say where I have no opinions.

"Not," he went on hastily, "that I would abridge the right of any freeborn Briton to express his views. Far from it. I have expressed dissenting views myself in my time, and on the floor of the House too. I cherish the right to dissent, for myself and for us all."

I seemed to remember vaguely that he had spoken out for Parliamentary reform, for abolition of the trade in slaves, even for the rights of Irishmen, some eight or ten years ago. I could not recall that he had done much for these noble causes recently.

"But some of these people, Arundel"—he tapped the print before him with a thin white finger—" some of these people and their friends—the Friends of the French Revolution—are going altogether too far!"

He looked at me sharply for a moment, as if to gauge my response. I had none, and I made none.

"It is one thing," he said then, slowly and portentously, "to express unpopular opinions. It is quite another to indulge in seditious communications with an enemy of the state."

"An enemy, sir?" I blinked as blandly as I dared. "I was not aware that England had an enemy at the moment."

He shrugged irritably and tapped the Gillray etching again, his bright-veined eyes still fixing mine.

"You do not know these people, Arundel," he said. "Paine, Priestly, the Reverend Dr. Price. Even Fox, and this MacFarlane woman with her beastly book. The best of them have simply been taken in. Swept off their feet by the enthusiasms of the hour." I looked at those softening jowls, those veined and disillusioned eyes, and I thought that the King's First Minister was safe enough from the enthusiasms of this or any other hour.

"But there are some among 'em," he continued inexorably, leaning toward me as he spoke, "that are far worse than that. And far more dangerous to this nation."

He paused. He was breathing rather more heavily than he had been, and the nascent strawberry blotches stood out more clearly on his cheeks.

"They have their radical clubs, their pamphlets, and their catechisms. They communicate with each other regularly, Arundel, like those Committees of Correspondence in the American colonies twenty years ago, before the insurrection there. And they communicate directly with their foreign mentors, the Jacobin Clubs in France."

Mentors like Citizen Jacques Machaud, I thought, with some distaste.

"Some of them communicate through the public prints, sir—you'll know who I mean. Some of 'em in person. And some of 'em"—his voice lowered, his eyes glittered more redly still—"in more devious and more dangerous ways.

"These are not inconsiderable persons, Arundel." He stabbed at the Gillray print once more. "Peers of the realm. Preachers. Members of Parliament. Not the sort of people one can proceed against with the—ah—dispatch that one might like. And yet some of them—some of these English Jacobins—are foreign agents pure and simple!"

I like a touch of melodrama as well as the next man. "Perhaps I will take that glass of port after all, sir," I said huskily.

He poured for me. Not, I noticed, for himself.

"What I am about to say, Lord Christopher," he continued slowly as he poured, "is in the strictest confidence. The strictest confidence."

I signified my understanding and waited.

"You declared a moment since," he continued, "that you were not aware that England *had* an enemy. By which I take it you meant that we are not at war."

"You take my meaning quite correctly, sir."

"And so we are not. I pray God that may still be true this time next year."

"As do we all, I'm sure."

"But Austria's at war with France, and Prussia too. And these are uncertain times. Uncertain times."

I agreed that the future was far from sure, and awaited the usual sermon on the sad state of the revenues. But he was not to be distracted from his new obsession.

"This is no time, in short," he said, "for England to be

weak. For the country to be riddled with secret enemies, like a termite-ridden house."

"Surely, sir, no Englishman—" I began as deprecatingly as I could.

"This next and last," he cut me off, "is known only to myself and the Cabinet—and to one terrified clerk in the War Office." He plucked a key from his watch chain, unlocked a small drawer at the right side of his desk, and handed me a hefty yellow packet, unsealed. His hand, I was startled to notice, was shaking slightly as he held it out.

I slid out the sheaf of papers contained in the yellow packet. It was a letterpress copy of some sort of report, written in a professional secretary's hand. The substance of it swam before my eyes as I riffled through the pages.

Eighty-one battalions currently in commission for the defense of the realm—but nineteen assigned for the defense of the West Indies, nine for India, *et cetera, et cetera*. A total of twenty-eight Line Regiments for the defense of Great Britain and Ireland, together with the Cavalry and the Guards. But even of these, many of meager complement, some little more than skeleton regiments. The new recruits of little use. The Militia unpopular—rush for substitutes. Volunteer Associations to be depended on only for local defense and for repressing disorders. Total troops available for the defense of Great Britain by the end of the present year: 17,013 men. . . .

Seventeen thousand men. Had I not heard that the French were mobilizing a hundred thousand troops against the German powers along the Rhine?

"It is a Report," said Pitt, "of the wretched condition of the British Army. It is a Report intended for His Majesty's Cabinet only, to be held in utmost secrecy. And," he added ominously, "the original of it is missing."

"Missing, sir?"

"Stolen from the War Office!" His voice came cracked

and harsh, and higher still. "Stolen almost a week ago, with the express purpose—we are sure of it—of conveying its contents to the French!"

"But who—"

"Some wretched suborned underling in the Department stole it, evidently. But he has gotten it out of the City long since. He has passed this paper on to someone else. Someone who will attempt to convey it out of England and across the Channel at the first opportunity."

"But why not simply carry it out of the country himself?"

A look of irritation crossed Pitt's florid countenance.

"Come, come, Arundel, we are not such fools. As soon as the document's loss was detected, we checked into the whereabouts of every clerk and charwoman who had any possible access to it. No such person has passed through any Channel port, or will be allowed to do so.

"No, the villain must pass it on. Will have passed it on by now, to someone who could take ship for France with ease and without suspicion. To someone who could be prevailed upon as a matter of principle—of *principle,* sir," he emphasized, his mouth twisting with distaste, "to put such a document directly into the hands of Dumouriez or Talleyrand in Paris."

"Surely you do not suspect—"

"I have no alternative, sir," he said stiffly, "but to suspect these people!" He stabbed at the Gillray one last time. "These Friends of the Revolution. These eminently respectable folk, who have made such a habit of crossing the Channel to visit their fellow Jacobins in France, to see how the Utopia of tomorrow is taking shape in the bloodstained streets of Paris today.

"What hapless port official would question the departure of a celebrated statesman like Charles James Fox for foreign parts? Who would dare to search the baggage of a gentleman, sir, or a *lady* even, of impeccable repute?"

Who indeed? I thought. I had never had a bag of mine so much as touched, beyond obsequious eagerness to help my servants carry them on board ship, on any foreign voyage I had ever made.

"It is indeed a most unpleasant situation, sir," I said, sliding the papers gingerly back into the yellow packet. "I am flattered that you should think my advice and counsel in the matter might be of some assistance—"

"It is not your advice and counsel I have called you here for, Arundel." The tone and the look made it painfully obvious how ludicrous this notion was. "It is your more material help I hoped to enlist this evening."

"My help, sir?"

"In my measured judgment, Lord Christopher, you are the perfect man—the only man—who can recover the Army Report before it falls into the hands of our enemies abroad."

"I, sir? I am the—" Surely there could be no worse choice than I in all England for a mission so sensitive and so—political!

"The perfect man, sir," Pitt pursued inexorably.

I was, for once in my life, nonplussed.

"Think, man!" His voice rasped like a schoolmaster with a singularly inept pupil. "No member of this Government, no person known to be beholden to a member of the Government, no Tory in the land, and damned few Whigs can get close to these people now. They draw in upon themselves, these English Jacobins. Profess to see themselves beleaguered, beset on all sides by enemies. Only the most notoriously *nonpolitical* man in England could get close enough to any of 'em to watch, observe—" he hesitated. "—To search even . . ."

My distaste must have showed on my honest Irish features. I have been called many things in my time, but it had never before been suggested that I should take up sneak thievery.

"You must know, sir," I said carefully, "that I am no close confidant of any of these gentlemen. I have not even the honor of many of their acquaintance. And then, there are so many of these Friends of the Revolution. The membership, the leading men in the Radical Clubs even, must number in the—"

"We are aware of that, Arundel. We do not ask you to survey the effects of every radical in England."

"Ah."

"We have our ways of narrowing the range of suspected persons. Closing the circle, you might say, till it includes no more than a handful of names. Three, two, one perhaps. It would only be when this winnowing was accomplished that we would ask for your help in the discreet recovery of the missing document."

"I see." Somehow I was immensely relieved not to be asked for a decision in the matter at once. Not to be asked to "sign anything," as the tradesmen say. Or had I, I thought suddenly, already signed on, simply by sitting there and listening?

Mr. Pitt locked away the yellow packet in his little drawer. The perspiration had dried off his ruddy forehead. His tone was crisp and businesslike once more.

"I shall be in touch with you again, Arundel. Probably within the week."

Then he stopped suddenly and stared at me, his face suffused with genuine alarm.

"But, Arundel—you have not touched your port!"

13

Over the Precipice

The next three days passed like a sluggish stream drifting toward a precipice.

It was the middle of August, and London—fashionable London—was emptying out. Everyone was off to a country seat, or a tour of the Lake Country and the North, or to Bath or Brighton or some newly discovered watering place, to enjoy the sunshine and the sea. The Park was deserted, White's a bore and Brooks's worse, the Opera not worth hissing. I snapped at Jeremy, slept overlong and restlessly, and brooded through the days.

Then, that last night, there came a quickening. The stream of life—if the reader will forgive me—flowed more rapidly. I could hear the roar of the approaching falls.

The lamplit streets of London were loud with streethawkers' cries that night, crowded with jostling mobs and chairs and carriages. Whether it was the madeira in my veins or the brooding thoughts that suffused my brain, the faces that pressed past me seemed uglier and more surly than I had ever seen them.

The Rose Tavern loomed up at last. Old Leather, the waiter, met me smiling at the door and ushered me inside.

"Will ye be seeing Sally Love, sir? Ah, I thought so. It's been a while, sir, but I'll not be forgetting. Nor will she, I'll wager, eh?" He nodded and made shift to wink—a rather grotesque performance, since his eyes were noticeably crossed. "Nor will our Sally indeed!"

The scene within was bedlam, full of smoke and loud

talk and laughter. The girls sat about a splintery table in the center of the room, laughing and jesting, fondling and fumbling in the pockets of two or three intoxicated young gentlemen who sprawled half conscious among them.

"Arun-Arundel!" called one of the latter, striving futilely to sit up, falling back into his chair. "Welcome sir to—to Par'dise!"

It was Danforth, eyes glazed with drink, asprawl in the arms of Sally Love. His coat and shirt were open to the caresses of the girl who bent over him, stroking his naked chest with one hand while with the other she deftly loosened his gold watch from its little chain.

"Your servant, Danforth!" I hailed him cheerfully enough. "And yours, mistress, as well," I added. I took Sally's hand—the one that was so busy about Danforth's watch—and kissed it ceremoniously.

"La, sir!" she protested. 'Ye do me too much honor, good Lord Kit!"

The black girl behind her, the one they called Mrs. Jamaica, laughed richly, showing white, stained teeth. "Ah, Kit's a 'squire, he is," she bleated through her mirth. "Kit knows how to treat an honest girl, don't he, Sally?"

"To be sure he does," Sally smiled freeing her hand from my dampish kiss but giving up on the watch for the moment. "We have not seen ye this year, I think, sir. I hope me lord is not offended wi' us?"

"Quite the contrary, Mrs. Love!" I assured her. "Quite the contrary, I'm sure."

"You want her, Arundel?" Danforth inquired blearily. "Take her, take her, sir, my compl'ments! But see—see here—the treat we are to have. Ar'tine—Aretine's to do her p-postures!"

And so she was. The most celebrated posture woman in Drury Lane was even then slipping off her stockings. Her loose gown showed no underclothes at all beneath the open bodice. Leather was just bringing in the great pewter tray upon which she would perform. It would not be long before we would have a treat indeed.

Things moved still more rapidly after that, blurring into a flickering stream of sensations, bombarding all my senses.

There was the smell and sweetish taste of gin. A great deal of gin. There were the fantastic poses of the unbelievable Aretine. Then there was a stairway swaying under a pair of legs that more or less obeyed my orders, a low room with bricks showing through the plaster, and a bed that creaked and sagged alarmingly as Sally's strong arms lowered me down upon it. After that, for a time, there was Sally only. My old Sally, that knew more ways to wake a dead-drunk man to pleasure than any highborn wanton in Pall Mall.

Through a greenish haze I watched her fold my clothes with some care as she hung them over the chair beside the cold hearth. Watched with a sigh but no protest as she removed my own pair of watches and secreted them somewhere about the fireplace. I did not see where, for the green haze thickened sometimes so that I could not see at all. Then Sally dropped her dress and came over to the wretched bit of ticking that served her for a bed.

There was none like Sally Love. I lay there staring glassily up at the drifting ceiling, and felt her fingertips graze and stroke and stroke and graze. Her hands, her hair, her mouth. Till I was awake once more, and aflame with desire. Till I caught her up by a tangle of slatternly hair and rolled her over and came down upon her, foaming like a stallion for my Sally Love.

We coupled three times to my memory. And the last time at least, her mouth was open too, spewing joyful blasphemies that more than matched my own.

The next clear memory I have is of reeling homeward through the midnight streets. The narrow lanes were empty now, save for the snoring drunkard, the scuttling footpad, the yellow curling fog of London. Now and again a shout, a savage drunken laugh, a sudden scream, unexplained and probably unexplainable, split the blackness. And then the cobbles would rise beneath me and crash excruciatingly against my battered knees.

Then at last, thanks to the benevolent providence that cares for such cases, I found myself in my own front hall. A single lamp lit poor Jeremy in shirt and nightcap, trying urgently to tell me something. More than one thing, it seemed, and all of the utmost importance. But the reek of London was strong upon my shirt and breeches, and my head shuddered to the forge blows of some nightmarish invisible blacksmith. I wanted only to collapse on the Turkey carpet at my feet—and sleep.

Instead, I held a letter in my hand. Jeremy's nimble irritated fingers were tearing it open, cracking the great red-wax seal. And I was reading meaningless words in a familiar precise penmanship:

Downing Street, August 14th 1792

My dear Arundel,

With regard to our pleasant conversation of the 11th, I regret to inform you that the mutual friend of whom we spoke on that occasion has *already departed the kingdom,* apparently en route to Paris.

I trust, however, that if you take the packet boat in the morning you will be able to overtake the *Lady Barbara MacFarlane, of Holyrood House, Berks,* at Calais, or as soon thereafter as possible. I depend upon you to carry out the commission we discussed, *vis-à-vis* this impetuous young woman, with discretion and dispatch.

I am, sir,

Yours,
W. Pitt

"The packet boat in the morning!" I mumbled, crumpling up the paper disgustedly and staggering against the nearest swaying wall. "Man's mad. A gen— A gennelman mus' have a decent night's sleep." I had something like two days in mind.

"That's the *other* matter, sir," said Jeremy, more petulantly still. "There are these two—gentlemen—to see you, sir. They insist they are here, with a coach and six, to see you to the morning boat at Dover!"

"Dover? But Dover's six—eight hours—"

"I realize that, your ludship. They say the boat will be stayed until we come."

"Impossible!" I straightened my shoulders and did my owlish best to look the picture of virtuous indignation. "And just who—who are these gentlemen that are so insistent?"

Jeremy looked sniffily over his shoulder, and I followed his gaze, focusing for the first time on the firelit interior of my parlor. There, standing to rigid attention between me and my own warm fireplace, were two strapping young fellows in the uniform of officers of His Majesty's Navy.

"The boat will be held, sir," the youngest of these unreal apparitions snapped with crisp authority. "But the sooner we set out the better. May we be of service with your packing?"

I remember nothing more.

BOOK II

Château d'Eauville

14

Well Met in a Heathen Land

I saw Lady Barbara MacFarlane next by moonlight in the shadow of the Gothic cathedral at Amiens. Once more, a milieu made for tender avowals and passionate exchanges. Once more, I failed to seize the time.

I glimpsed the cathedral first from the dusty highway, a gray mass huddling above the steep-roofed houses of that ancient provincial city. Then our hired coach was in the narrow streets themselves, and I lost sight of the great twin towers, the spire above the crossing. There were only the more homely and domestic sights and smells and sounds of that part of Picardy.

The shadows of the summer evening were settling fast. The moon was just emerging above the housetops as we swung into the courtyard of the little inn on the Place Notre Dame, the central square of Amiens.

There, looming vast across the eastern side of the *place*, was the cathedral once again. A huge pile of weathered stone, all crockets and finials and dim statuary, it dwarfed the houses, the chestnut trees around the square, and the inn itself.

The coachman and postilion we had engaged at Calais saw to the stabling and feeding of the horses. Jeremy unpacked a few things in our candle-lit chamber and began the usual inquiries as to whether *une dame anglaise* had passed that way recently. And I set out to stretch my legs with a stroll in the cool of the evening.

The Place Notre Dame of Amiens was named for the

cathedral and dominated by it, and it was inevitably toward this massive relic of the past that I walked. I proceeded at a leisurely pace, squinting idly up at the moon-gilded Gothic spires overhead. I paused for a moment in front of the central portal, gazing up at the colossal images of medieval kings with which the west front was liberally garnished. There was a melancholy tone to the moonlight on that ancient stone that I found quite touching on an empty stomach.

"So your passion for things Gothic does in fact go beyond artificial ruins, Lord Christopher!"

I started and turned. Another figure stood in the shadow of the west front, contemplating the cathedral by moonlight. A slender girl with a cool, crisp voice and gleaming auburn hair.

"Lady Barbara! Well met in a heathen land!"

"A heathen land, sir? And by what right does a confessed libertine condemn the French for heathens?"

"A slip of the tongue, madame, for which I hasten to apologize. The French are the finest cooks in Europe, and the acknowledged arbiters of fashion. The people that invented champagne, *boeuf bourguignon,* and the new transparent bodices surely sit close to the right hand of God!"

"The right hand of *that* God, sir?" Lady Barbara glanced up at the great stone figure of the *beau Dieu d'Amiens*, dimly visible above the central portal, magisterially grinding a lion and a dragon underfoot. "Or of some pagan divinity of your own devising?"

I shrugged. "There must be some deity somewhere to reward such national genius. May all good Frenchmen be rewarded in a Mahometan paradise with flowers and fine wines and beauteous *houris* for the blessings they have conferred upon mankind!"

She did not respond to my sally. She raised her eyes

still further, to the solemn parade of kings across the vast facade, far above us in the darkness.

"There are twenty-two of them," she said after a time. "And that but a fraction of the kings that have reigned over this land since Charlemagne."

"Fascinating, madame," I replied, mildly surprised at her interest. "*Sic transit gloria mundi*, as the prophet says."

She turned upon me once more, her green eyes flashing in the darkness.

"Has it crossed your mind, sir, that the last king that will ever reign in France may be sitting in the Tuileries this minute? That the reign of crowned and sceptered tyranny may be ending all over Europe now, in our own time, and beginning in this nation—?" She checked herself, shrugged her slim shoulders, and twirled the light silk parasol swinging in her hand. "But I forget myself, sir," she said dryly. "You are the man who is not concerned with politics or principles or the fate of nations. Let the heavens fall, so there be ale at the Beefsteak Club, and a play at Drury Lane!"

"Madame, I must protest! A *good* play, please! I should not turn my gaze from the fall of empires for anything less than Sheridan, or Goldsmith—"

She sighed, and a smile flickered across the pale oval of her face. "Will nothing compel you to take life seriously, Lord Libertine?"

"Perhaps, my lady, if I might have the pleasure of escorting you back to your inn, you could yourself accomplish that laudable enterprise. An inspired word or two, they say, may do wonders with the most unregenerate sinner."

"My lord, all the words in Dr. Johnson's dictionary would not suffice to work the miracle of your conversion. Yet I will accompany you, since unless I am mistaken my inn is the same as your own."

"Surely some deity somewhere smiles upon me, madame! And may I venture further still, and ask if even such diametric opposites as we two might share a late supper at the *table d'hôte* this night? We shall have roast duck and a fricandeau of veal, I understand, with cucumbers and mushrooms."

"Very well, Lord Libertine." She chuckled. "I shall surrender to your Epicurean code. Thus far," she added, "and no further. Roast duck and fricandeau of veal it shall be."

"And a mushroom, madame?"

"And a mushroom too, sir. But there I draw the line!"

I bowed and offered her my arm, and we strolled back together toward the inn.

I had been three days in France—familiar enough ground to me from many an earlier visit—but I still felt vaguely astonished at finding myself so suddenly translated from the familiar purlieus of Hanover Square and St. James's to this foreign strand.

Prime Minister Pitt's emissaries had been as good as their word. They had dumped me into a closed carriage and, driving post all night, had got me to Dover by midmorning. The Dover-to-Calais packet boat had indeed been kept waiting—much to the vexation of the other passengers—and the afternoon cross was uneventful. Or so Jeremy had informed me. I had spent most of those first hectic twenty-four hours sleeping off the debauches of the night before.

The following morning we had engaged an open berlin to take us south to Paris, on the track of Lady Barbara MacFarlane.

I was still quite unclear as to exactly what I was doing in France. My first impulse, on awakening in my room at Dessin's Hôtel d'Angleterre in Calais, had been to shout for Jeremy and take passage on the next boat back to Do-

ver. But fragrant black French coffee and delicate crois-
sants, served by a charming *fille* of the house, had done
much to soothe my sense of outrage at Pitt's high-handed
treatment. And when Jeremy brought word that Lady
Barbara MacFarlane—*la belle Anglaise* as M. Dessin
described her—had departed only the day before on the
road to Paris, my mind was quickly made up.

The most beautiful woman in the world was not to be
let go for a mere matter of affronted dignity and minis-
terial highhandedness. Whether her ladyship had in fact
purloined any documents, what precisely I should do
when I overtook her, I did not know. But by God, I
would overtake her!

Three days later I found myself walking across the
Place Notre Dame in Amiens with her ladyship upon my
arm. Walking, though I did not know it, straight into yet
more of those misfortunes which seemed to dog my footsteps from the first moment that I ever clapped eyes upon
the lady of Holyrood House.

15

Captain Patch Again

We entered the innyard in silence. High dark walls
loomed on one side, the black maw of the stables on the
other. Ahead, the warm firelit windows of the inn beck-
oned. We proceeded cautiously in the thicker darkness,
working our way gingerly around a crumbling fountain in
the center of the courtyard.

Suddenly Lady Barbara stopped and cocked her head
toward a row of coaches lined up along the stable wall.

"That is my carriage yonder," she said in a low, steady

voice. "And unless I am much mistaken, there is someone in it."

I picked out the heavy post chaise at the front of the rank. There did indeed seem to be a sudden movement, a muttered exclamation from within. I started toward it. Lady Barbara's hand caught at my arm.

"Wait, sir! It may be a—"

It was.

Even as she spoke, a man flung open the carriage door and lunged toward us. Two others burst from hiding behind the vehicle, brandishing weapons. And a fourth, a small, hunched figure, hurtled with a muffled shout off the top of the coach itself.

"We've got 'er this time, Cap'n!" a familiar voice hissed in muted eagerness as the pocky-cheeked man in the red greatcoat lunged for Lady Barbara MacFarlane.

"Aye, lads," rumbled a huge ill-shaven rogue with a black patch over his eye, as he thundered down upon me. "But *quiet*'s the word, mates, quiet and quick, or we'll 'ave an inn full of Frenchies on our backs!"

I sidestepped Captain Patch's bull-like rush, and the sheer force of it carried him past me and over the edge of the dilapidated stone fountain to disappear with a mighty splash in the waist-deep water.

"Noo then, your lairdship," the lean, narrow-faced Scotsman called Figgis began, "I'll hae a word wi' ye mysel', since I see ye've left your sword cane safe beyond the Channel!" He leaped for me like a ferret, his long dirk gleaming in the moonlight. But I caught him with a stiff right hand that sent him rolling on the hard-packed earth, his blade flying off into the night.

A crack and a howl next drew my attention to the chunky redcoated fellow—called Fag, as I remembered—who had lunged for Lady Barbara. He was there, all right—reeling backward, clutching at his ear, roaring with pain as the slender girl laid her furled umbrella furiously across the side of his head.

"Have you got me then, you rogue!" she taunted him. "By God, I do not think so!"

I felt a flash of exultation, a flush of triumph mounting to my cheeks. We were doing splendidly. And there were only four of them this time. Which reminded me—a moment too late—to wonder where the little hunchback might be.

"On 'em, then, Trip!" growled Patch, breaking the surface of the fountain with a splash and a roar behind me.

I had scarce time to wonder bemusedly just how the diminutive Trip might be expected to bring down such a solid-built man as I am, when a manure fork came swinging out of nowhere at my face. I leaped back, protecting my face with my forearm, tripped over the edge of the fountain myself, and went over backward into the brackish waters.

When I floundered to my feet, wiping the slime and froth from my eyes, all was transformed.

Crookbacked little Trip, balancing on the side of the fountain, immediately clapped two pistols to my head. "I 'ave 'im, Cap'n, I do indeed!" the shrunken gargoyle crowed. "One move, and I'll blow 'is brains to the devil!" Patch himself grinned brutally—a gold tooth glittered—and laid his naval short sword across my Adam's apple.

Beyond his hairy ear I saw that Lady Barbara too was faring ill indeed. Fag had her spread-eagled across a carriage wheel, one fat sluglike hand upon her throat. With the other he was tearing open the bodice of her gown!

"Inside the corsets, Fag!" called Captain Patch, a leer suffusing his heavy, unprepossessing countenance. "They'll all keep valybles in their stays these days. But gently, mind—gently! 'Is lordship will not 'ave 'er 'armed!"

I heard a woman's strangled cry, the sound of tearing

fabric—and then a croaking chuckle. "This 'un keeps naught in 'er corsets, Cap'n!" called Fag. "She 'as no corsets on!"

Patch and Trip would not have been human if they had not turned their heads.

With a single sweep of my arm I sent Trip caterwauling in his turn into the water. One of his barkers discharged itself into the air with a tremendous report as he vanished into the murky depths. Meantime I struck up Captain Patch's sword blade, vaulted out of the fountain, and charged for Fag, who now stood grinning down at Lady Barbara, half swooning at his feet, her gown torn open to the waist.

I scooped the fat rogue off his feet and flung him squealing into a horse trough a dozen feet away. Then, hearing a heavy tread behind me, I locked both hands into a single massive fist, swung round, and clouted Captain Patch full in the face. He went over backward into a tangle of pitchforks and buckets and other hostler's gear.

The little villain Trip was just emerging from the fountain, blowing like a whale, and Figgis had recovered his dirk and was coming for us in his turn. But Lady Barbara, who had either been feigning altogether or else possessed remarkable powers of recuperation, was rising too—with a pitchfork in her pale, determined hands. *By God*, I swore once more, *but we have the rascals now!*

I had scarce thought it when a shot crashed out and a ball went whistling past my ear.

I froze in my tracks.

The inn door was open, and lanterns were dancing toward us through dark. There were shouted questions: "*Qu'est-ce qui se passe? Qu'est-ce qui arrive là?*"

I caught the unmistakable Irish accents of the faithful Bridget: "My lady—O my lady, are you killed then?"

And then a second English voice, even more well-known, much hated, and totally unexpected here: "Lady Barbara! We shall be there momently!"

I heard Patch lurch to his feet and hiss an urgent order to his band, and Fag cursing as he extricated himself from the splintered water trough. I made a grab for Figgis as he bolted past me, heading for the innyard gate, and let go an oath or two myself as he vanished into the night.

A second shot crashed out.

"Hold, you villain," called Lord Mortimer Durward, "or I'll drop you where you stand!"

"Durward!" Lady Barbara called, clutching her tattered bodice across her bosom. "Lower your pistol, sir! It is Lord Christopher. Our real assailants are escaping!"

"Nay, madame—have escaped, I think," I sighed disgustedly, knocking water out of one ear. "Thanks to his lordship's timely intervention." For Fag and Captain Patch had faded into the darkness after Figgis, and I knew that Trip had slipped out of the fountain and melted into the night as well.

"Thanks to my intervention, sir?" said Durward testily, stepping out of the cluster of inn servants and gawking guests who now grouped around us with flickering lanterns and a gabble of eager protestations. He was impeccable as usual, not a hair of his powdered periwig out of place, a double-barreled pistol drooping languidly from one hand. "Come, come, Arundel. I've just saved your life, I think!"

"My lady!" wailed Bridget, clasping her ladyship in a tearful embrace. "Are you hurt, ma'am?"

"Lord Mortimer." said Lady Barbara, setting her distracted maid firmly to one side, "justice requires that even the devil have his due. It was Lord Christopher who saved my honor, sir. And indeed, between the two of us, I think we had the scoundrels well enough in hand well before you intervened."

Durward's response was smooth and perfect.

"I am sorry, sir," he said, bowing with just the proper

touch of condescension, "if I have done your—ah—gallantry an injustice. I am sure your well-known skill at such knockabout play was more than equal to the occasion." He scarcely sniffed at "knockabout play" at all.

I longed to knock him down, to call him out, to do for him at last. Instead, I turned a cool shoulder on him in my turn, and spoke to Lady Barbara.

"I regret, madame, that this affair has deprived me of your company for supper. May I hope, however, that if your ladyship is sufficiently recovered by morning, we may perhaps breakfast together before departing?"

She turned gray-green eyes full of innocence toward mine. Her auburn hair was a sweet tangle about her bare white shoulders. The bruises upon her lovely throat showed clearly in the lantern light, and the hand that held her ruined gown together across her breasts was trembling very slightly. Yet she smiled as sweetly as if she were presiding over tea in her own drawing room.

"My dear Lord Christopher, I am sure Lord Mortimer and I will be happy to join you for *supper*, as soon as you please. I doubt if it will take me longer to change to a fresh frock than you will require to find dry clothing for yourself!"

In point of fact, she was half through her soup before I could get back to the dining room.

16

In Which Sundry Motives Are Superficially Explored

"Tell me, my lady," I asked, "what is it that brings you into France in such tumultuous times as these?"

I was breakfasting with his lordship and my lady at a

table under a shady chestnut tree outside the front door of our inn, overlooking the Place Notre Dame. It was a sunny morning, with twittering birds in the branches overhead, and peasants in pantaloons scurrying about the square. Across from us, old women in shawls drifted in ones and twos into the cathedral.

"Tumultuous times, sir?" replied Lady Barbara. "I see no tumults."

"Not here in the provinces, madame, I grant you. Though we have passed soldiers enough on the roads. But they say in Calais that the fighting has broken out again upon the Rhine frontier, that there is more bloody work in the streets of Paris—"

"They say a great many things!" the girl snapped, looking me straight in the eye. "I am weary of hearing what 'they say' in Calais—in London—everywhere. Wearied unto death of slanderous rumors, sir! The only way to *know* what is going on in Paris is to go and see. And that is precisely what I propose to do!"

Her eyes held mine with that straight, unblinking gaze that had such a power to intimidate me. I smiled at her as winningly as I might and turned my attention to her unlikely traveling companion, whose purpose in following her to France I could only too clearly guess.

"And you, sir?" I asked Lord Mortimer. "Surely so staunch a Tory as yourself can have no desire to challenge the common tale—that the Revolution is expiring in civil and foreign war?"

"You are quite correct in that assumption, Arundel," that impeccable conservative responded. "I should like nothing better than to see the whole insane adventure come to a sanguinary end. But you are quite *in*correct— as usual—in your suggestion that I would rather live with comforting illusions to that effect than face harsh realities. *If* the revolutionary regime should be on the brink of collapse, no man will be quicker than I to cheer. But staunch adherence to firm principles does not exclude the love of truth. Like Lady Barbara, I go to see for myself!"

It was remarkable how Durward could turn the simplest statement into a sermon. The Church of England lost a noble ornament, and society at large gained an unspeakably sanctimonious bore, when Mortimer Durward opted for the secular life.

"Lord Mortimer and I have had our disagreements and misunderstandings in the past," Barbara MacFarlane explained in clipped tones, "personal as well as political. But we *are* both people of principle, I think. And we both long to know the truth about the great events in Paris these last years. So we have resolved to travel there together, to look with what objectivity we may, and to see for ourselves."

She spoke as calmly as though she were referring to a stroll down to Hyde Park to see what *they* were wearing this season. I recalled to mind tales of heads on pikes and hapless *aristos* hanged from lampposts by the howling mob. I tried to remember what I had heard of the ingenious new device for beheading men mechanically we had all heard so much about—"Dr. Guillotin's invention," as it was called in horrified whispers everywhere. And this slender, stiff-necked, unconscionably self-assured young woman was resolved to see for herself!

I sat at my ease under the ancient chestnut tree, gorging myself on crusty rolls, blackberries and cream, and scalding black coffee. I was actually feeling quite smug myself.

For I had already accomplished my prime goal for that morning, and that quite casually, at the outset of our conversation. I had simply suggested that, since we were so happily if *unexpectedly* come together, we might travel on together in company. We should thus save the expense of two carriages, multiply our strength against brigands or other hazards of the road, enjoy each other's society, *et cetera*.

I had other, more reprehensible motives, of course. For I had been up quite late the night before, devising and conceiving. The hunt was on again, the fair quarry full in sight. And none of it had anything at all to do with misplaced War Office documents, or the future of the Revolution in France!

Lady Barbara, then, had agreed to my proposal most willingly. Lord Mortimer had assented with as sour a grace as I can remember, even from him. And I, this fundamental goal thus easily accomplished, sat back on my rustic bench, dabbed my lips with a spotless *serviette*, and talked complacently of other matters.

"And you, Arundel?" Durward's voice rasped unpleasantly against my ears. "What is it that brings *you* to France at such an—ah—unpropitious time?"

I looked at him, saw him gazing blandly back. I felt Lady Barbara's eyes upon me now as well. And I began to think very fast indeed.

"Why, what would bring any man to Paris, Durward?" I chuckled, laying on my broadest Irish grin. "The *Comédie*, the *Opéra*, the races! The wines! And the food, Durward, food fit for the gods!" I smacked my lips. "The galleries, music! Some of the finest faro tables in Europe! What else, eh?" I winked, implying further dimensions of pleasure not mentionable in present company.

Lord Mortimer's slightly protuberant eyes fixed uncomprehendingly on mine. I could see sheer disbelief breaking across Lady Barbara's face. I spread my hands and smiled.

"It is a pleasure trip for me, sir. Pleasure pure and simple!"

"Then this is not the country for you, I think," rasped a half-familiar voice from somewhere just behind my left shoulder. "The new France is no longer a playground for gentlemen of pleasure."

I turned in my seat and beheld the dark, intense face of Citizen Jacques Machaud.

Lady Barbara was the only one of the three of us who was not startled. "Durward," she inquired tranquilly, "you remember Monsieur Machaud? Pardon, *Citoyen* Machaud. You met in London, I believe."

"And again in Calais, madame," said Durward stiffly, "as he was leaving your own apartments, I believe." He bowed curtly. Machaud responded with equal coldness. They reminded me of nothing so much as a pair of fighting cocks stalking each other around the ring.

Then Citizen Machaud turned to me.

"And this," said Lady Barbara diplomatically, "is Christopher Arundel, whom you may also recall from London. He too proposes to visit Paris—though for reasons quite unconnected with politics."

"I remember *Milord* Arundel quite clearly," said Machaud. He spoke the fatal *milord* with a cold contempt, the contempt of the dedicated Jacobin for aristos everywhere. I would have been just as happy if he had not remembered me so clearly, somehow.

Once again, as in the gilded splendor of Lady Arbuthnot's ballroom, I felt a nasty chill at the sight of this stocky, dark-complexioned Frenchman with the hot, impatient eyes. He looked downright portentous, standing there in the square at Amiens, one hand behind him, the other spread across his belly in the familiar politician's pose. He was clearly about to make a speech.

"I should like to welcome you all to France," he began stiffly. "For the sake of Citoyenne MacFarlane, a true citizen of the world." He bowed very slightly in her direction. "Citoyenne MacFarlane, whose voice was so eloquently raised on behalf of the Rights of Man in your own country during my brief visit there. Who was so kind a hostess to me, a stranger in your land."

Lady Barbara nodded and smiled faintly in response.

"For her sake, I should *like* to welcome you—but I cannot do so." Machaud's forehead ridged, the skin glistened drum-tight across his cheekbones. He was the embodiment of stern republican virtue. "Instead, I must urge you to terminate your stay in France as soon as possible, and to return to Engalnd with all dispatch. If you stay on, it will be at your own risk. And that risk, I must warn you, is a very substantial one indeed."

Lady Barbara looked up quickly. "But surely, Citizen Machaud, the traditional hospitality of the French—we have been most warmly and courteously received thus far—"

"I regret, Citoyenne MacFarlane, that neither the natural courtesy of our nation nor your own high reputation among us can guarantee even your security much longer. Let alone that of your traveling companions. Especially in Paris, *citoyenne*, you will find things much changed. The righteous indignation of my people boils very close to the surface now."

"My dear Monsieur Machaud!" protected Durward. "Certainly you can't expect us to turn right round and return to Calais!"

"That is precisely what I should advise. Or at the very least, to give Paris a wide berth and take ship perhaps at Le Havre. As soon as possible, sir."

"Ridiculous." Durward sniffed. "Is France surrendered into the hands of bandits and riotous mobs, then, that the safety of peaceful travelers cannot be assured? What are things come to, when a uniformed officer of the French Army tells us we are not safe upon the roads of France?"

"It is not I who warn you, sir!" Machaud's voice rose sharply. "It is the French people!" He leaned upon the breakfast table and slammed a white-knuckled fist between the plates and coffee mugs. "The French people, sir, who have been put upon so long—who will be put upon no longer!"

Now, I do not like to be harangued. And I was beginning to think that Citizen Machaud was as insufferable a prig as Lord Mortimer was. Yet I am a peaceful man when my Irish temper is not roused; hence I sought now to smooth the waters a bit. For Machaud's olive skin was actually pale, and Durward's bulging eyes were veined dangerously with scarlet.

"Gentlemen, if you please," I murmured. "There is a lady present. Surely this is not the place for politics. Let us complete our breakfast—I hope Citizen Machaud will join us?—and then over more coffee, and perhaps a pinch of snuff—"

"I have not time to break my fast, *monsieur le milord*," snapped the Jacobin, "nor any intention of lolling here over coffee, or dulling my head with snuff. We Frenchmen have other work to do in the world! I must continue on to Paris on the people's errand."

I saw his chaise behind him now, the other side of the chestnut tree. The horses were lathered already, at mid-morning. I wished fervently he would return to his carriage and be gone.

"But I warn you once again that you go in peril of your lives if you go on." He was back in his oratorical posture again, one hand spread across his belly, one leg slightly advanced. "The people of this country have suffered much from your sort, *monsieur le milord*"—he seemed to be focusing all his wrath upon me now, rather than upon Durward—"and the time has come for vengeance!"

Suddenly Machaud raised his hand, fumbled inside his coat, and flourished a printed handbill in front of us.

"Have you seen this?" he demanded angrily. "This declaration from the *soi-disant* Duke of Brunswick, that commands the German mercenary troops gathered upon our frontiers? Have you seen the insolent threats and menaces he dares to offer to the new regime—to the whole French nation?" He fumbled out a piece of paper—a formal proclamation of some sort—and began to read aloud:

" 'That if the least violence be offered, the least further outrage be done their majesties the king and queen—I shall inflict upon those who deserve it the most exemplary and ever-memorable avenging punishments, by giving up the city of Paris to military execution and exposing it to total destruction. . . .'

"The people of Paris have read this insult to the nation, sirs—and they have answered it! On ten August last—not a week ago—the Tuilleries was attacked, Louis' Swiss Guards put to the sword, Louis Capet himself imprisoned in the Temple!"

He flung the paper down upon the table. "We shall never accede to such impudence, sirs! And we shall have our vengeance for it on the Austrians, the Prussians—" His voice sank to a hoarse whisper. "We may even come to London one day soon, and have a word about it!"

Then he turned upon his heel and stalked off across the square toward his waiting carriage. Jeremy, coming from the stable, stepped aside to let him pass, then came on over to the table under the tree, looking puzzled and suspicious.

"Was there something in the food, then, sir," he inquired anxiously, "as made the gentleman ill? 'E looked as if 'is stomach 'urt 'im something ferocious, sir."

Lady Barbara looked acutely unhappy, Lord Mortimer muttered about infernal insolence, and I enjoyed the first hearty laugh I had had that day.

17

In Which the Most Beautiful Woman in the World Steps into My Snare

Lady Barbara fell quite easily in with the next step of my insidious scheme. Indeed, Lord Mortimer himself provided me with precisely the opening I needed to set my complot in motion. He could not have served my ends more perfectly if he had been my sworn confederate instead of my dedicated foe.

But I approached the matter slowly and deviously. I began by allowing most of the day to pass before undertaking anything beyond that first simple agreement to travel on in company.

It was a pleasant ride, all things considered.

There was room for six on the leather seats of our berlin, and more than space enough in the wicker rack at the rear for their baggage on top of ours. The five of us fitted in quite comfortably, the two parties facing each other. Bridget's potato-plain Irish face was set in her usual expression of dyspeptic disapproval. Jeremy kept squinting back into the baggage rack to see that the Frenchies had not "done something" to the bags at the last post change. Lord Mortimer pointedly ignored me (and of course the servants) and spoke only to Lady Barbara. Lady Barbara spoke cheerfully enough to everyone. But her mind was clearly on what was to come, on the world of high principles in action that awaited us in the Paris of the Jacobins.

Meantime, the dark forest of Chantilly closed about us

as we rolled south through Picardy. Green aisles of oak
and elm and beech spread out on either hand, and luxuri-
ant summer foliage sometimes brushed the swaying coach
itself. Rich moist smells of pine needles and damp earth
and scattered wild flowers filled our nostrils. It was dark,
mysterious country now. Romantic fairy-tale country, that
drew the mind away from the real world into a twilight
realm of fantasy.

My fantasies, as usual, were all under the patronage of
Eros.

She sat across from me, gazing into the woods beyond
the open window, conversing casually with Lord Mortimer. From time to time she exchanged a word with
Jeremy, who did not seem to be thawing in his attitude
toward the Judith of the Jacobins. I rested my head upon
the brocaded back of the seat, affecting to drowse.
Beneath lowered lids I devoured her beauty at my leisure,
mile after delectable mile.

For many minutes I could not take my eyes off one
particularly vulnerable spot at the base of her throat. It
was a tiny pulse in the hollow where the clavicles met.
The skin seemed unbelievably smooth and tender there. I
imagined how that skin would feel under my caressing fingertips, beneath my lips. I could practically feel that slow
pulsing beat quicken under my mouth.

My eyes drifted downward, stroking her breasts and the
curve of her stomach under the close-fitting gown. I
paused in delightful titillation before the mysteries
concealed by so many layers of skirts and petticoats. I
gazed enraptured at the elegant shoe tips protruding from
beneath her gown.

And then back up again my eyes would wander. I
remembered her face beneath my drunken kisses that
night in the Gothic Ruin. The palm of my hand tingled
once more to the firmness of her breast, the swelling of a

nipple beneath the stiff white tulle. I even recalled with perverse pleasure the thrust of her hand against my chest, the jarring impact of her palm across my face, shoving me backward, rolling me ignominiously out upon the cold stone floor.

I should not be so foolish again. Never again so crude and boorish, groping and clutching in the dark. I must have been delirious with wine and desire to attempt so violent an assault at all, I told myself. Henceforth I should proceed with subtlety and sophistication to my end.

By this time, what with the swaying of the coach and the closeness of the unheeding object of my desire, I was in a truly lamentable state of excitement. My palms were sweating, my cock swollen painfully in the tight fashionable breeches. I decided I should do better to join in the conversation after all.

Lady Barbara was talking about her childhood in the wilds of Berkshire. Country fully as wild as this, but very different in kind, she assured us. Open downland, where you might walk all the afternoon and never see a tree. Fens and marshes along the river. Sheepwalks most of it still, though her father had labored mightily to turn it into flourishing croplands. She touched lightly upon some of his experiments in crop rotation and the use of fertilizing agents.

"He sounds an interesting sort, the Earl," I offered with an effort, trying manfully to focus on legumes and seed drills and new sorts of plows.

"*Eccentric* is the word most commonly used to describe him," she responded, smiling. "Few have such faith as he in turnips, or the Herefordshire wheel drill. He was something of a byword among the country gentry when I was a girl. Even the plowboys would laugh at his agricultural follies over their evening ale at the village tavern. None of it made the slightest difference to him, of course." Her face softened, remembering.

"And were his experiments successful?" I inquired politely.

"The turnips worked out quite well. The wheel drill, with seed- and manure-hopper appended, was a disaster."

"Ah," I said. "But then, an average of fifty percent in such experimental matters is not to be sneezed at, I think."

"He didn't really care, you know. He did it for the excitement of it. He loved to try new things. Still does, though he's past sixty now, and kept indoors much of the time by gout and rheumatics. He still hopes his investigations will benefit the county. And he still doesn't care a ha'penny that they chuckle over their ale about 'the mad new thing the owld Earl's trying up at Holyrood House!' "

Her eyes flashed with warmth and pride.

"And does the Earl share your political views then?"

He has no use for them at all," she answered cheerfully. "He is a rank backwoods Tory, when he bothers to think about such things. I believe he finds my own enthusiasms rather more amusing than anything else." She brushed a strand of hair back from her forehead. "Except of course when he hears that they laugh at me in London, and publish caricatures of me in the printshops. Then he grins like an old troll and tells me to 'stick to your guns, my girl, and give 'em a shot or two betwixt wind and water!' "

"Not a bad sort for a father."

"Indeed, sir"—she flashed me a straight look—"I have known few or none to match him."

What was there about Lady Barbara MacFarlane's "straight looks," as I came to think of them, that so daunted me? On this occasion a single level glance conjured up a sudden vision of an entirely new Barbara MacFarlane. Not the woman in her twenties whom I knew and lusted after, but the girl of ten years before. A girl galloping at

her father's side across the Berkshire Downs, her unbound hair blowing in the wind.

A strange image indeed for the mind of Lord Libertine
to hit upon. It took me several miles of winding road to
purify my lust once more of that enfeebling sentiment!

It was toward evening that Lord Mortimer gave me my
golden opportunity to advance another step toward my
goal.

"That Jacobin fellow may have been right, you know,"
said he suddenly, in the lengthening light of late afternoon.

"What," I responded in astonishment, "that flaming
revolutionary Machaud?"

Durward shrugged irritably. "It is possible for even a
flaming revolutionary to possess some modicum of mere
factual information."

"And for a flaming Tory to accept it at such hands?"
smiled Lady Barbara, obviously amused.

Durward chose to ignore her. "I merely suggest," he
said, "that no one should be better informed as to the
state of decay into which France has fallen than the root-
and-branch radicals who have brought her low. And this
fellow Machaud is clearly very close to the ringleaders
indeed."

"D'you expect the citizens of Paris to string you up
from the nearest lamppost at the first glimpse of your
well-cut English coat and impeccable fingernails?" Lady
Barbara was in a mood to banter, it appeared. But Lord
Mortimer would have none of it.

"If the good *citoyen* is to be believed, madame, no one
is safe in this hornet's nest Marat and Danton and this
Robespierre fellow have stirred up in the capital. My
God, if the Swiss Guards are massacred, not even the
King's own person is secure in this madhouse of a coun-
try!"

"Pray explain yourself, sir," said Lady Barbara, becoming serious now. "You do not propose that we should allow Citizen Machaud's impassioned warnings—quite understandable, of course, but surely somewhat exaggerated—to deter us from our projected tour of inspection? Fie, sir! When we spoke of this journey in London, you did not sound so faint of heart."

"I do not propose abandoning our enterprise, madam," he answered sharply. "I simply suggest what common prudence dictates: a touch of caution. A short stopover this side the capital. A week perhaps, no more. A rest from our travels, while we endeavor to learn more of the situation in the city."

"There is, of course," I interjected smoothly, scarce believing my luck, "always the Château d'Eauville. It is somwhere hereabouts, I believe."

"D'Eauville?" inquired Lady Barbara. "I don't believe I know it."

"I think," said Durward doubtfully, "that I have heard the name. A Countess d'Eauville is the current mistress of the château, I believe? She has a town house in the Rue St. Honoré as well, and quite sizable properties in the south."

"The very same," I answered cheerfully. "But she spends the summers at her château on the Nonette, in the westernmost depths of the forest of Chantilly. A fine old Gothic pile from the exterior, but thoroughly modernized within, I understand."

"Another Gothic Ruin?" murmured Lady Barbara, arching an eyebrow at me. "Surely not, Lord Libertine."

"Ah, well, a Renaissance foundation actually. But quite romantically medieval in appearance, I am told. I have never been there. But I have met the Countess d'Eauville a time or two in Paris, and she was most hospitable. Urged me to visit her here, in fact." I smiled ingenuously.

"I am sure she would never turn a coach full of weary travelers from her door."

"I have heard more of her," said Durward, hooding his protuberant eyes thoughtfully, looking even more like a longfaced frog than usual. "But I cannot recall precisely what."

"Really," I concluded winningly, "I believe she would be an ideal hostess for a few days of rest and quiet before plunging into whatever sort of hurly-burly they're having in the capital."

"I dislike to delay our voyage," said Lady Barbara at length. "I feel no need for *caution*, as Lord Mortimer puts it. Only an impatience to get on, to see for myself that great city poised on the brink of a new life." She sighed. "But for your sakes, gentlemen, I will agree to a short delay. Three days should suffice to reassure you, I hope. A week at the most.

"But after that"—her seagreen eyes turned suddenly full upon me—"after that it is my full intention to press on to Paris. Whatever rumors we may have heard by then. With you gentlemen—or without you."

And so the die was cast.

Just north of the town of Chantilly, we took a right fork in the road and followed a narrow lane through thick forest and gathering darkness toward the ford of the River Nonette and the secluded Château d'Eauville. I gloated all the way.

18

The Realms of Old Romance

The Château d'Eauville was a most romantic place.

Its situation was dramatic in the extreme. It was entirely isolated, miles from the main road, in the wildest part of the forest. There could have been no better place, I realized at once, for my purpose.

One emerged from the long tunnel of the trees quite suddenly upon the shores of the little River Nonette. Just across the narrow ford—little more than a trickle so late in August—clustered the village of Eauville. It was a drab little hamlet of unpaved streets and overhanging roofs, sagging with antiquity. Above the town loomed a towering chalky bluff, surging up dramatically out of the dark wood. And on top of this gigantic crag, pressed from below by evergreen oaks and flowering chestnuts, rose the pale-yellow towers of the Château d'Eauville.

It was a fantastic fairy-tale sight, rising thus above the river, the village, and the misty forest. A cluster of ramparts and balconies and steeply sloping roofs, topped by pointed towers and crocketed spires against the sky. Bizarre, unreal, bewilderingly out of time and place, it gave one an uneasy feeling of having wandered into the wrong world by accident.

None of this, of course, was visible to us that starry summer night when our little coach splashed across the ford, clattered through the sleeping village, and labored up the rutty road to the château. I noted only that the windows of one wing were brightly lit, those of the other dark and uninhabited. Then the postilion was holding the horses on the gravel drive and the coachman was stumping across the unlit *parvis* to lift the great iron knocker.

The footman who admitted us was dressed in an elegant livery of black velvet. He was also, I noticed, a strikingly handsome young man. He took our cards, bowed in silence, and withdrew, leaving us to cool our heels on the flagstones and admire the antique gargoyles on either side of the nail-studded door.

The black-clad servingman was back in a moment, however, to swing wide the ancient portal and bow us obsequiously across the threshold.

The vestibule within abandoned all pretense of medieval quaintness. There was a slender chair or two, in the fashion of the present reign, and an alabaster bust of a periwigged gentleman on a pedestal. A comely maid, dressed in black like her male compeer, dropped us a respectful curtsey as we passed.

The young man guided us across the little vestibule, opened a pair of double doors, and announced us.

The long, high-ceilinged room into which we next stepped had clearly been the great hall of Eauville in other, more spacious days. It was now an oversized salon, decorated in the latest Paris mode. The walls were white and gilt, with fluted pilasters, tall mirrors, and taller windows. A huge Italian marble fireplace with a very small fire in it filled the far end of the room. Glittering chandeliers hung from the coffered ceiling. There were Turkish carpets on the floor, and slender plush-covered chairs. On a slightly raised dais at one side of the room a dozen men in black-and-silver livery played a muted sequence of melancholy Italian airs. On the other side black-liveried servingmen and serving girls in low-cut gowns flanked a long table laden with sweets, coffee, liqueurs, and wine.

Between these two groups of obsequious servitors, the Countess's guests sat or drifted languidly about, conversing in low tones. There were no more than a score of them, ladies and gentlemen of the *haut monde* from purple-velvet slippers to snowy powdered hair. All of them, I realized suddenly, had a faintly unhealthy look about them. Their gowns and *culottes* were in the latest style—yet there was a *démodé* look to them, as though they were wearing this year's fashions with last year's wig. I even fancied I detected a furtiveness about their gaiety. They seemed to be constantly looking over their shoulders.

"*Mon cher* Arundel!" A woman rose from her seat before the vast ornamental fireplace at the far end of the great salon. "How many years since I have had the pleasure? And now at last you come to visit me. It is so good of you, in these unhappy times."

The Comtesse d'Eauville extended one pale, exquisitely manicured hand to be kissed, and I bowed over it with alacrity.

Charlotte d'Eauville was a thin, fine-boned woman of thirty-five or so. She had a small nose and a small mobile mouth, high cheekbones and a pointed chin. Her eyes were her most striking feature. They were large, black, and velvety, with an oddly Levantine look to them.

Her body, though not strikingly lovely at first glance, had an animal grace of its own. Her breasts were small and pointed, bared to the nipple by her swooping *décolletage*. Her hips were narrow, her waist amazingly slender beneath the clinging, translucent gown.

A meager body, really, and a face no longer young. And yet, if half the rumors one heard in the salons of Paris were true, this small, dry body housed a furious sensuality unmatched since the days of Borgias, or the decadence of ancient Rome!

"And these are your friends and fellow travelers? They are welcome to my house."

The Countess's eyes met Lady Barbara MacFarlane's.

A spark of instant enmity flashed across the gap between them. Each was a masterpiece of her own unique kind. They were as opposed by nature as velvet and tempered steel, or Greek wine and English ale.

Madame la Comtesse accepted Durward's hand with due reserve, diluted with just the proper touch of flattery. He was the distinguished English statesman, was he not? The well-known spokesman for the rights of the aristocratic orders everywhere? He was struggling with a modest prissy smile as she turned away to introduce two or three of her own guests.

She presented a seated gentleman first—the oldest, the ugliest, and by far the fattest.

"The Marquis de Brissac," she said. "My dear old friend, and an illustrious ornament of the old order himself. The new regime will look long before they find such another."

The Marquis de Brissac was a sluggish sack of a man, with sagging jowls and belly, pouchy eyes, a drooping red-veined nose. His chest and stomach gleamed with ribbons and orders of merit, civil and ecclesiastical. His fingers were covered with rings. His lips and cheeks were garishly painted, and perfume oozed thickly from him.

"*Mon plaisir, m'sieu,*" the Marquis lisped in an unhealthy whisper. "*Enchanté, madame, m'sieu.*"

"And this is the Graf von Teufel," the Countess continued, "a distinguished visitor from beyond the Rhine."

The Graf von Teufel, standing at her left flanked by a pair of gigantic white wolfhounds, bowed with a heavy, insolent air and said nothing at all. The Graf was a coldly handsome Teutonic type, as tall as I, though more heavily built. He had blond hair, pale skin, and opaque blue eyes. There was a cynical twist to his lips and a Nordic arrogance in his bearing that made me dislike him at first sight.

"His excellency," his hostess added, "is a metaphysician of sorts." I looked at the empty eyes and the restless wolfhounds and wondered what sort of metaphysics his might be.

"And this," the Countess concluded with a faint smile, "is the Baron de Franval."

The Baron stepped forward and made us all a leg. He was about nineteen, with pink cheeks and flaxen hair and a petulant, spoiled look in his light-brown eyes. His gestures were perfect as an orator's, his hands delicate as a girl's. His features were too perfect, his body too slender and elegantly proportioned to be real.

"Lady Barbara," he said, in a high-pitched boy's voice that scarcely seemed to have broken yet. "Lord Mortimer. Lord Christopher. I am so pleased."

We all expressed our pleasure in turn. Out of the corner of my eye I could see Durward's mind whirring away behind his bulging batrachian eyes. The Baron de Franval, as he must know, was the hereditary *seigneur* of a sizable proportion of Touraine, and one of the richest young men in France. Unless, of course, the Revolution had expropriated him since I was last in the country.

I wondered if Durward was aware that young Franval was also one of France's most flagrant sodomites. It was unlikely that the Revolution had done anything about that.

"But come, will you not join us for sweets and coffee?" Charlotte d'Eauville led us down the glittering salon. Servants in black placed chairs for us with those already grouped in front of the marble fireplace. "Some lemon cakes, perhaps? Or apricots?" And then, to the serving girl at her right: "Marie—*des bonbons!*"

I settled myself carefully in my chair before I looked up at the girl who now hovered at my side, offering a tray of sugary delicacies. Marie had coarse black hair and a peasant girl's peaches-and-cream complexion. There was a lushness about her which triggered a surge of raw greed in my still unregenerate soul.

"Vous voulez quelque chose, monsieur?" she said. Would I care for something, sir? Would I indeed!

She kept her voice down to the proper servitor's murmur. But there was a directness in her phrasing and a cheerful impudence in her gaze that warmed my heart as it stiffened my cock. Marie was the only genuinely likable person we had met since we had arrived at the château.

"You admire my people's unusual livery, Milord Arundel?" Charlotte d'Eauville's voice intruded upon my appreciative revery. "It is for mourning, sir. The whole establishment here has been in mourning these three years past."

She smiled enigmatically. When I stammered out some attempt at condolences, the nearest guests burst out laughing.

"It is for a suicide we mourn, sir," she added suggestively.

"Ah," I said, none the wiser.

"The suicide of the night of August fourth."

Franval giggled, old Brissac chuckled throatily, the Graf von Teufel split his arrogant cheeks in a haughty smile. I began to feel somewhat nettled.

"It is August fourth of 'eighty-nine the Countess refers to, perhaps?" said Lady Barbara coolly.

"But of course, madame."

"The night the more enlightened French nobility themselves voted to abandon some of their more anachronistic feudal rights and privileges," Lady Barbara explained to me. "Including," she added, "their patents of nobility themselves, as I recall."

"That is substantially correct," said the Comtesse d'Eauville. "The night three years ago when the ancient aristocracy of France committed suicide."

"Shocking business, shocking," murmured Durward. I

could feel Lady Barbara's eyes hardening, her combative spirit bracing itself.

This was an ill omen for my master plan, which depended upon at least a week of relaxing, lulling quiet at the Château d'Eauville. I began to search about for a soothing response to the Countess's unpropitious humor. But it was the Countess herself who came to my rescue.

"But no more of our misfortunes here, my English friends. You see that we enjoy our titles still, and our property as well, here in the forests of Chantilly. There are ways of managing things in this world still." She smiled. "Not even these Jacobins are immune to politics."

"Yes," said the Baron de Franval eagerly. "Do tell us again how Talleyrand managed that sale of guns, Brissac! Or Danton's latest indiscretion with the ladies . . ."

"*Ah, oui, M'sieu Talleyrand*," the Marquis whispered. Then he was off on a long, involved tale of intrigue and financial chicanery involving the chief diplomatist among the new leaders of France. But it was at least a highly nonpolitical story, in which Talleyrand's nominal allegiance to the new order played no part. I settled back with a sigh to my coffee and my lemon cakes. Lady Barbara's eyes were combative still, but I could meet her gaze more casually now.

If we could but stay off politics, and revive the spirit of the Berkshire Downs, I should have her in a week!

19

Countess Charlotte in Bed

I laid the whole tangled matter out for Jeremy before retiring that same night. It was time: his sulky injured silences were becoming more than I could bear. And now if ever, here within the walls of the Château d'Eauville, I would need his help.

He was somewhat skeptical at first.

"You expect 'er ladyship to fall into your arms in this 'eathen place, when she wouldn't put up with so much as a peck on the cheek in London?"

"With the help of the Countess, Jeremy, I do. Charlotte d'Eauville is the most notorious woman in Paris! Mistress of all the amorous arts, by all accounts. We shall have music, moonlight in the gardens, perhaps a fête in the woods hereabouts. And in such a setting! Why, the very walls reek of fair ladies and gallant courtiers and medieval romance! I shall be blameworthy indeed if I cannot bring her to bed!"

"Meantime ransacking 'er ladyship's baggage for this rutting piece of paper she 'as purloined from the War Office?"

"*May* have purloined, Jeremy. But some search surely must be made—with your good help, of course."

"Yes, sir," said Jeremy, brightening visibly. "I shall do my duty right enough there, sir. As any trueborn Briton should!" He drew himself up to his full five feet and a few inches and tucked his chin in like a soldier on parade.

"I had no notion you were such a patriot, Jeremy!"

"I 'ope I 'ave never given you cause to think differently, sir?"

"Oh, none at all, none at all," I hastened to reassure him. "But to the matter at hand. I shall do my best to draw the lady away, and you must watch your chance with Bridget. The time must come when you will have unimpeded access to her ladyship's bags and boxes. And then at least we may inform the King's ministers that their suspicions are groundless."

"Unless they aren't, sir."

"Unless they aren't, of course."

Somehow I found it difficult to believe that so mili-

tantly principled a person as Lady Barbara MacFarlane
could possibly betray her country's secrets to the enemy
on the eve of war. But then, of course—a still small voice
would whisper—there is the possibility that the lady's
principles do not include any particular reverence for
George III and Merrie England.

But damn it all, what matter? Damn her principles,
damn the War Office Report, damn the precious wager
even. Damn all but that fantastic body, breathing peacefully in an antique four-poster only a short hallway and a
single flight of stairs away!

"I shall speak to the Countess now, Jeremy," I decided
abruptly, "before she retires. Lay our amorous intrigue
before her and plead frankly for her help. If rumor does
not lie, we shall have the rarest bawd in France laboring
to advance our cause before this night is done. And then,
while the lady and I dally in the gardens or wander in the
woods, you may slip in unobserved and rifle her effects at
your leisure, for the honor of King and Country."

Jeremy bowed in silence. But his eyes were bright. I
could almost hear the sound of a distant drummer.

I clapped him on the back and set out upon my own
crucial mission, threading my way through the labyrinth
of the old château to the Countess's apartments.

Countess Charlotte d'Eauville reclined in gauzy splendor on her high canopied bed. Her chamber was hung
with deep-purple silk, frescoed with rosy nymphs and
goddesses, lit by silver candelabra. Two charming maids
in close-fitting, lowcut black—one of them the sensuous
Marie—attended her hair and to the gown she had just
slipped off. A handsome strapping page in black livery
was clearing a white-clothed table by the window. The
window itself was tall and arched, standing open to the
gardens and the fragrant summer night.

The table, I noticed idly, had been set for one only.

Somehow that seemed unlikely, considering all that I had heard of the lady of Eauville.

Countess Charlotte propped herself up farther in her bed and smiled at me.

"Madame," I began circumspectly enough, "I hesitate to call so late. Especially after having intruded so precipitously upon your sylvan sanctuary—"

"Nonsense, *mon cher* Arundel!" She waved her maids away and summoned me with a regal gesture to a chair drawn up beside her bed. "I have heard so much of you, desired so long to know more of you. The sooner the better, as you other English say."

"You are too kind, ma'am."

"No, no. It is you who honor this rustic retreat of mine. But come—tell me of your journey. And what you think of our poor nation now."

Her small mouth curved in an inviting smile. Her pitchy Levantine eyes told me nothing whatever of what was really passing behind them.

"Your country is indeed much changed," I temporized. "Yet summer is as lovely as ever in Picardy. And French women as beautiful."

"And English gentlemen as disposed to take advantage of them?"

"Madame does *my* poor country too much honor. We are for the most part a tongue-tied race, scarce able even to take proper advantage of the ladies of our own land. Without surrendering to matrimony, that is to say."

"Which is of course a violation of the rules of the game."

"Ruins the sport of it, at any rate."

It seemed we understood each other.

"Maurice!" the Countess called to the servant still pottering about with candlesticks and silver at the table by the window. "You may leave the fruit and wine. And tell

Catherine and Marie I shall have no need of them till later. I will ring."

Maurice bowed and left, closing the door silently behind him.

Now it would be foolish to claim that I had not noticed the distinctive charms of Charlotte d'Eauville. Indeed, it would have been very difficult not to have noticed them. The silken nightdress and the gauzy lavender peignoir concealed none of her fetching figure. Her small brown nipples jutted dark against the silk. The contours of her limbs molded the swooping skirts of her gown. As the last servant left and the door closed, I could not but be aware that only a couple of layers of tissue-thin cloth lay between me and that taut, slender, legendary body.

"Allow me to be frank with you, madame," I said in a businesslike tone. "I am not here purely by chance, nor simply to partake of your excellent hospitality."

"Vraiment?"

"You see before you, ma'am," I declared with a hand upon my heart, "a helpless victim of Eros' dart. A man writhing—writhing, madame—in the grip of unrequited passion. A helpless slave, in short, of Love."

"Formidable."

"It is my hope, Madame la Comtesse, that here, in this idyllic retreat, far from intruding eyes and the censures of society, my passion may at last find some response. If, that is, I may appeal to your own delicate sensibilities to aid two star-crossed hearts to become one."

"Ah."

She tapped her lower lip with one white finger, settled herself more deeply back into her pillows. Her dark hair, unbound, was a lustrous tangle about her face. The faint smile never left her lips—and never reached her eyes.

"Your charming *Anglaise* has refused to make you happy then."

"Alas, madame, she offers me no hope."

"Is the rejection personal to you, or is it a matter of scruples?"

"Scruples and conscience, ma'am, upon my word."

"Too bad she is not French," the Countess murmured. "The nuns would have cured her of any such foolishness long since."

I recalled vaguely having heard that Charlotte d'Eauville herself had enjoyed the advantages of a convent education. And had been seduced immediately upon her emergence from the nunnery.

"But there is still hope, evidently." Her thin cheeks dimpled. "We shall arrange picnics, do you say? *Fêtes galantes*, intimate suppers to speed your courtship."

"Madame is more than kind."

"And of course the château, its gardens and environs are entirely at your disposal. There are quiet alcoves about the castle, glades and groves in the parks and woods quite suitable for amorous dalliance."

"I am most grateful, madame. If the other wing of the château is as unpeopled as it seems, for instance, the lady and I might derive much joy from the opportunity to explore it. There is nothing to kindle amatory excitement, I find, like unused chambers, perhaps a lonely tower room—"

"The older wing, *malheureusement*, is closed and sealed now. It is very decrepit, really. I should never forgive myself if there were an accident."

I started to reassure her, and then stopped. The smile was still there, but I detected something in her eyes for the first time. It was the merest flicker of emotion, indefinable and quickly gone. But it told me there was no use inquiring further about the other wing.

"I am sure, ma'am, that the château and the forest round about will provide romantic settings enough to melt the most icebound heart. And once again, my gratitude. I knew my confidence in your kindness and delicacy of understanding was not misplaced."

I rose as I spoke, quite satisfied with these initial arrangements, preparing to depart.

Still smiling enigmatically, the Countess extended one bare white arm, and I bent to kiss her hand. I felt the skin warm beneath my lips, then a sudden movement, and the fingers tingling across my cheek, brushing through my hair. Her hand slid around to the back of my neck. With a sinewy strength I would never have expected in so elegant, fine-boned a woman, she pulled me forward, sprawling across the bed.

Across the bed—and across the Countess d'Eauville!

The perfumed flesh of her breast and throat came under my cheek. Then she locked her powerful fingers in my hair, yanked back my head, and crushed her mouth against mine.

I had—I must admit it—seldom been boarded so furiously before. Her mouth was open, her tongue inviting. Her thighs were hot and shifting under mine, her loins grinding slowly against my own. I was on fire in a moment, meeting her thrust for thrust in two.

Rumor had exaggerated not one iota. Countess Charlotte's talents were beyond compare. She teased, she tantalized, she responded, she resisted. She gave herself in sudden abandon, then drew back with a slow seductive longing that drove one wild. I gasped, panted, clawed for her. Her half-naked thighs clung passionately to my clothed ones, slid lingeringly away.

I lurched to my feet and began to tear at my clothing.

The countess sat up in the bed and reached for the tasseled bell rope that hung ready to her hand. Still smiling, she pulled gently at the cord. She was not even breathing heavily.

"I wish you all good fortune with your green-eyed puritan, monsieur," she said tranquilly. "And if at any time monsieur should feel the need for relaxation, of surcease from your so romantic quest—perhaps we might speak further."

My fingers stammered to a halt among the buttons of my vest. My eyes, glazed with lust, refocused slowly as she brushed the translucent fabric down over her naked thighs, drew the covers up.

'Marie," Charlotte continued serenely, "will show you to your chamber." I swung awkwardly about and saw her there, materialized in answer to the bell. She stood just inside the door, her eyes sparkling at my obvious discomfiture. Her heavy breasts gleamed in sculptured perfection above the swooping neckline of her black gown. My fingers twitched convulsively at the sparkle in her eyes, the slight inviting sway of her hips.

"Conduct Milord Arundel *chez lui*, Marie," I heard the Countess say behind me. "And then perhaps you might look in upon Monsieur le Marquis de Brissac. To see if his excellency requires anything before retiring."

"*Certainement, madame.*"

Marie bobbed a devastatingly low curtsey to her mistress. I broke out in a cold sweat.

"I shall see you tomorrow, then, Lord Christopher," the lady of Eauville continued conversationally. "We do not rise early here. But you have only to ring and order whatever you would like to break your fast. Perhaps in the afternoon we might all forgather for a stroll about the gardens?"

Baffled, at bay between these two lush bodies, I managed a hoarse affirmative response.

"*Très bien.*" The Countess smiled. "Sleep well then, sir, and dream of your heart's desire."

She turned away and reached for a scented bonbon from a little silver tray on a side table by the bed. I grunted an acknowledgment and followed Marie's swishing skirts out the door into the dim corridor beyond. I was so dazed, in fact, that I didn't even think to reach for the narrow waist swinging so enticingly up the hallway before me until it was too late, and she had left me—another devastating curtsey—at my door.

I stumbled into my chamber and plopped down on the nearest chair. Jeremy had left my nightshirt lying across the bed and retired to his own room on the floor above. I was alone with a cold sweat, an ache in the groin, the call of a night bird outside the window.

I sucked air in over my lower teeth and wondered what that hideous old toad de Brissac would do with the extravagantly endowed creature who was even now rapping demurely at his door. I wondered what the passionate Countess would do with herself the rest of the night—if in fact she planned to spend the rest of it alone. And I wondered how in God's name I was to keep a clear enough head to accomplish anything at all in this Mahometan paradise into which I seemed to have stumbled.

20

Lady Barbara on a Swing

I leaned on a marble balustrade around the terrace and gazed down into the little garden below, where Lady Barbara strolled among the lime trees. I watched her pale-green skirts brush the gravel path. I absorbed the gentle sway of her waist, the set of her slender shoulders, the almost roguish tilt of her broad summer hat. And I congratulated myself on the Machiavellian ingenuity that had brought me so close to success.

For I was close, there could be no doubt of it. Everything about Lady Barbara's demeanor revealed a woman relaxed, yet sensuously stirred by the subtle charms of the Château d'Eauville.

She turned now, her slim figure outlined against a scarlet bank of rosebushes, to look up at the spires of the château, pale yellow against the morning blue. She saw me there on the terrace then, resting my elbows on the stone balustrade and gazing down at her. She inclined her head sedately enough in greeting. But the smile that played about her lips and shadowed her sun-warmed cheeks had a touch of mischief in it, and more than a hint of genuine gladness at the sight of me.

I bowed to her in turn, and indicated my intention to join her on the lawn.

This proved to be more time-consuming than I had expected. There was no direct access from the terrace to the little garden ringed with lime trees. It was necessary to reenter the château, and then to find one's way through a tangle of ancient passageways and winding stairs to the level of the garden and thence out upon the lawn. By the time I had accomplished this feat, with the help of more than one obsequious black-liveried servant, Lady Barbara was no longer alone.

The young Baron de Franval, pink-cheeked and voluble, was apparently broaching some sort of project to my lady as I approached across the grass.

"Arundel!" de Franval gaily included me in his invitation. "You must come too, and see it. The most delightful bower Madame la Comtesse has created. In the grove just below the garden here, perfectly charming. And the swing—you *must* see the swing!"

He clapped his hands and looked so childishly eager, even for a youth of nineteen, that Lady Barbara and I could only exchange tolerant smiles and acquiesce,

"It is just this way, down these stairs. Mind the vines along the wall." He hastened ahead of us, a handsome lad in a velvet coat and satin breeches, snowy lace at wrist and chin, a great diamond on his left hand flashing in the sunshine. Then we passed into the shadow of a gnarled beech, through an open gate, and began a vertiginous descent down a long zigzagging flight of stone steps.

The escarpment on which the château stood, which towered so impregnably above the village on the river side, sloped somewhat less precipitously here at the rear of the castle. The bower to which de Franval led us was perhaps halfway down, one of an intricate series of terraces, gardens, views, and promenades on many levels between the castle above and the dark forest below.

The stairs were slippery with moss and moisture. Lady Barbara and I descended carefully. She rested one hand upon my arm, and once at least clutched more tightly at me for support when a broken step threatened to give way beneath her. I felt her closeness, smelled the freshness of her hair.

"Here—here we are. I can't think how you haven't seen it sooner. *Délicieux*, is it not?"

Delicious—and insidiously sensual, like everything else about the Château d'Eauville.

There was an old stone bench, wider and longer and altogether more capacious than any sitting couple should normally need. There was a carnal quality about the naiad, arms stretched upward, *cuisses* indolently parted to reveal a good deal more of her sculptured charms than anything I had ever seen in an English garden. The whole bower had an indefinable air of intimacy about it. It felt more like a scented boudoir translated out of doors than any natural glade.

"It is lovely," said Lady Barbara.

"Very pleasant indeed, sir," I agreed politely.

"Come, come, mademoiselle!" de Franval burbled on. "You must try this swing. It carries one ever so high up among the branches. It is like flying. Intoxicating. Come, you must!"

With a glance of mock despair at me, Lady Barbara submitted to the Baron's importunities. She sank into the little swing. De Franval pulled on the long leather thongs, and the swing began to move. Listening to his cries of vicarious delight, watching his soft hands and flashing eyes as his efforts propelled her higher and higher into the trees, I felt not the faintest touch of jealousy. With women, at least, his lordship's pleasure was obviously so totally untinged by desire that the most besotted lover could have felt no spark of resentment.

"Exquisite." The feebler, faintly ironic voice of the Marquis de Brissac intruded on my ruminations. "A lovely pair of children, are they not?"

"Children, Monsieur le Marquis?" I could not help but challenge him. "Surely not children!"

The Marquis tilted back his head to watch Lady Barbara's flying figure, skirts and petticoats fluttering seductively as she rose among the branches. Her laughing face flashed past us, swinging back, then rising once again as de Franval released the leather thongs. The old roué's neck wrinkled like a tortoise's as he watched her rise and fall.

"Children at heart, Milord Arundel," he wheezed. "All young people are still children in their hearts, is it not so? So it seems at least to those of us that have reached a certain age. We who feel the chill of the grave already upon us, m'sieu, we can only warm ourselves at the fires of their youth, and envy them their childish hearts." He tilted back his head once more, to watch my lady rise into the foliage, laughing at the leaves against her face. "She has lovely hair," he added gravely, in his wheezing whisper. "Hair like a Titian portrait—like a Renaissance madonna. There is fire and passion in your Titian hair, beneath the chastity and coolness."

He left his phrasing deliberately ambiguous. He might as easily have been talking about Titian madonnas as about the lady in the swing. But I knew with violent certainty that he was contemplating the fire and passion that lay banked behind the flying hair and sparkling glance of Lady Barbara MacFarlane. And I felt a sudden quite uncharacteristic surge of righteous indignation at those hooded old eyes, soiling the virginal Lady Barbara with God knew what licentious meditations.

Before I could decide whether to push de Brissac into the lily pool, a burst of laughter from the slope below turned our attention elsewhere.

There was the brief bay of a dog, another burst of laughter, and a scuffle of running feet—two pairs of running feet—coming up the steep path from the forest of Chantilly. There was a final smothered cry just beyond the screen of flowering vines on that side of the grove, and then a sudden silence. The pursuer had clearly caught up with his prey. The silence lengthened. De Franval turned to look that way too, and then Lady Barbara, still rising and falling on the ribboned swing.

There was a gasp, a laugh, a renewed scuffling in the underbrush, mingled with the worrying sound of excited dogs. Then the maidservant Marie exploded, disheveled and laughing, into the clearing. The Graf von Teufel surged after her, his two white wolfhounds nipping at her heels.

Marie pulled up, gasping with surprise, at the sight of us. But her smile was as broad as ever, and she made only a token gesture at drawing her bodice back up over one naked shoulder. The Graf whistled his dogs to a stiff-legged standstill and surveyed us arrogantly, in his cold Teutonic way, as though we had somehow intruded upon him instead of the other way round. Then he saw the Lady Barbara, and a smile split his palely handsome face.

"*Messieurs—et madame*," he said, without a trace of a German intonation, bowing infinitesimally from the waist. "*Enchanté*."

We acknowledged his greeting with various degrees of a bow. Lady Barbara, slowing to a stop now, inclined her head graciously. Her rumpled hair, her color attractively heightened by the sun and the exercise, her slightly disordered skirts and heaving breast would have drawn any man's admiring gaze. The opaque blue eyes of the Graf von Teufel fixed on her like a serpent trying to mesmerize a sparrow. There was another brief, heavy-breathing silence.

Marie swayed gently back against her former pursuer, her eyes cast down demurely. The Graf fondled one half-bared shoulder as absently as one might fondle a child.

"Madame s'amuse, j'espère?" he inquired heavily.

"Yes, indeed, sir," Lady Barbara answered briskly. "I am mightily well entertained. Monsieur le Baron has just shown me this excellent swing, and I have been exploiting his two good arms shamelessly ever since."

"I hope," said von Teufel, "that I may entertain you myself before you take leave of us, madame. And that you will not hesitate to exploit my own two arms as well as the fortunate Baron's."

His cool smile, his words fairly dripping with innuendo, were transparently suggestive. Still Lady Barbara smiled serenely up at him from her seat in the gently oscillating swing.

"I shall certainly accept your offer, monsieur," she answered cheerfully, "if ever the pleasures of the forest of Chantilly should wane. Which truly does not seem likely to me! It is so beautiful here!"

She rose from the swing as she spoke, flung back her head and stretched her arms wide to the fragrant summer foliage that closed us round. I saw her breasts go taut under her gown, her fingers spread and flex in the ardor of her desire to possess it all, to absorb the whole murmurous world of summer into herself. My throat went dry with a very different sort of desire.

She laughed and settled back upon her heels, her arms falling to her sides. When she looked round at us, every eye in the little clearing was riveted upon her. Even Marie, I could have sworn, ran the tip of her tongue provocatively along her lower lip with a look of approval that was more than admiration for the fashionable perfection of *la belle Anglaise.*

It was a moment heavy with sensuality. The grove oozed pure honey-sweet lust. Even I—dare I confess it?—felt slightly suffocated by it. Only Lady Barbara MacFarlane seemed totally oblivious.

"Are we not to have a picnic this afternoon?" She broke the panting stillness brightly. "Did I not hear the Countess say so, Lord Christopher?"

"Ah—indeed, madame, I believe so," I responded with some confusion. "A short voyage down the Nonette to an island of some sort. Quite idyllic, I believe she said."

"Ah, yes," the Marquis de Brissac murmured in that strange half-whisper of his. "Our own little Île de Cythère. A charming place, charming."

"The Island of Cythera?" said Lady Barbara. "The island where Venus was born—here in the heart of Picardy?"

"The isle where Venus rose naked from the sea," smiled the Graf von Teufel, still absentmindedly fingering Marie's shoulder, now completely bare beneath his heavy hand. "It is the Countess's name for it. The brushwood folk below"—he nodded disdainfully in the general direction of the village—"call it l'Îlot du Cochon, I believe. Pig Island, you would say. Eh, *Kleine?*" he added, looking down at the servant girl. "Is that not what they call it—down there?"

He pinched her shoulder brutally, and she gasped with pain. Or was it pleasure, after all, that brought that sudden intake of breath? Nothing seemed to be what it seemed at first in this perverse place.

"*Oui, monsieur*," Marie replied in her usual muted tones, "*l'Îlot du Cochon*."

"Oh, but the Countess is quite right to have renamed it," the Baron de Franval cut in. "It is lovely—lovely. You will adore it, madame, I know you will." He smiled brilliantly at Lady Barbara and all but clapped his hands with glee. "So we are to go this afternoon! I must find Jasmin, and tell him!"

He made a leg to all of us and hurried off through the trees, toward the stone staircase that led back up to the château.

"Jasmin?" said Lady Barbara doubtfully. "Who is Jasmin? Have I met him?"

"I do not believe so, madame," the Marquis responded gravely. "Jasmin is Monsieur le Baron's *valet de chambre*. His—ah—body servant, do you say in English?" His prunelike jowls quivered with licentious mirth.

"Jasmin," said Lady Barbara. "What an odd name."

"All of the Baron de Franval's body servants have odd names," said the Graf von Teufel. "He names them himself. It is a whim of his. The one he had last year was called Hyacinth."

"How extraordinary," said Lady Barbara. And then, to me: "Will you walk back to the château with me now, Lord Christopher? If we are to go sailing on the river this afternoon, I must have my parasol, and Bridget must unpack some shoes more suitable than these."

I hastened to offer her my arm. I bowed briefly to the gentlemen, she smiled brightly at all and sundry, and we set out upon the short path to the foot of the flagstone stair. The Graf and the Marquis stayed behind with Marie.

"They are an odd lot, Lord Christopher," mused the lady beside me as we walked, "aren't they?"

An odd lot! Dear God. I suddenly heard Lord Morti-mer's voice once more, as I had heard it over the green-baize table at White's that evening three short weeks before: *There is such a thing, Arundel—there is such a thing as innocence!*

21

"Fête Champêtre":
or, A Voyage to Venus' Island

"Milord s'amuse?" the Countess murmured to me, as I sipped chilled wine and admired the tall cypresses swaying in the breeze. It was the same question the Graf von Teufel had asked Lady Barbara that morning. And my answer was substantially the same:

"Indeed, ma'am. I have seldom enjoyed myself more."

The Isle of Cythera—or Pig Island—looked much more like the former than the latter. But one suspected that the ingenious hands of the Countess d'Eauville's gardeners had had more to do with its carefully designed charms than the hand of Nature and Nature's God.

L'Île de Cythère was a verdant jewel, rising from the river just beyond the rushing waterfall at the confluence of the Nonette and the Somme. The river flowed wide and slow here, and the island was quite isolated in the middle of the stream. Its banks were as grassy as the Countess's lawns, its trees as landscaped as her gardens. Picturesque crags mounted majestically to a hilltop crowned with a highly unconvincing bosky grove of carefully pruned evergreens and Italian cypresses. In the heart of the grove there was a small, round Doric temple, where we sat. There were benches inside, and a sculptured Venus with *putti* clambering about her marble limbs.

It was ideally suited for an *alfresco* meal, just as the Countess had promised.

We sipped a sparkling vintage cooled in a nearby well, munched cold fowl and cheese and cakes. There was louder laughter, and more furious gossip still. Gentle breezes dispersed the sultry late-August heat, and the servants brought us fresh strawberries washed in well water. We all felt delightfully rustic. Somebody was inevitably reminded of the queen's *charming* little peasant village behind the Petit Trianon, on the grounds of the palace at Versailles.

After the meal the gentlefolk wandered somnolently off in twos and threes among the trees, leaving the servants to finish the not inconsiderable remains of the feast. It was a drowsy afternoon, and most seemed desirous of a shady nook to nap in for an hour or two.

I took advantage of Lord Mortimer's temporary involvement with a sleepy viscount over a question of genealogy to slip quietly away with Lady Barbara.

"You know, Lord Christopher," she announced a propos of nothing as we strolled up a forest path, "I really do not think you are quite the villain you're cracked up to be!"

"Indeed, madame?"

"I have never heard it said, for instance, that you imposed your will upon maidservants and peasant girls—the helpless of this world. As the gentlefolk of the Château d'Eauville so clearly do."

So she had noticed more than I gave her credit for. I wondered how much more.

"Indeed, Lady Barbara," I said, "I have not made a practice of it." There would be little challenge in such paltry intrigues, I providentially managed to refrain from blurting out. Nor little pleasure either, with such green girls and helpless wenches as the von Teufels of this world batten on.

"In fact, sir, from all I can tell, the only real victim of your most reprehensible escapades is your own unfortunate self."

"Madame?"

"Who has lost his fortune by your gaming, sir, but you yourself? Who will one day succumb to gout and liver from too much wine, but you? And who is demeaned by the profligate reports of your—*amours* is, I believe, the fashionable term—but Lord Christopher Arundel himself?"

"Well, madame, put that way—"

She paused on the path and turned to me, one hand upon my arm. Her face, shadowed by the wide summer hat, looked up at me with what was clearly a half-humorous twinkle now. And was there—I would have sworn there was—a glimmer of affection there as well?

"I think, Lord Christopher," she said, "that we might be friends."

"Lady Barbara—I dare to hope so."

The glint in her eyes, the firmness of her hand upon my sleeve jolted my passions awake in an instant. I sought to press my own fingers quickly over hers. But she gave my forearm a friendly squeeze and took her hand away.

"There is a charming prospect over the river just here, madame," I said hastily. "Shall we not sit down on yonder mossy bank and contemplate Nature's handiwork? Or," I could not forbear to add, "the ingenuity of the Countess's landscapers at any rate."

"Madame la Comtesse may have designed the mossy bank," Lady Barbara answered cheerfully, "but Nature made the river."

She settled herself gracefully upon the soft green turf, and I scrambled down beside her. The place was indeed suspiciously like a wide deep couch, sculptured to the human form, backed by nodding ferns and shaded by a flowering tree.

"Now tell me, Lord Christopher." Her cool voice cut through my feverish fantasies. "What do you think of *me?*"

"Why," I stammered, "as a most beautiful and spirited young woman, madame. And—ah—a most intelligent one."

"Really, sir." She seemed amused.

"I have no objections, madame," I assured her earnestly, "to intelligence in man or beast."

She shook her head with a little sigh and a rueful smile, like an adult with a child that seems incapable of learning. Unhappily certain that I had said the wrong thing, I fumbled for words. And all the while, I longed only to be fumbling for her lovely body in the pale-green gown.

"Alas," she interrupted my labored efforts abruptly. "I seem to have forgotten my book. May I prevail upon you, sir, to remount the path and fetch it? I must have left it on the pedestal of Venus in the small rotundo."

With a nervous smile and a silent curse, I rose and set off up the hill, feeling marvelously frustrated and ill used. I hurried, slipping on pine needles, eager to fetch the wretched book and get back before the lady's relaxed, warm mood should wane.

Then, perhaps halfway to my destination, I heard the first low moan.

It was a moan of delight, a cry of love. Or more accurately, a cry of pleasure—the ultimate pleasure of a woman writhing in sexual congress. And it clearly emanated from the trembling throat of the Countess Charlotte d'Eauville.

I glimpsed her a moment later. Indeed, I almost stumbled over her.

On my left, jutting dizzily out over the river, was another of those unconvincingly convenient nooks, this one carpeted with violets and curtained with ivy. And this one was inhabited. I caught a glimpse of Countess Charlotte, her head flung back above the moving water far below. Then the broad back of one of her faceless black-clad servingmen cut off my view. I heard him breathing heavily as he labored over her lean, quick body.

"*Ah, Jean-Paul,*" she whispered avidly against his ear, "*mon Dieu, que je t'aime—que je t'adore—ah, ça—fais ça, mon cher, mon chéri—*"

I saw his impassive peasant face over one husky shoulder as he worked her methodically toward her climactic moment. I could have sworn he was the one called Jean-*Louis.* I was also certain that she did not give a tinker's dam what his name might be.

After that it was sighs and murmurs all the way. The Island of Cythera was living up to its name.

Threading my way through the trees to the little round temple, I heard the girlish giggle of the Baron de Franval. I did not have to look behind the flowering juniper on my right to know that the faithful Jasmin was keeping his master company. I wondered vaguely where the Marquis de Brissac and the Graf von Teufel might be—and the rest of the company, and the rest of the servants. As if in answer to my unspoken question, a sweet voluptuous cry came echoing up the wooded slope. Somewhere below me on the hillside they were all finding their own sorts of entertainment. I pursed dry lips and hurried on.

Marie sat alone on the marble base of the statue of Venus in the center of the Doric temple, finishing off a plate of *marrons glacés.* Her gown clung, revealing the smooth sculptured magnificence of her body. She popped a last sugared chestnut into her mouth and licked her lips like a cat.

"*Vous voulez quelque chose, monsieur?*"

"*Ah, non, mademoiselle.*" I grinned. "*Tant pis pour moi.*" I immensely preferred Marie's frank concupiscence to the involuted theology of self-indulgence that seemed to be the prevailing mode at Eauville. But my mountainous lust for Lady Barbara would brook no rivals that day. There was only one thing I needed from Marie now. *"L'autre milord anglais—le seigneur Durward— vous savez où il est allé?"*

"Par là, je crois," she answered, gesturing negligently toward a path which ran roughly opposite to that down which Lady Barbara awaited me. *"Je crois qu'il vous cherche."*

I was sure he was looking for me. Luckily, looking in the wrong direction.

I snatched up a slender volume bound in limp leather from the marble two inches from Marie's left thigh, blew her a kiss, and hurried back down the way I had come. I chuckled as I walked, and rubbed my hands together like a miser contemplating his buried hoard. It was an absolutely beautiful summer afternoon.

Lady Barbara lay sound asleep beneath the fragrant dogwood, one cheek resting on one sun-browned arm.

I sank down beside her, hot-eyed with desire, hands trembling with lust. Her eyelids fluttered slightly, but she did not wake. A lock of her lustrous hair moved in the breeze. She sighed once in her sleep, and smiled like a happy child dreaming.

I am not a monster, more's the pity. So I sat there through the long afternoon. All around me the forest was alive with unimaginable delights. Beside me lay the most beautiful woman in the world, more beautiful and more helpless than I had ever known her. And I sat there, shuddering with passion, perspiring with desire—and paralyzed by what my Irish grandmother would no doubt have called my better instincts.

Until that moment I honestly did not know I had them.

22

The Confidential Agent

The Countess's elegantly decorated barge glided into the landing at the foot of the single street of Eauville just as the westering sun disappeared behind the towering ridge above. There were, as it happened, neither carts nor coaches enough to carry us all up to the château in comfort. With some thought of walking off the frustrations of the afternoon, I volunteered to ascend on foot.

So, to my surprise, did Lord Mortimer Durward.

I accepted his company with a resigned sigh. He had seethed through the somnolent homeward voyage, his eyes darting suspiciously from Lady Barbara to myself like a nervous *duenna* that has been caught napping with her charge. And this, I realized as we trudged up the rutty track beneath the trees, leaving the patched and peeling village behind us, was my first moment completely alone with Durward since I had caught up with the pair of them in France. It promised, in short, to be a head-butting, horn-locking confrontation of the first order. After a momentary inward groan I realized that nothing would suit me better.

He came to the point directly.

"You have not forgot our wager, I see, Lord Christopher." His smile was as sour as lemons and as insidious as serpents.

"I have not, sir. I am here, as you see. In spite of your best efforts to the contrary."

"I beg your pardon, sir?"

"You surely don't expect me to believe, Lord Mortimer, that this precipitate departure for France within a week of our wager is a mere coincidence?"

"Sir?"

"Come, come, my lord! It would be remarkably difficult for even so experienced an amorist as my humble self to cast much of a spell over the lady once the English Channel was safely put between us!"

"And you imply that for this reason—?"

"Imply? I'll say it to your face, my lord. It was a shrewd stroke, Durward, but it has come to nothing. As will all similar devices to the same end. For I shall have her, by God, though hell itself should bar the way!" It was an uncharacteristic flash of romantic fustian, I admit—but nowhere near so far off the mark as it sounded that peaceful afternoon in the forest of Chantilly.

"I am sure you will do your best to have your lascivious way with her, Lady Libertine." Durward kept his totally unconvincing smile firmly in place. "I am also sure that I shall do my best to protect her ladyship's honor from your unprincipled designs." He looked straight at me and did not blink an eye.

"Her ladyship's honor?" I snapped. "Or your own stake in the matter?"

"There is nothing in our wager, sir, to prevent my taking a hand in the game. I fully intend to act in her ladyship's behalf, as any gentleman would do under the circumstances."

"No one would ever accuse you of a lack of gentility, Durward."

"She is an English lady traveling alone through this barbarous land, beset by footpads, threatened by a rebellious people, prey to any rakehell that should come upon her. Why, it is no more than my duty, Lord Christopher, to offer her what security I can. If you were not so casually contemptuous of principles yourself, sir, I am sure you would understand my view."

His froglike eyes met mine unflinchingly, and his prim little smile never wavered. His dishonesty was so total, his hypocrisy so natural that I think he almost believed what he was saying himself. I knew at once that from this point on it was open warfare between us.

Had we not come in sight of the château that moment, with Madame la Comtesse waiting for us smiling at the gates, I should certainly have thrown Patch in his teeth, accused him to his face of plotting kidnapping, forced marriage, or worse—and taken the consequences. Or rather, reveled in them, since the consequences of such an accusation must inevitably have been pistols at dawn, the long deferred settling of all our accounts over the years of taunt and jeer and mutual contempt. A still small voice in the back of my brooding Irish soul told me we would surely come to that, and my bloody Irish heart leaped up at the thought.

While I was dressing for supper that evening, Jeremy gave me a low-voiced, conspiratorial account of his day. It had been no more successful than my own, when all was said and done. But somehow I got the distinct impression that he had enjoyed it a good deal more—frustrations included.

Jeremy had found the servants of the Château d'Eauville eminently corruptible. Especially if they were given to understand that an affair of the heart was involved, all doors opened magically. In no time Jeremy had a key to Lady Barbara's chamber and a watch set on Bridget's room abovestairs. We were not halfway to Cythera that afternoon before my inestimable man had penetrated Lady Barbara's boudoir and was rifling energetically through her things.

"It's in the corner, your ludship, down the hall and down the stairs. A rare fine view it 'as, out over the river. I could see your punt most of the way to the rutting island." He handed me my shirt, looking uncommonly pleased with himself.

"Ah." Somehow the notion of Jeremy, busy about his espionage, pausing to look down upon the boat where I was paying ardent court to the unsuspecting Lady Barbara irritated me.

"I went through 'er ladyship's things as thoroughly as I could, sir, without breaking into anything, or disarranging what I couldn't conveniently put back. I'm not much for 'andling chemises and cosmetics."

I grunted. A stevedore's lad from East London would evidently have little experience of ladies' boudoirs.

"But I did rummage a bit in 'er ladyship's bags and boxes. Looked in the clothespress and the *escri-toire*. Even thumbed through 'er ladyship's books, sir, to see if she'd anything inserted betwixt the pages," he added, his eyes alight with enthusiasm for the chase.

"And you found?"

"Well, your ludship, there was a letter."

"A letter?"

"A letterpress copy of something 'er ladyship 'ad sent some days ago—to judge by the date," he added shrewdly. "I found it in the little writing desk by the window."

"I hope you didn't purloin it, Jeremy."

"No, sir. But I did take the liberty of committing the general drift of it to memory, sir." He paused dramatically once more, this time ostensibly to help me on with my vest.

"And the general drift of it was?" I asked, grimly determined to get the worst out of him at once.

"Well, sir, it was addressed to *Thomas Paine, Esq.,* in Paris. That would be *Tom Paine*, sir." He paused to let the significance of this sink in. "That's the firebrand, sir. The republican leveler that 'as fled 'is bond in England to sit in the French Assembly with them Jacobins, sir."

"He wouldn't be the first man to break his bond in England. But do get on with the *letter*, man!"

"Yes, your ludship. 'Er ladyship requested to know the state of things in the capital, sir. 'Ow strong Mr. Paine would expect the new National Convention to be, when it meets in the fall. 'Ow safe the streets might be from 'excesses by the populace, rightly if per'aps extravagantly indignant at the injustices perpetrated upon them by the Owld Regime.' Those were 'er very words, sir. I committed *that* to memory exact."

He looked self-righteous and shrewd at once, a ludicrous combination on his sharp-featured Cockney face. Jeremy's natural passion for intrigue, heightened by his newfound sense of patriotic zeal, was making him almost unbearable.

"You forget," I snapped impatiently, "that that is precisely why we intruded upon the Countess's hospitality in the first place—to learn the condition of the capital before pressing on. Have you nothing more damning than that to show for all your prying?" I was practically certain that he had not.

"One more thing only, your ludship," said Jeremy. "There was the chest, sir."

"The chest. What chest, man?"

"The little inlaid chest with the silver lock, sir. A jewel case, I took it for when I first noticed it among 'er ladyship's bags in the carriage, sir."

I remembered it. A small inlaid casket, silver-mounted. About the size of a government dispatch box.

"Well, what about it, man?" I snarled at him. "What was in the silly box, then?"

"I don't know, sir."

"You don't know?"

"No, your ludship. But I did ascertain this much, sir: *it do not rattle, sir.*"

"It do not *rattle!* That is the sum and substance of your afternoon's espionage?"

"Yes, sir," he responded. "But it did seem uncommon odd, sir, that a casket full of jewelry should not rattle, sir. Not so much as a clink or a tinkle."

"Ah. But then, why should it, after all? Thick velvet lining, no doubt, with each piece properly stowed—"

"Not so much as a tinkle, sir. Only a bit of a rustle, if you take my meaning."

"A rustle. A glove case, perhaps, or handkerchiefs—"

"A stiffish rustle it was, your ludship. Like paper, I should say, sir. Much more like paper than cloth."

"Well, well!" I yanked my neckcloth into place and cursed the fashion that required it. "Perhaps her ladyship has more than one correspondent, Jeremy, and prefers to keep her more personal letters away from prying eyes."

"Per'aps, sir."

"And this is all your confidential mission has netted us, then? A handful of books, a thoroughly understandable inquiry addressed to an English friend at Paris—and a mysterious *rustle!* Hardly hanging evidence, Jeremy."

"No, sir." His tone was injured and sullen as he knelt to buff my shoes. He obviously felt his news was being vastly undervalued.

"Very well, Jeremy, I shall make some shift to check into the matter of the little casket myself," I said magnanimously. "Mustn't let a rustle go unchecked, where the safety of the nation is at stake."

"Yes, sir!" He perked up at once. "No, sir, we assuredly must not." His narrow shoulders squared once more, and his chin sucked in, like a grenadier's on review. "For King and Country, sir!"

For peace in the family and a happy valet, it seemed little enough to do.

23

The Inlaid Casket

The time came at last to strike.

It was the night before our scheduled departure for Paris. Lady Barbara evinced all the symptoms of having succumbed as thoroughly as she was ever likely to do to the sensuous charms of the Castle of Eauville. That very night she took two full glasses of sparkling vintage with her supper, exclaimed over the quality of the delicately spiced meats provided by the Countess's cooks, and stroked the Graf von Teufel's white wolfhounds with a langorous sensitivity to their stiff white fur that quite charmed me. I even fancied that she cast a warm glance or two in my own direction in the course of the evening!

Politics and principle seemed all but forgotten, the sensual side quite regnant. The tender trap, in short, was all wound up, ready to spring.

I allowed sufficient time and more for the good Bridget to prepare her mistress for sleep and to return to her own cubbyhole under the eaves. Then I had Jeremy comb my hair and retie my queue with care, applied a dash of rosewater to the bosom of my coat, and set out for a midnight visitation to my lady's chamber.

Alas, I had, as usual with Lady Barbara, disastrously miscalculated. For one thing, I had not counted on my lady's ridiculous contention that early retiring and early rising significantly improve the character and constitution. I had also failed once more to be prepared for one of those disturbing intrusions from without which haunted my long and increasingly desperate pursuit of Lady Barbara MacFarlane from beginning to end.

The result of the first of these miscalculations was immediately apparent: my lady was sound asleep when I arrived, with pounding heart and panting breath, at her chamber door. The second error of judgment was also clear enough at once—or should have been to a less feverishly single-minded man than I had become. For Lady Barbara's door was open.

Not at all a likely thing, to come tiptoeing down a midnight corridor and see a long vertical strip of flickering candlelight where a lady's chastely closed portal should have been. Even in my high state of excitement, I realized that. I touched the door with my hand, and it gave at the touch. A strip of light perhaps two or three inches wide expanded to a full view of the room within.

The room was dimly lit by a lantern standing on a small table by the wall. There was a suit of armor at one side of the sleeping alcove, and broadswords crossed above it. Picturesque hammer beams showed across the ceiling. The furniture was dark and heavy, quite unlike the slender, elegant Louis Quinze chairs in my own chamber. It was all very modishly medieval; I wondered for a moment if I had stumbled into the wrong room in the dark.

But the gowns that showed through the open door of a wardrobe in the corner were familiar enough. So was the wide summer hat settled almost jauntily on a wig stand near the bed. And so, I realized with a totally inappropriate throb of the heart, was the little silver-mounted chest dimly visible on the shelf of the open wardrobe.

Now, I thought with totally uncharacteristic cunning, was clearly my best chance. The château slept. The redoubtable Bridget was in the servants' quarters two floors above. Lady Barbara's canopied four-poster was still and quiet, the curtains drawn, in its alcove on my left. And there stood the fatal chest, its silver fittings glimmering feebly in the lantern light. It would take but a moment. . . .

I stepped boldly into the room. I was reaching up to pull the casket down—held it indeed between my finger-tips—before even the most striking anomalies of the situation began to dawn upon me.

Why *had* the door been standing ajar? What was that lantern doing on the table—a dark lantern, I noticed now, open only a slit to provide the barest minimum of illumination? And what were those two heavy, dirty, indisputably masculine boots doing behind the swaying dresses in the wardrobe?

"Lord Libertine once more, by God!" the familiar voice of Captain Patch hissed hoarsely behind my back. "Roll 'im in the scuppers, mate—we 'aven't a moment to lose!"

My lady's elegant gowns gyrated wildly, and the pockycheeked face of Fag peered grotesquely out at me through the crinolines, a horse pistol in his hand. "Why didn't Figgis tip us a wink?" the stout villain in the red coat rasped irritably, extricating himself from the wardrobe with what alacrity he could manage.

"Never mind why, lad. Lay 'is bloody lordship out proper, and let's be after 'er ladyship before the castle's down upon us!"

I saw the pistol come up in blank-eyed astonishment. I heard the hall door crash to behind me, and the captain's heavy stride across the floor. I dodged awkwardly to one side, to avoid either Master Fag's shot or Captain Patch's impending spring upon my back. I lost my balance completely in the attempt, and reeled against the nearest wall. The roar of the pistol filled the room, and Patch howled with pain.

Staggering off the wall, I squinted through a cloud of acrid powder smoke to see the captain clutching at a bloodied arm and volleying curses at his mate. But any hope that the rogues might take out their wrath in mutual bloodletting was dashed at once. For Patch, with a final

bitter verdict on his henchman's ancestry and likely prog-
eny, swung back to me at once.

"There—there—" he cried, inarticulate with rage,
pointing furiously at me, the final cause of all his troubles.
His dark ill-shaven jaw worked ferociously as he whipped
out his short seaman's sword—it was his left arm that was
injured—and came for me. Fag, his pistol empty, reversed
it and followed his chief, swinging the long-barreled
weapon like a bludgeon.

The inlaid chest, I realized suddenly, was still in my
hands. I flung it at their heads. It missed by half a yard,
and then they were upon me.

I got a knee into Captain Patch's groin, and that
slowed him up somewhat. But I had had too much experience of his indestructibility to expect any injury less than
mortal to deter him for long. And then Fag's gun butt
slammed me a glancing blow across the temple. Glancing,
but quite hard enough to do the job.

I seemed to fall very slowly. There was ample time to
smell the reek of fish and garlic on Captain Patch's
breath, the smear of dung on his comrade's battered scarlet coat. I hit the floor with a resounding thwack, rolled
over, and saw a suit of armor come crashing down upon
me.

Beyond the rain of falling metal, the stout rogue with
the pockmarked face swung into view. He was hoisting
the small inlaid chest above his head, about to dash it
down upon me. A blue-coated arm reached out and
stopped him with a curse.

Patch himself was glowering down at me then, his tattered tricorne set awry, his greasy eyepatch shadowing
half his swarthy cheek. "Bloody rutting Macaroni!" he
spat between yellow teeth. "But we've no account to kill
'im. *She's* the one we're after—"

Something else exploded against my head—a boot toe,

perhaps? More falling metal? And then things went completely out of joint.

There was a series of concussions, like a cannonade, or fireworks over Vauxhall. A flash of fire, and wheeling suns. Another face was peering down at me out_ of the star-flecked darkness—a shifting physiognomy with planets whirling through it. First it was a sighing Jeremy, then a triumphant Durward. And then it was the face of Mr. William Pitt, Prime Minister of England. His strawberry-marked cheeks were flushed as usual with port, but his eyes glittered with that cold contempt for which he was so justly famous. He hefted the inlaid casket and shook his head, gazing down at me where I lay, sprawling on the floor of his book-lined study in Downing Street.

A pretty mess you've made of it, Arundel! he said in his sharp, unpleasant voice. *The nation stands in peril, on the very brink of war. And there you lie, giddy with lust, blinded by desire, flat on your back under the heel of a pair of ruffians. And the chest as tight sealed up as ever! Most distressing, Arundel, most distressing!*

The blackness swirled away, was sucked suddenly up into a wild shriek of terror.

The room lurched back, and the blessed casket slammed painfully into my chest. Dropped, rather than thrown, it seemed. For there went Fag and Patch, retreating desperately down the room before the outraged advancing figure of Lady Barbara MacFarlane. Her flaming hair was wild, her white nightdress swirled about her legs. She was swinging a two-handed broadsword round her head.

"Villains! Poltroons! Catchpole cowards, have you no stomach for more perilous work than bludgeoning a helpless man? That, sir—and that—for your hire this night!"

I saw Captain Patch stumble through the door, with his mate clawing after him. The massive sword blade slammed splinters from the doorpost above their terrified faces.

"Lord ha' mercy!" wailed the pockmarked scoundrel, vanishing from sight. I heard footsteps pounding down the hall, and saw Lady Barbara turn back toward me, eyes flashing in the lantern light. Then the darkness came back over me with a rush, and swirling constellations.

24

The Transports of Love

I awoke with my broken head cradled in Lady Barbara MacFarlane's lap. She was dabbing at my temple with a bloody rag and crooning what sounded like some sort of barbaric Gaelic lullaby. On one soft cheek, I saw to my amazement, there gleamed an indisputable tear.

She stopped crooning the minute I opened my eyes.

"Lord Christopher!" She brushed the telltale moisture from her cheek. "I thought they had killed you!"

"Indeed not, ma'am." I managed what I hoped was a devil-may-care smile. "My thick Irish skull has survived worse drubbings. But I am mightily sorry if my misfortune has given you any unhappiness!"

"I should be sorry to see you injured on my account, sir," she said quickly.

"No fear, ma'am," I began, starting to get up. But the pain that shot through my battered cranium then caused me to fall back into her lap once more. "If I might rest but a moment."

"Don't move!" she insisted sharply. "Not till your injury is bandaged up." I was glad enough to comply.

Still cradling my head in her lap, she leaned forward

over me, plucked up the hem of her nightdress, and ripped off a broad strip of cloth. This she folded length-wise into a thickish bandage. Elevating my aching head with care, she began to bind up the multiple cuts and con-tusions inflicted by gun butts, boots, and various pieces of knightly armor that lay scattered around us on the floor.

I had never been so close to her, in the purest physical sense of the word, as I was at that moment. Her fragrant breasts hovered only inches from my face. Her thighs were firm and warm beneath my cheek. Only the thinnest of fine muslin separated her flesh from mine. Even while her hands labored with their customary cool efficiency over my injuries, lust blazed up in me. Despite my aches and pains I began almost timidly to caress one white-swathed thigh.

She took no notice.

"There. Does that feel better now, sir?"

Her voice was crisp as ever. But was there the faintest tremor in it?

"Much better, Lady Barbara." I twisted about in her arms to gaze up at her face. "If I might rest but a mo-ment more—"

"Most certainly, sir."

I looked up at her, and suddenly I began to laugh.

"Lord Christopher," she said in bewilderment. "Are you quite all right?"

"Oh, yes, my lady! Oh, I am indeed, and never better!" I rose up on one elbow, bringing my face close to hers, laughing still. "Never better in my life, I assure your la-dyship!"

The ridiculousness of the situation swept over me uncontrollably. The ludicrous formalities, the inane re-straints that kept us still apart, with only the thickness of the thinnest cloth between us, seemed to me the funniest thing I had ever experienced. I stretched up, kissed her on the nose and on each of her baffled eyes, and collapsed chuckling into her lap once more.

"I am so comfortable, my lady," I declared positively, "that I think I shall not move from here until a physician is summoned to pronounce upon my various infirmities."

"A physician? But there is none at the château, nor in the town either."

"Then one must be sent for! A specialist from Paris! Indeed, I do not think I may with safety move my head from hence until the king's own surgeon shall have offered an opinion!"

"I think," said Lady Barbara, "that you are not so badly hurt as I first feared, sir."

"Madame, I protest! I am on fire with fevers! And feel how irregularly my poor heart beats!" I seized her half-resisting hand and thrust it under my shirt, upon my naked chest.

"I believe," she said firmly, "that we may with safety move the invalid after all."

"Never, madame! I shall swoon. My health will never recover from such cavalier treatment!"

But she was already rising, and helping me to rise as well. One surprisingly strong arm encircled my waist. The other—I noted with a wicked thrill—remained still inside my open shirt, though hauling at my torso in a purely functional manner, to get me on my feet.

Still protesting, I stood dizzily beside her now. She helped me toward the nearest piece of furniture, a low, carved oak chest of medieval vintage, strewn with incongruous Oriental cushions.

"If you must move me, ma'am," I began cunningly, "perhaps the bed—"

"Sit down, sir!" she ordered, lowering me into a sitting posture among the pillows. "Your head will clear in a moment, I dare say. In the meantime I shall fetch Bridget and send her for your man."

She turned away as she spoke. She was all business. And suddenly so was I.

Shrugging off an undeniably real stab of pain, I leaned forward and stretched out one arm to encircle her slender waist. I hauled myself giddily erect and swung her round to me, breast to breast, my eyes looking down into hers.

"Lord Christopher!" she gasped.

"Lady—Barbara—MacFarlane," I answered her. "Of Holyrood House, in Berkshire."

"Sir—"

"Madame?"

"What—what would you do?"

"Why, ma'am, just what I have longed to do every moment since I had the pleasure of making your ladyship's acquaintance—up a drizzly alley just this side of Hog Lane, Cheap, as I recall!"

And I kissed her on the mouth.

It was not a great kiss, not even a particularly passionate one, at least on her part. There were no Roman candles, no pyrotechnics bursting in air. Nor was there any of that platonic sublimity which our more genteel romancers frequently attribute to that holy of holies, the First Kiss. But it was, to put it mildly, a moment of some significance in my life.

I shall therefore attempt to be as specific and particular about it as memory permits.

Her lips were full and strong, her mouth not overlarge. Her lips had just parted, as though she was about to speak, when my own came down upon hers. Both our mouths stayed open as we kissed.

For she did respond. Her lips were cool, not feverish with desire, but they did press back. Her mouth did move, rather slowly and experimentally than quick with ardor, but it did move under mine. I felt her breath sigh between her small white teeth to mingle with my own.

Then her arms slid slowly up around my neck, and I

felt all her slender loveliness come against me. Her perfect breasts flattened against my chest, her belly against my seething loins.

All the impulses, Lord Christopher, if I am any judge, murmured a voice from the distant past—White's clubrooms, on that fatal night. Oh, what a prophet was the Reverend Dr. Throgmorton!

We kissed, then—*we* kissed, I say—for perhaps a hundred breathless seconds. Our lips explored—lips only, reader, I must be exact. Our arms were about each other, our upper bodies pressed together. I could feel the pressure of her breasts, and she must have felt the swelling hardness of my instrument belowstairs.

A hundred seconds of beginning. Slow, cool, exploratory, maddening.

And then she drew way.

"O my lady!" I was the one gasping now. "You know I care for you!"

Her seagreen eyes looked back at me, gleaming faintly in the light of the abandoned dark lantern. I could see her bosom rising and falling in the clinging nightdress. Her face seemed faintly flushed, though I could scarce be sure in the dimness.

Her lips parted to speak.

"I think Lady Barbara knows well enough how much you *care* for her. Lord Libertine!" The harsh, sarcastic accents of Lord Mortimer Durward shattered the moment like brittle glass. "And *how* you care, I'm sure!"

Durward strode into the room, fully if hastily dressed, carrying a streaming candle in one hand.

"As you care for all your *victims!*" His reedy voice slashed at me like a fencing foil.

Lady Barbara took a step back, looked at him and back at me.

"As you care for all the innocent maidens who have fallen under your hands down the years! All the good

wives who have betrayed their sacred vows for your lascivious embraces! All those celebrated conquests that
have gone to swell the monstrous rakehell reputation of
the king of libertines!"

I turned around and hit him in the face.

"Lord Christopher!" Lady Barbara raised a hand in
shocked protest. Her eyes were wide, her lips still
parted—but clearly not with passion now.

Durward reeled backward out the door, slammed satis-
fyingly into the opposite wall of the narrow corridor. I
staggered against the nearest wall myself, dizzy once more
with pain. But I had still command enough to get out the
words:

"At your service, Durward—with any weapons you
may choose! Only let it be now and here, this coming
morning and this present place!"

Then I keeled over in a swoon once more. I had barely
time to notice that Lady Barbara MacFarlane, standing
not a yard away, did not raise a hand this time to help me
as I fell.

25

I Fall from Grace Once More

"If I may say, so, sir, I believe you have outdone even
yourself this time."

"I think you have said so before, Jeremy."

"Yes, sir." He adjusted the bandage around my brow
with quite unnecessary vigor. I wondered which hurt
worse: the injuries inflicted by Captain Patch, or the
swollen, bleeding hand I had slammed into Lord Mortimer's protruding teeth with such carefree abandon.

"The inlaid casket," Jeremy went on inexorably, "remains unopened. The contents still entirely unknown. And the nation, sir, the nation still in peril!" He yanked the bloody bandage taut with a final flourish. "Am I right, sir?"

"Damn the casket!" I snapped with quite justifiable irritation. "And damn your clumsy hands! That's my head you're mucking about with, not a bale of cotton on the East India Docks!"

"You've also missed your rutting chance with 'er ladyship—am I right again?"

"What could she say, man, with Durward standing there wiping the blood off his mouth and staring at me with those fishy eyes of his? And then the good Bridget popped in, and the other servants a moment after—"

"And then, of course—begging your ludship's pardon—the other gentleman did make a point or two. About the innocent maidens and good wives, I mean to say. Do you think it might appeal to 'er ladyship as an argument, sir?"

I thought of Betsy Murrain the barrister's wife, and Lady Arbuthnot, and Sally Love at the Rose in Drury Lane. Innocent maidens and good wives were not exactly the terms that leaped to my lips. But to Lady Barbara MacFarlane's?

"Durward will regret his precious points, by God," I said aloud. "In precisely four and one-half hours from now, in the woods below the lime-tree gardens." I gloated happily for a moment over the vision. I had longed for years to get that supercilious aristocratic prig on the other end of my barkers. And now the time was come. I glanced fondly down at the gleaming long-barreled pistol in their velvet-lined case upon the table, and a warm glow of anticipation flooded over me.

" 'Er ladyship, as I recall," Jeremy broke in on my revery of blood and carnage, " 'as for some time been a strong advocate against dueling, sir. Before *The Rights of Women* and *The Vindication of the Chimney Sweeps,* she did a famous tract called *A Gentleman's Honor: or, the Barbarous Practice of Dueling Exposed.* Or some such." He sniffed. " 'Owever, it's called, I don't think she'll be waiting with open arms if you come back to breakfast with Lord Mortimer's blood upon your 'ands."

I gave him what I hoped was a withering glance. But I did remember the damned tract now. That, and the shocked dismay on Lady Barbara's face as I hurled my challenge at Lord Durward.

"Of course," added Jeremy thoughtfully, turning his attentions from my bandaged head to my skinned and swollen fingers, "you may not 'ave that problem at all, sir. If this 'and swells up any more, you'll 'ave the deuce of a time even pulling a trigger. It may be *your* blood on *'is* conscience in the morning, sir."

"You're a wonderful consolation to me, Jeremy," I sighed.

He laved my stinging hand in the cold water of my shaving basin. He wrapped two badly chewed-up fingers in strips of cambric handkerchief. But I could tell that he had more to say. I waited sourly for him to say it.

"While you've been lollygagging around at 'eathen ceremonials and letting the casket slip through your fingers, sir," he announced presently, "I've been dredging up a bit of intelligence of my own. I thought it might be of interest to your ludship."

I shrugged morosely. His "intelligence," I shrewdly guessed, would have to do with the wretched business of the Army Report, about which I could increasingly care less.

"There's someone come to the castle, sir. Come up from Paris, to see 'er ladyship the Countess Dooville on urgent business."

"From the Parisian chapter of the Ancient Order of Sodom and Gomorrah, I suppose."

"I wouldn't say so, sir. The servants took 'im straight to madame's own chamber, not to the chapel where the rest of 'em forgather, as I understand it. I expect 'e's still waiting for 'er now. A gentleman of some importance, I should guess, to be shown straight into the Countess's own boodoir."

"And what precisely have the Countess d'Eauville's liaisons to do with this silly espionage business, pray tell?"

"I don't know that, sir," the little Cockney answered, his small black eyes bright with the London street passion for intrigue. "But if we were to make our way quietly down the back stairs, we might examine the gentleman's 'orse in the stables—a great foaming bay it was, sir; I saw 'im riding up in the moonlight. And then if we slipped round by the rose garden under 'er ladyship's boodoir window—"

"—We could easily get our heads blown off by an outraged lover!" I cut him off wearily. "I have difficulties and to spare, as you yourself have so trenchantly made clear, without that sort of thing into the bargain."

"Yes, sir!" Jeremy shut his mouth and turned frigidly away. I knew I should be out of favor for days to come.

My loyal servant finished undressing me in silence. He brushed my breeches and folded them, flung my shirt onto the laundry pile, drew the curtains of my bed, all without another word. His cheeks were stiff with disapproval, his meager shoulders squared with a sense of patriotic duty—the patriotic duty I was so flagrantly neglecting.

But my mind dwelt gloomily on my own manifold personal problems. I had no time for public business. Or for indulging Jeremy's natural aptitude for plots and counterplots, As he opened the door to return to his own quarters on the floor above, I called final instructions to him.

"Be sure to wake me an hour before dawn, Jeremy. I'll clean and oil the pistols myself."

"Yes, sir."

He bowed coldly and went out. I tumbled into bed, with a scant three hours' sleep between me and a very difficult morning.

But I was not to have even that much rest before I faced Lord Durward across two pistol barrels and twenty yards of forest glade. For my adventures were not yet over for that unlikely night at the Château d'Eauville.

It was an odor that awakened me. A thick familiar fragrance that I had smelled before. A mingling of musky perfume and something stronger—the hot sweet stench of a woman's body at the highest pitch of sensual arousal.

I rolled over dreaming of Mahometan angels, pried my eyelids apart, and stared up into the taut, fine-boned features of Countess Charlotte d'Eauville.

She had drawn back the heavy hangings of my bed and stood looking down at me. Her eyes were dark and fathomless as the midnight Nile. Her thin aristocratic nostrils dilated slightly as my eyes opened, and her lips parted just enough to reveal a glimmer of milk-white teeth. She wore the same pale lavender peignoir she had had on when I had come to her bedchamber our first night at Eauville. But this time she clearly wore no nightdress beneath it.

"It is cold, *mon cher* Arundel," she said tranquilly. "Have you no room for me in your bed?"

This, as the reader may recall, is a highly moral tale. A tale of regeneration, of the rise of a fallen man from the lowest ranks of moral turpitude to some sort at least of grace. And here was I, the hero of this pilgrimage, fresh from the arms of my beloved. Fresh, indeed, from our first kiss. Surely even so notorious a weak vessel as I am would not fall from Lady Barbara's virginal embrace into the arms of a wanton courtesan? Surely, the right-thinking reader will suggest, not even Lord Libertine could be so crass? Surely not?

But then, the right-thinking reader has perhaps never beheld the Countess Charlotte d'Eauville standing all but naked beside his bed.

I did resist—let me have so much credit at least.

"Madame!" I said, sitting up in my nightshirt. "I have had the most extraordinary misadventures since I saw you last at supper. As you may have heard?"

"I am informed there were prowlers," she murmured, seating herself on the edge of my bed. She ran one forefinger across my cheek and down my neck. "It is shocking. I cannot apologize sufficiently. But in these mad times . . ." Her finger wandered down over my somewhat hairy chest, to the limits of the open neck of my nightshirt.

"I fear," I said, "that Lady Barbara's chamber was badly disarranged in the melee. A suit of antique armor was, in fact—"

"And you were injured," she whispered, taking my bandaged hand in hers. "But not too seriously, I hope?" She laid my hand upon her thigh. "I should hate to think that the celebrated Lord Libertine was permanently incapacitated under my roof."

"No—ah—permanent injury, madame, I am happy to report." My fingers twitched of their own accord, lying there on that slender limb, half visible through translucent silk.

Her eyes had been cast down since she had seated herself, looking at my half-bared chest, at my injured hand. Now she raised her head, shook back the dark cascade of straight black hair, and looked me in the face.

"I have done all I can, Lord Christopher," she said, "to help you with your reluctant Lady Barbara—have I not?"

"You have, ma'am. I am most grateful." I spoke tersely. Credit me with this too, reader: I could no longer speak comfortably of my beloved in the presence of the bawd I had engaged to help me win her!

"And tonight your lovely puritan has once more rejected your advances, *n'est-ce pas?*"

"Not exactly, madame," I began nervously, wondering if she had heard of Lord Mortimer's intervention at the crucial moment. "It was not precisely what I should term a *rejection*—"

"But you *were* in her room this night, milord. And now you are here, alone. And the *belle Anglaise* sleeps virginal still in her own bed. Is that not so?"

"It is," I answered unhappily.

"I think, Lord Christopher, that I have done all I can to help you with your amorous campaign."

"You have been most kind."

"And now, *mon chéri*, I must ask you to be kind in turn." As she spoke, she raised one hand to the drawstring at the neck of her single garment. The slightest of tugs, and the peignoir fell open to the groin.

"Madame?" My tone rang false even to me.

"You may take it, if you wish, as an ancient custom of the country. A form of that famous *droit du seigneur* which the French nobility at least have striven so hard to keep alive in these lamentably traditionless times. *Droit du seigneur* —or *droit de la châtelaine* in this case, perhaps. One which I always insist upon exacting from my more interesting guests before they leave." She shrugged the peignoir off her shoulders.

"Leave!" I croaked. "Indeed, I fear we must be on our way to Paris soon. Lady Barbara has heard from an acquaintance of hers that there is at least a lull in the disorders there—"

"We shall all leave tomorrow, or the day after at the latest, for the capital. I am closing down the château for the rest of the summer and returning to the city for the season. It may be the last social season in Paris for many a day." She drew back the bedcovers as she spoke. "Tomorrow or the next day, we shall go. But now it is tonight!"

She pulled my tangled nightshirt from between my legs and bent to kiss my resurgent cock.

Pity poor Master Cock, dear reader! A full fortnight without indulgence, half of it amid all the temptations of this palace of sensual delights. This night alone had exposed the tall man belowstairs to cruel and unusual strains almost beyond the endurance of mere flesh. When the Countess's thin lips, gentle as eiderdown, touched that red Hibernian head, all resistance ended.

Charlotte d'Eauville, as I have intimated more than once, was a small woman, with slim hips and small tight breasts and an incredibly narrow waist. But there was a fire in that dry little body. A fire that blazed into a roaring conflagration as we came together.

Before the moon went down outside the window and the stars paled into dawn, I believe that I penetrated the Comtesse d'Eauville through every possible orifice. I am sure that she offered them all.

And there was more to come.

The moon was down, the false light just glimmering in the east, when I heard the latch lift and my door creak open. I looked up from the Countess's quivering body, expecting to see Jeremy, come early to awaken me. But there was a rustle of skirts instead, and Marie stepped into the circle of guttering candlelight beside the bed.

"*Madame!*" she said in her low voice. "*Il est ici! Chez vous, et fort impatient!*" Whoever it was must be very impatient indeed, I thought, if the urgency of Marie's tone was any gauge.

Countess Charlotte rolled her head on the pillow to look at her maid, and muttered an unladylike expletive.

"He says," Marie went on, "that he must see you instantly!"

It must be Jeremy's mysterious visitor, I told myself. A jealous lover, as predicted. I glanced about, located my pistol case on the table, and tried to recall whether I had loaded the weapons or not. He must be a man of importance, I thought, to cause the usually impeccably discreet Marie to break in thus upon her mistress's tryst.

But the Countess Charlotte simply laughed aloud and raised herself upon one elbow.

"*Qu'il m'attend, chérie*," she said: Let him wait. And then, reaching out one slender patrician hand: "*Viens ici, toi! Viens, Marie! C'est un homme, celui-ci!*" She squeezed my hairy thigh, her dark eyes smoldering. "*Formidable! Viens, toi aussi!*"

I tried to respond becomingly to the compliment. But verbal responses were clearly not in order. For in a matter of seconds Marie had slipped off her own low-cut black gown and scrambled demurely into bed beside us.

So I forgot about the mysterious visitor, and the impending confrontation with Lord Mortimer, and indeed about everything at all except these two enthusiastically female bodies. For another hour or so, there was nothing in the world but the three of us. Nothing but those sugared slits and thrusting tits and throbbing buttocks, nothing but hands and mouths and tangled hair and intertwining limbs.

They were like cats, insatiable of caresses and of milk; and they drained me finally of both.

But a cold unfeeling congress underneath it all, the hopeful reader adds? Quite so, quite so. And there was a part of me that knew this, even while we rolled and gasped and cried out and tore the bed apart. A part of me that felt the emptiness, if you will, of this meaningless encounter in the dark. We were animals in heat, no more.

But the tall man belowstairs did have a wonderful time.

26

Pistols at Twenty Paces

Two hours later I stood under a greenwood tree in the forest of Chantilly and made ready to blow Lord Mortimer's brains out at last.

It was five o'clock of a crisp summer morning, the red sun just filtering through the trees to incarnadine the little glade. The four of us went through our paces with the ritual precision of schoolboys preparing for a fistfight in a corner of the yard.

I had drawn the Graf von Teufel for a second. Durward had perforce engaged the Baron de Franval (whose title outranked von Teufel's, even if he was a blatant sodomite). There was no physician present, and no other witnesses.

We had drawn lots for the position and the word, and my man, von Teufel, had won both. We had primed our weapons in each other's presence. De Franval and von Teufel had paced off the distance—twenty steps—and placed us as the German would have it, me beneath a spreading evergreen oak, Durward under a nondescript elm.

We now stood facing each other across the damp grass, listening to von Teufel remind us of the particulars agreed upon.

"I shall have the honor of presiding," the Graf declared in his precise Teutonic French. "I shall first inquire if each gentleman is ready to begin. This being so, and so acknowledged, I shall proceed to give the word to fire. The word agreed upon shall be the English term *'Present!'* " His agateblue eyes glistened at the prospect of impending carnage.

"Each gentleman shall have two shots. A snap or a flash will be counted as a shot. Neither party shall move from his position until both shots have been discharged. Unless of course a single shot should prove sufficient to incapacitate one or the other from firing a second time."

I was fully resolved that one shot should prove sufficient.

I did not, of course, actually intend to kill him.

Much as I despised him, had despised him for a prig and a hypocrite for all the years I had known him, I felt no particular passion to rid the world of him. The world liked him well enough, with his pompous talk of Toryism and the honor of his class, and the world was welcome to him. I desired merely to wipe the supercilious smirk off his face when he looked down his high beaked nose at me personally. A shot through the shoulder should suffice for that I thought. There is nothing like a heavy-caliber pistol ball at twenty paces to wipe the smirk off a man's face.

And then too—happy thought—his injured lordship would undoubtedly find it necessary to abridge his journey as a result. He would surely return home posthaste, to put himself under the care of a civilized English physician. Lady Barbara and I would thus be left to go on alone—to Paris or wherever. Paris was certainly not my first choice. Perhaps her ladyship might be prevailed upon to travel south instead? The Alps, perhaps, or Italy?

"If you are ready, then, Milord Dur-var?"

"I am," that unfortunate responded stiffly, raising his pistol.

"Are you ready, Milord Arun-del?"

"Most assuredly," I answered. Italy, I decided, would

be a bit feverish in late summer. The Swiss Alps, then: Zurich, or Geneva?

My barker came up easily, the engraved barrel flashing briefly in the sunrise.

"Present!" said Graf von Teufel.

"Stop this nonsense at once!" said Lady Barbara MacFarlane, breaking through a last tangle of ferns and sapplings at the clearing's edge. Behind her, plowing more slowly through dewy pines and crackling underbrush, came the unhappy Bridget, calling after her mistress to wait for her, Jesus and Mary, and it was all folly surely.

Lady Barbara stepped briskly into the glade, cheeks high-colored, eyes flashing. She was dressed as for a picnic in a light-blue frock, with her wide summer hat swinging from one arm. In three strides she was between us. Or more precisely, she was in front of Durward, and looking haughtily back up my pistol barrel into my own stricken eyes.

"Put it down, I say!" she snapped.

I lowered the heavy weapon instantly, thanking whatever gods might be that I had always eschewed a hair trigger.

Poor Bridget stopped at the forest's edge, her eyes round with horror at the sight of the gleaming pistols. She stood knee-deep in ferns, wringing her hands and muttering her Romanish prayers.

"This is disgraceful!" Lady Barbara actually stamped her foot. "Grown men acting like—like spoiled children. Civilized human beings settling their differences like barbarians out of the Dark Ages!"

I had a quick vision of Lady Barbara herself the night before, flailing away at Patch and his henchman with a two-handed war sword. But I had the sense to say nothing. This was a different Lady Barbara from the woman I had held in my arms not five hours before.

This was the author of *A Gentleman's Honor: or, The*

Barbarous Practice of Dueling Exposed. Of that, I realized with a silent groan, and of so much else beside. This was the vindicator of chimney sweeps and Jacobins and no end of other marvelous causes. This was the intrepid lady who spoke her piece in political clubs and embarked upon quixotic quests to "see for herself" how the Guillotine worked!

And all the sensuous influence of Eauville was gone, vanished, shattered at a stroke.

"I had, of course, intended," Lord Mortimer was saying, "to withhold my fire. In order that my opponent might have every opportunity to reconsider, to draw back from this folly."

"I have no doubt of it, Lord Mortimer," said Lady Barbara. "For all our differences, you are, I think, a man of principle."

Dear God.

"As for you, Lord Christopher—I really have no words!" It was a straight look and a half she leveled at me then, a look more terrifying than any pistol barrel.

"My lady—" I began desperately, futilely, hopelessly.

"No words, sir! I saw you strike this gentleman down, who had done nothing but what any gentleman would—step between a notorious rake and his intended victim!" She had at least the grace to blush. It was the only hope left to me that catastrophic morning.

"I saw you press, nay, *force* this villainous duel upon him! And I saw this moment past, in your very eyes, sir, the joy with which you would have cut him down! The barbarity of it, sir! The barbarous lust to murder your fellowman that I saw in that square, stupid, ugly *Irish* face of yours not a moment since—it passes understanding, it passes belief!"

She tossed her head, her copper-colored hair flashing in the sun.

"I leave for Paris today, as soon as my things can be

got ready. The Countess will give us a carriage, I am sure. May I count upon your company, Lord Mortimer?"

"Of course, my lady!"

"Shall we return, then, to the château? Some of us at least have more important things to do than play at swords-and-daggers in the dew!"

And that was that.

Lady Barbara and Lord Mortimer set off toward the castle arm in arm, with Bridget muttering in their wake. De Franval and von Teufel shook their heads and rolled their eyes at the *folie* of *les Anglais* and then went off about their business—von Teufel after his wolfhounds, the Baron de Franval in search of his valet. I was left alone in the forest glade, with only a sleepy bird or two for company.

Suddenly I was very tired.

I emptied my pistols carefully and returned them to their case. I brushed the dew off my coat, flung that garment over my shoulder, and left the glade to the birds and the brightening day.

A pretty mess you've made of it, Arundel! a voice echoed in my weary brain. Jeremy's or Prime Minister Pitt's, I could not remember which. I could not even recall which of my recent disastrous failures whichever of them had been speaking of. But it was true, all true.

I did not wish to overtake the others, so I circled round the looming ridge on which the Château d'Eauville stood and approached it from the front, up the winding road from the village and the river. I was plodding up that rutty track, all but asleep on my feet, when the pounding of hooves intruded upon my walking dream. I looked up bleary-eyed and saw a rider round the bend of a deep gallop, clattering down the road from the château.

Rather by instinct than by any clear, conscious recognition of my danger, I flung myself sideways into the bushes, out of the path of the big bay horse. I had only a glimpse of the rider before I crashed into the thorny tangle of gorse and brambles, and lost consciousness of all but more bumps and bruises and the outraged sense of being all the world's victim. But that single glimpse was sufficient to give me something to wonder about all the way to Paris.

For the galloping rider with the swarthy cheeks and cold impatient eyes—the Countess's mysterious visitor, now clearly on his own way back to the capital in considerably greater haste than she—was the Jacobin Jacques Machaud.

BOOK III

Place de la Guillotine

27

"Allons, Enfants de la Patrie"

As it happened, we did not set out for Paris until the following morning, a full twenty-four hours later. It took the Countess that long to set in train the closing down of the château. Her guests used the time in packing to depart for their own scattered domains, and in clucking over their hostess's folly in returning to the city "under the present circumstances." Lady Barbara—so Jeremy learned from Bridget—spent the extra day fuming over the delay. As for me, I slept clock around and awoke refreshed, ravenous, and almost eager for the journey.

There were seven of us in the coach.

Jeremy, who was convinced the entire affair was being horribly botched, was a veritable Banquo at the feast. He had laid out my clothes in silence that morning, served my usual barbarically heavy breakfast without a word, and packed without consulting me. He sat stiffly in his corner of the carriage, austerely withdrawn, throughout the whole half-day's journey to Paris.

The estimable Bridget stared pale-faced and apprehensive out the window as we swayed and jounced along the road toward that citadel af Antichrist itself, the center of the Revolution. In the end I could not forbear to ask what troubled her. I was informed that the light of the Gospel had been quite put out in Paris, right and wrong confounded, and the bones of a wicked old man named Voltaire set up to be worshiped in the Church of Our Lady—and wouldn't any Christian woman worry, to be pounding pell-mell down the road to such a place? She turned her puffy pudding face resentfully toward her young mistress as she spoke.

Lady Barbara was polite and cool and totally uninterested in me. She sat with her hands clasped firmly in her lap, gazing out the window on her side of the coach. Her bold, mad, quixotic journey was nearing its end; she was apparently beginning to wonder just what she would find there. Her eyes never once met mine from Chantilly to Paris.

Even Lord Mortimer Durward seemed to feel the mounting tension. He gnawed his lower lip, drummed his thin aristocratic fingers on his knee, and shrank back into his seat like a snail every time we passed an official carriage or a detachment of troops. I gazed at him beneath lowered lids, trying to guess what might be going on behind that pale forehead, those pale batrachian eyes. He had accompanied Lady Barbara across the Channel to keep her out of my hands. Indeed, if the hovering presence of Captain Patch and his bullyboys in the background was any evidence, Durward had hoped for an easy abduction and forced marriage with himself, perhaps in the English church at Calais. But Calais was far behind us now. Things were decidedly getting out of hand. I got the distinct impression that Lord Mortimer Durward was regretting his own ingenious ploy.

The Countess d'Eauville had brought but a single maid with her—lush, moist-lipped Marie, of course. That placid daughter of the people sat contented as a cow through the day, her buxom beauty undimmed by the slightest glimmer of thought. She nibbled on things, tended quickly to her mistress's wants, and generally seemed quite unaware that, to use another of Bridget's vivid expressions, we were all galloping hell-bent into Belial's gripe.

That left only the Countess herself for me to converse

with. And even she seemed less than enthusiastic about the present journey. Her responses were monosyllabic and considerably less witty than usual. I wondered what the stiff-necked Jacobin Machaud could be to her, a daughter of the most ancient and decadent aristocracy in France. I had given up the importunate-lover explanation the moment I saw who her secret visitor had been—a point for Jeremy. But the object of Citizen Machaud's visit remained mysterious. I hazarded a guess that he might be her prime contact in the new regime, and that even her remarkable immunities might be beginning to crumble as the Revolution gathered momentum. That would explain the secret visit and the unlikely return to Paris—to mend fences, bolster her unique position as one of the few of the old nobility to ride out the storm. It all made quite good sense, really.

Or so I thought at the time.

Paris, they say, is all things to all men. They also say a great deal more about it—mostly claptrap. In fact, it is a great gray sooty modern city, with a few splendid palaces and boulevards where the wealthy live and disport themselves. A city like any other, in short: nine-tenths uninhabitable, the other tenth the heart and soul of modern civilization.

We reached Paris about three that afternoon.

There were some differences between the old City of Light and the new one. The new national colors—red, white, and blue—were prominently displayed everywhere. The mendicants who thrust taloned hands at us as our coach inched its way through the bustling streets brightened their rags with the largest tricolor flowers I have ever seen. The prostitutes who strolled arm in arm in the Palais Royal gardens all wore red-white-and-blue ribbons in their mobcaps. The tricolor flag fluttered in the sultry gray air above the Bastille itself, that massive mon-

ument to the worst excesses of the old order, gutted by
the Paris mob on that fatal fourteenth of July three years
since.

But Paris was still Paris, I thought, as we turned south
to the river and I glimpsed the towers of Notre Dame
above the housetops. There might be fewer fine carriages
like our own in the tangle of wagons and carts and fiacres
and barouches that jammed the streets. But the stench
and din and general dinginess of the largest part of the
City of Light remained unchanged.

We rattled on along the Seine, leaving the medieval city
behind. The Hôtel de Ville gave way to the mighty palaces of the Louvre and the Tuileries. When we swung
north once again at the far end of the Tuileries Gardens,
we were in the heart of the modern, civilized city.

It was there that I got my first real shock.

We were crossing the vast tree-fringed Place Louis
Quinze, dedicated to the memory of the present mon-
arch's inglorious predecessor. Only an empty marble
pedestal remained of the royal statue in the Place Louis
Quinze now. In its place a tall, gaunt, wooden scaffolding
rose against the sky.

I glimpsed it only briefly before we veered to the left
once more, into the Rue St. Honoré at last. Not enough
time, certainly, to see the machine clearly or to understand its workings. But time enough to recognize, with a
cold chill up the spine, the terrible engine of which we
had all heard so much that summer.

"*That*, I believe," said Lord Mortimer nastily, "is the
famous achievement of the Revolution your Jacobin
friends boast of so enthusiastically. The finest flower of
the democratical spirit—"

"Mary and Joseph preserve us!" whispered Bridget,
white to the lips. "It's the knife! The mechanical headsman!"

"Precisely!" snapped Durward. "Dr. Guillotin's invention for extinguishing human life more rapidly and more efficiently than ever in human history before. I understand," he added caustically, looking at Lady Barbara, "that the partisans of the Revolution justify it as the most humane means ever devised for eliminating the enemies of the state."

Lady Barbara did not answer. Her eyes and ears were engaged elsewhere.

Along the northern edge of the Tuileries Gardens came marching a detachment of troops. They were a sun-browned, swarthy lot, in the usual ragtag uniforms, liberally decorated with tricolor sashes and cockades. They were armed with an unimpressive array of ancient muskets, fowling pieces, even cutlasses and scythes. They were weary and dusty to the knees. But they were singing as they swung along under the trees toward the Place Louis Quinze—the Place de la Révolution, as it was now officially called. The words of their marching song reached us just as we turned off out of the square—words bellowed out in the rich nasal accent of the South of France:

> *Allons, enfants de la patrie,*
> *Le jour de gloire est arrivé!*
> *Contre nous de la tyrannie*
> *L'étendard sanglant est levé,*
> *L'étendard sanglant est levé!*

The whores in ankle-length frocks promenading under the trees in the Tuileries Gardens waved and applauded. The cheerful detachments from the sunny South waved back and doffed their hats, white teeth flashing in their bronzed faces.

Aux armes . . . citoyens!
Formez . . . vos bataillons!
Marchons, Marchons! . . .

It was, I must admit, a catchy martial air. Quite up to "Rule, Britannia," or even "The White Cockade."

"It is the marching song of the Marseilles regiments," Countess Charlotte commented dryly. "I understand they are singing it all over Paris now. And the troops marching north to defend the frontiers have carried it to the Army of the Rhine."

We had just creaked to a stop in front of the long yellow-brick facade of the Countess's Paris mansion, at the far end of the Rue St. Honoré. A final distant chorus of *"Allons, enfants de la patrie"* still reached us from the square several blocks behind.

"It is the marching song of liberty!" said Lady Barbara MacFarlane suddenly. "It is the battle song of a New World aborning!" Her voice was husky, and the eyes she turned upon me at last glinted with tears of emotion.

Then the Countess's liveried servants poured out of the front doors, in considerable confusion because they had not been warned in advance of her ladyship's intention to return so early. We all alighted from the carriage, stiff and sweaty from our journey, and were escorted with much bowing and scraping and many obsequious apologies into the Hôtel d'Eauville.

28

Paris in the Reign of Robespierre

Paris in the reign of Robespierre. It has a ring, a decided ring. Unfortunately, it is not strictly speaking, true.

I understand that there is a National Convention in Paris now, and that the Jacobin faction are emerging as the masters of it. Nor is there any question that Maximilien Robespierre is the master of the Jacobins. They call him "the Incorruptible," and expect he will be the savior of France. Certainly he is a simon-pure Revolutionary: and in the Republic of the Revolutionaries, his eventual triumph seems assured. Once poor Louis is done away with, Citizen Robespierre will no doubt emerge as the Cromwell of a kingless France.

No doubt. But it was not so when we reached Paris in those last tense days of August, 1792.

Robespierre did not yet reign, though his name was on everyone's lips, eclipsing even such celebrated tribunes of the people as Danton and Marat. In fact, nobody reigned in Paris that hot, muggy last week of August. Invading armies were poised upon the frontiers, counterrevolutionary conspiracies were rumored everywhere, and there seemed at first glance to be nobody at all in charge of affairs in that nervous, fearful, beleagured capital.

Louis XVI, Marie Antoinette, and the royal princes were sequestered in the Temple Prison, their lives at the mercy of the Revolutionaries. But the Revolutionary leadership itself was hopelessly divided—moderate against extremist, would-be republican against constitutional monarchist, Jacobin against Girondist. Independently of such factional and ideological disputes, there were the personal feuds of one ambitious tribune against another; most notably, perhaps, of Danton against Robespierre. And beneath it all seethed and bubbled the most volatile and unpredictable force in the Revolution: the Paris mob.

An incisive analysis, is it not? Pithy, sweeping, to the point. Every word of it came, of course, from Lady Barbara MacFarlane. On those rare occasions when she would speak to me at all, she lectured me on politics.

That last-mentioned element in the mix—the Paris mob—was particularly worrisome, even to Lady Barbara. They were "the People" to her, never "the mob." But they worried her nonetheless.

"It is the Commune of Paris," she explained earnestly, sitting in a window niche overlooking the street our second morning in the city. "The poor citizens of this miserable capital, whom you and I will never see, but from a moving carriage, or through a parlor window, as we do now."

She gazed pensively out through the panes.

I looked at the grubby faces drifting past. Three years ago, they had stormed the Bastille with their bare hands. Two weeks since, they had massacred the King's Swiss Guards to the last man. What, a breathless world wondered, might they not do next?

I shrugged and looked at Lady Barbara instead.

Her lovely eyes glistened, fever-spots of excitement glowed in her otherwise paling cheeks. But I could not forget the warmer flush on those same cheeks, the warm, strong arms sliding around my neck that night at Eauville. I watched her lips move, spilling out eloquent words, and I remembered those same lips under mine.

Somehow I could not believe that she cared nothing at all for me, and everything for the Great Experiment.

"It's clear as daylight, sir!" Jeremy would remonstrate with me as he handed me my nightshirt. "She's one of 'em—'eart and soul! She does naught else but talk of 'em, visit with 'em, attend their rutting clubs and assemblies and what not. Why, only a blind man could doubt it!"

"And the precious inlaid casket, Jeremy? Has she hastened to deposit that token of her sympathies upon the rostrum of the National Assembly, with the compliments of The Friends of the People in London?"

"Ah, sir, and that's even more mysterious, if I may say so." He was the confidential agent again, voice lowered conspiratorially, beady eyes darting suspiciously toward every shadowy corner. "The little silver-mounted chest, sir, 'as *disappeared!*"

"Indeed? You've been poking through her ladyship's things again, have you?"

"I 'ave my ways of keeping track, sir." He drew himself up, spoke portentously. "There's two things I do know, sir. The chest 'as gone from 'er ladyship's room. *But it 'asn't left this 'ouse!*"

"Ah? Light-fingered servants, would you say?" I shook my head, mimicking his own characteristic deprecation of our hosts. "These Frenchies—"

"I wouldn't say that, no, sir."

I grew weary of the game. "Very well, Jeremy. If it's not the Countess's servants, then who has got the silly chest?"

He answered hollowly, in a voice even fuller of dark portent: "*I don't know*, sir!"

I gave up and went to bed.

About one thing Jeremy was quite right, however. Lady Barbara did spend immense amounts of time in what Prime Minister Pitt would undoubtedly have regarded as suspicious company.

She visited the National Assembly, then in its concluding days. She spent long evenings at the radical *salon* of Mme. Rolland, a bright-eyed aggressive woman who surrounded herself with young fanatics and henpecked her husband, a moderate minister in the government. She visited with the English exile community in Paris, among whom Tom Paine—who had in fact jumped bail before his treason trial could convene in England—was the regnant lion. And she attended the long wrangling oratorical contests that passed for political meetings at the Jacobin Club of Paris.

Her escort to many of these functions, I discovered early on, was the mysterious Jacobin envoy to London, Jacques Machaud. Somehow that disturbed me.

"Surely you have not let your fancy settle upon so poor a fellow?" I queried jocularly our third evening in Paris, as she awaited his coming in the intimate rococo drawing room off the entrance hall. "He has not half the force of our recent acquaintance the Graf von Teufel, nor a quarter the grace of the young Baron de Franval!"

"Citoyen Machaud," she answered tartly, "is a man of lofty principle. Not vulgar force or false effeminate grace, as you call it. His interests, sir, are in public matters only—not private ones. Something I am sure you find quite incomprehensible."

"Bravo, Citoyenne MacFarlane!" The harsh unpleasant voice of Jacques Machaud scattered my pleasant ruminations. "The celebrated Lord Libertine—is that not how you are called, sir, in your own country?—must learn that all the world does not despair of human goodness and the progress of the race."

Machaud stepped into the little gilt drawing room, smart and simple in his army uniform and red-white-and-blue sash. He looked, I thought, remarkably blatant in that subtly sensuous room, rich with curlicues and velvet and half-naked shepherdesses in plaster and fresco.

"Lord Christopher is not the sinner he seems, Citizen,"

said Lady Barbara, to my surprise. "He is only a doubter. Perhaps we may open his eyes in spite of himself." She spoke gaily. But did I perhaps detect a hint of hope behind her words? I clung to the thought.

"It is possible, Citoyenne," answered Citizen Machaud, sober and unsmiling as usual. "But it is not probable. I do not think your Lord Libertine gives much attention to the general welfare. And in Paris today, in the new order of society, nobody cares for anything else!"

I tried to catch my lady's eye, to warn her once more: *Never trust a man that claims to have no private interests.* But she was at the door already, preparing to depart for a night meeting of the Assembly. Machaud gazed at me speculatively with those soft, brown, strangely impatient eyes of his. His swarthy cheeks were damp as usual with sweat. There was a half-smile on his lips. Then he inclined his head infinitesimally—a massive concession to the effeminate customs of the old order for him—and the two of them were gone.

Decidedly, I did not like Citizen Machaud. He showed up too frequently, in too many connections, for it to be entirely coincidence. Staring at the empty door, I began in spite of myself to wonder once more about that damnable inlaid casket.

29

Countess Charlotte Speaks Her Mind

I discussed the differences between the old Paris and the new with a pair of faded strumpets I had known well (and often) during earlier visits to the city, three and more years before. We sat over coffee in the colonnades of the Palais Royal, remembering my last visit, in the long-ago spring of '89.

"Ah, Milord Christopher," sighed Fanchon, "times are not the same. Would you believe they have sent a minister of the government down to make speeches at us? To tell us we must display true republican virtue, and there should be no more prostitution? So now all the *filles de joie* are *filles de la Révolution*, and we must offer our favors first to the cheapest *sans-culotte*, the dirtiest provincial soldiery on their way to the front." She pouted and sipped her heavily sweetened coffee.

"It is true," agreed Georgette, fingering her ringleted hair, which spilled over her forehead in the new republican fashion. "Even the leaders of our profession, even Papillon and the Amazon go only with delegates to the Assembly and the officials of the Commune."

"We should love to see you again, Milord Arun-del," Fanchon hastened to explain. She was perhaps eighteen now, with orange hair and plumpish painted cheeks and a simpering eagerness to please which had increased markedly since I had seen her last. "But now—even to drink *café* with you in public is an act of folly. Is it not, Georgette?"

Georgette nodded. "It is true," she said. She fingered her ringlets and watched the drifting crowds, the men in army uniforms, the *sans-culottes* in blouses and pantaloons, moving along under the trees. In the public gardens beyond the colonnades, an impassioned orator was shouting and waving his arms.

"You come back to Paris another time," Fanchon urged me. "Come back in six months, in a year. It will be all right again in a year, won't it, Georgette?"

Georgette shrugged and watched the crowds.

Another late afternoon I found myself at the Temple itself, the medieval fortress in the marais quarter where

King Louis and Queen Marie Antoinette and their royal offspring were imprisoned. The street in front of that crumbling complex of ancient buildings was full of soldiers and gawkers, in about equal numbers. King Louis's enemies clustered openly about the gates, savagely eager for a glimpse of "Citizen Capet" taking his evening constitutional in the Temple yard. The king's few supporters stood inconspicuously at a distance, gazing at the gray-stone towers that held the head of the house of Bourbon and the Austrian princess he had married.

I may as well confess right here that the street outside the Temple was as close as I ever got to seeing the unfortunate monarchs of the French. This must make me practically unique among foreign visitors to the city at that time, all of whom seem to have enjoyed lengthy and intimate conversations with Louis XVI and his unhappy wife.

In a city where no one cared for anything—or spoke of anything at least—save the general welfare of mankind, my own highly personal aspirations found little sympathy. Lady Barbara herself never alluded to my earlier importunities, or to her own half-formed response. Jeremy was entirely consumed by the mystery of the inlaid casket and kindred matters, and had no time for intrigue of any other sort. Even Countess Charlotte, I discovered to my surprise, now took an uncharacteristically jaundiced view of my *affaire de coeur*.

Madame la Comtesse d'Eauville seemed far less sanguine in Paris than in the country. She spent more time receiving strategic leaders of the new regime than she did entertaining her few remaining aristocratic friends. She was often waspish, seldom witty, and generally not the Countess Charlotte one had known before.

Her opinion of my own affairs came to light one evening as the two of us sat alone over wine by candlelight, waiting for the others to gather for supper. I had been mooning like a rejected lapdog over my lady of Holyrood House all that afternoon, to Charlotte d'Eauville's obvious irritation. Now she spoke out suddenly with a quick switch of her ivory-handled ostrich fan.

"Her ladyship will be down directly." She sniffed. "You need not fret so obviously."

"Madame?" I queried, startled from a melancholy meditation on my lady's eyebrow.

"Your green-eyed *Anglaise*. She will be with us soon enough, for you to mope and slaver over to your heart's content!"

"Madame is too harsh," I protested feebly.

She rose abruptly from her chair and paced away across the *salon*, her fan slashing the air before her almost viciously.

"It is not flattering, you know," she said in a low voice, her back half-turned, "to offer—all that I have and am— and to have it spurned for an English virgin!"

It was startlingly unlike the sophisticated Lady of Eauville even to raise such a subject in the drawing room, let alone to speak with such unaccountable emotion. I stammered, strove to formulate an acceptable pleasantry. But she cut me off once more.

"What charms I have to offer, monsieur, have pleased some of the most discriminating tastes in France!" Her voice was snappish and querulous. "The noblest names, the most exalted ministers of state have vied for my favors."

"I can well believe it, madame!" I responded honestly enough.

"But the celebrated Lord Libertine," she continued obliviously, her face still turned away, "has other interests!"

"Alas, madame, the incomprehensible ways of the human heart—"

She swung back to face me then, shadows shifting un-

der her cheekbones, her thin patrician nostrils dilating
with mingled anger and desire.

"I shall have you for myself, Arundel," she whispered
savagely. "As I have my Jean-Pauls and my Jean-Louis.
As Franval has his Jasmins and his Hyacinths. I shall
have you for my own, so long as it shall please me!" Her
little teeth showed in a mocking, feral smile. "For you
and I are of a piece, Lord Libertine, as you yourself must
come in time to admit once more. When this foolish infat-
uation with your English Joan of Arc shall have passed
and gone!"

Once again I labored to answer her, and once again she
cut me off. This time with a laugh, as she turned away
and strolled to the nearest window.

"But see, milord," she said in a lighter, cooler tone, as
Lord Durward entered the room behind her, "they are
dancing a carmagnole in the Place de la Révolution, and
singing some new hymn to La Sainte Guillotine. Shall we
not open the window and listen?"

30

A Moment of Madness
in the Rue St. Honoré

Our fourth evening in the city, Lady Barbara announced firmly that for the good of my soul she would
take me to see some small portion of the Revolution in
action that night. We should attend a séance of the Jacobin Club and a soiree of the more moderate element at
Mme. Rolland's. I was grateful to be spared the Assembly
at least. Quite cheered, in fact, with the prospect of

spending an entire evening in her ladyship's company, and without Lord Mortimer. I was quite cheered, that is, until it developed that we were going to the Jacobins in company with Citizen Machaud.

The Paris Jacobins met nightly in an ancient Jacobin monastery across the street from the Palace of the Tuileries, only a few blocks down the Rue St. Honoré from the Countess's great house. The three of us strolled down the street together, Machaud exchanging fraternal greetings left and right with every out-at-elbows citizen we passed. He was, it seemed to me, extremely well-known among the People.

The notorious Jacobin Club turned out to be one of the dullest institutions ever devised. So far as I could tell, it was little more than a political caucus or strategy meeting. The most extreme root-and-branch men in the Legislative Assembly forgathered there every night to lay plans for their parliamentary maneuvers in the next day's session of the Assembly. On this particular evening, these hot-eyed radicals wrangled interminably over a draft decree on the redistribution of communal village lands. I would soon have dozed off if the medieval hall had not been so drafty and the voices of the fraternal Revolutionary leadership so loud and querulous.

Afterward, Lady Barbara and I set out for Mme. Rolland's alone. Citizen Machaud, it appeared, was not of her Girondist persuasion. I cheered up considerably at this news.

"And you, madame?" I inquired as we strolled across the twilit city, both of us properly garnished with tricolor ribbons and cockades. "Are you of Mme. Rolland's persuasion?"

She shrugged slightly.

"I am a stranger here," she said. "I have no right to condemn one point of view"—she came within an ace of saying 'faction'—"and praise another. But I must confess that I feel most comfortable with the circle of Mme. Rolland's salon. Her husband, the Minister of the Interior, is a man of no consequence, a nonentity. But some of the English exiles gather there. And they are all moderate-minded people, I think. We share concerns in common."

She paused a moment and then went on, in a lower, more vibrant tone. "That means a good deal to me, sir: to share concerns with others. It is long since I have enjoyed that feeling of fellow work, of fellowship with others of like mind in this world."

I glanced down at the earnest set of her head, the momentarily lowered eyelids, the cheekbones flushed and slightly more prominent than they had been a week before. I remembered the caricatures in London printshop windows, the snide remarks in Parliament, the jokes about the Judith of the Jacobins. I realized suddenly that it could not have been the pleasantest life in the world, being the Vindicator of Women and the Champion of Chimney Sweeps.

"I am glad, then, ma'am, that you have found such friends," I said impulsively. "Even for a little while."

Lady Barbara stopped between a bakery and an aromatic sausage seller's and looked up at me. And I looked down at her.

It was not a romantic moment in any normal sense of the word. The street was narrow and cobbled and as dirty as the streets of Paris always are. The air was thick with plebeian voices, plebeian laughter, a child squalling, the mingled smells of sausage and baking bread and unwashed bodies. Lady Barbara's face blurred in the thickening shadows of the evening.

But it was as if I saw her for the first time.

It was—how shall I say it? it was a *human* face I looked at, not a *woman's* face. Lips made for speaking, not for kissing only. Eyes that saw, and a mind behind them that understood and felt and feared. The clear, exquisite features of a woman who was also a fellow mortal in this uncertain world.

I looked into those wide eyes, and—upon my soul I swear it—I felt myself quite lost. That frank level gaze of hers overwhelmed me as no more wanton glance had ever done. A great free ocean seemed to beat behind the seagreen eyes of Lady Barbara MacFarlane, and I was lost and swept away.

It was a moment of pure madness, unlike anything I had ever felt before.

"My lady," I heard myself say then, "you must know that my attentions to yourself are not—what Durward called them in your chamber that last night at the château. You must know that, whatever I have been, whatever I am in large measure still, yet my intentions toward your ladyship, my hopes at least and dreams, are not mere lechery and love of conquest."

I paused for a dozen heartbeats, sucked in a lungful of spiced sausage and *pâtisserie*, and finished in a rush.

"You know that I care more for you than I have ever done!"

"I am not insensible of your—affections, sir," she answered candidly, gazing back at me there in the open street. "Nor am I lacking in some warm feeling for yourself."

"But then—my lady—may I not dare to hope—?"

"Lord Christopher. You know, you must know now, that I could never care—completely—for any man that did not honor high principle at least as much as his own sensual gratification!"

My crestfallen look seemed to touch her heart, however. For she extended a hand at once and pressed my own, a quick smile on her lips.

"Yet we may still be friends, my lord, I think?"

I bowed in silence—for once I had the wit to say nothing at all—and we walked on.

It was, I think, the beginning of the end for the great free soul that had been Lord Libertine.

31

Dr. Guillotin's Invention

Meantime, the city around me hurtled on to its fate.

I had developed no particular interest in the tall gaunt apparatus popularly known as *la Guillotine* (or, to others, as *la Louisette*, depending upon which eminent physician was assigned credit for its devising). In this lack of interest I was practically unique in the metropolis—indeed, I sometimes think, in the civilized world.

The machine stood, as I have said, only a couple of blocks down the Rue St. Honoré from the Countess's palatial abode, in the vasty reaches of the Place de la Révolution. It had been set up just that summer, and had already claimed its first victim, a nonpolitical malefactor whose execution had been delayed for some time in order that he might have the honor of being first beneath the knife. This had taken place only a few weeks before our arrival. There had been a considerable number of mechanical decapitations since, increasing numbers of them for political offenses. Not surprisingly, there was a vast deal of general interest in this latest revolutionary wonder.

I had seen crowds at public hangings before, of course. I had philosophized as sardonically as the best wits of our time over the happy throngs that accompanied a popular highwayman on his last ride to Tyburn Hill. But there was something particularly horrifying about the Guillotine and the mobs that clustered round it.

Perhaps it was the *science* of it.

The thing had been calculated to a nicety, so one of the Countess's Jacobin visitors enthusiastically informed me. The vertical posts were of the precise height, the massive blade of the exact weight required to smash through flesh and muscle and the odd cervical vertebrae with sufficient force to sever a human head from the trunk. It had been pretested scientifically, he explained proudly, on sheep. And then on human corpses.

The blade too—now there was scientific ingenuity for you.

"All blades cut like a saw, you know," my interlocutor enthused. He was an eminent *philosophe* of the second generation, I had been told: a round-faced man of fifty, bald on top, with dirty gray hair falling to his shoulders and small square spectacles perched upon his nose. "All blades cut by virtue of the slanting surface, whether it be the multiple serrations of a saw edge, or the cross-sectional sloping of an ordinary knife. A plain horizontal edge, no matter how narrow, would in theory be incapable of cutting butter!" My informant beamed at this thought, and pushed his unsteady spectacles back upon his nose. "The cutting edge of the blade of Dr. Guillotin's remarkable invention is slanted at precisely the correct angle to achieve the effect for which it is intended—painlessly, almost effortlessly. It is a beautiful example of the scientific spirit, of human reason applied to one of those practical problems which the old regime dealt with only by the crudest, most primitive *traditional* methods." Meaning, apparently, the headsman's ax or sword.

Other details, equally morbid and unappetizing, filtered to me from other sources.

The horizontal board upon which the victim was strapped, face down, before his head and neck were run

through the little hole beneath the blade, was not, it
turned out, the work of modern scientific minds at all.
Maître Sanson, the royal executioner—now chief executioner for the new regime—had suggested this refinement
on the basis of his own long years of experience with
those very traditional methods the *philosophes* derided.
The victim, Sanson had informed the proper committees
of the new government, is the weakest link, the chanciest
element in any execution. The victim tends to be nervous.
He moves. And the slightest movement of the head, in
the moment before the blade strikes, can mean the difference between a clean decapitation and a botched job. If
the blade strikes the skull or the big bones of the shoulders, half-a-dozen strokes may be required. There would
probably be a great deal of unseemly writhing around. It
would be a mere butchery, rather than the inspiring, even
instructive public spectacle the government wished to
present to the people.

Hence the board. The victim should be lashed down,
Master Sanson had explained, and the board slid into a
fixed position, bringing the neck inexorably under the
knife. There was an implacable logic about it, even if the
source was tainted with the crude rule-of-thumb tradition-
alism of the *ancien régime*. So the board was built into
the new machine.

I learned also about the crucial function of the bran
sack.

The notion was widespread in England that the severed
heads of the victims of this new revolutionary horror fell
into baskets of some sort. One visualized a wicker market
basket. Such was not in fact the case. Each head, after
being briefly displayed to the multitude, was quickly de-
posited in a sack half filled with bran, to absorb the blood
that continued to flow from the severed extremity (if that
is the right word) for some time. Sawdust or any other
absorbent material would do as well, a grizzled *aficionado*

explained to me one afternoon, squinting up at the machine. But bran was cheapest, and did the job as well as any. The new government knew the value of a sou, he nodded cannily. Wasteful expenditure had been one of the besetting sins of the old order.

I never, I may say, attended an execution in the Place de la Révolution—Place de la Guillotine, as we all came to call it.

But I heard them. One could not help but hear, even indoors, at the Hôtel d'Eauville. The roar of the multitudes, singing, chanting, whooping with glee as the dripping head was held up by the hair for their inspection, carried far up the Rue St. Honoré. It could be heard in the front parlors even with the windows closed:

> *Ah! Ça ira, ça ira, ça ira,*
> *Les aristocrates à la lanterne!*
> *Ah! Ça ira, ça ira, ça ira,*
> *Les aristocrates, on les pendra,*
> *La liberté s'établira,*
> *Malgré les tyrans tout réussira!*

The verses could be rendered very freely, with some of the verse of the gay country dance tune to which they had been written:

> *Aristos to the lamppost!*
> *Aristos, hang them all!*
> *Liberty's on call!*
> *Tyrants all shall fall!*

or something of the sort. The sense was considerably violated, particularly in the last line, but the spirit came across intact. It was the famous two-word tag on the chorus that gave me trouble. *Ça ira!* "It'll be all right!" "We'll pull it off!" "We shall bring it to pass!" The Great

Experiment shall succeed, the world be made over on a foundation of true principle at last.

All very noble, no doubt, and straight from the great throbbing heart of the people.

Prudence and a squeamish stomach kept me away from executions. But I did often enough look up at the Guillotine as I passed through the Place de la Révolution. And one evening I saw another gazing as I was, for long silent minutes. Somehow it gave me pause.

I have, I may safely say, nothing of the romantic or Gothic temper in me. Despite my poetic vocation and my Celtic ancestry, I have never been visited by any intimations of impending fatality or doom whatever. But gazing up at the Guillotine that day, I experienced precisely that.

I glanced idly from the infernal engine to my fellow gawker and back again. Abruptly, our mutual musing seemed to link us, to bind us one to another as though an invisible umbilical cord had suddenly come into being between us. It was as though both of us saw our destiny there, both our fates writ black against the sky in the hard, ungainly outlines of Dr. Guillotin's miraculous invention.

He was an ordinary-looking bourgeois citizen, my fellow meditator on mortality—if, in fact, he was meditating on any such thing. A lawyer by his dress and manner, rather somber and introspective in his bearing. Certainly not gauded up with any of the elaborate patriotic paraphernalia of many of the tribunes of the people I had met—the military uniforms, the saucer-sized cockades, the tricolor sashes and ribbons. And yet I knew at once that if ever there was a tribune, this was he.

Then I heard the voices behind me, murmuring in awed whispers.

"*C'est lui!*"

"He comes here often, and stands and looks at it. For

minutes at a time. For a quarter of an hour together sometimes, and never says a word."

"And then he goes away."

"C'est lui—l'Incorruptible!"

I came to myself with a positive shiver and turned hurriedly away. For it was in fact Maximilien Robespierre, the only time I ever saw him. A very different sort indeed from the hearty, human, eminently corruptible Danton, who dined so cheerfully on the Countess d'Eauville's venison. If he and Danton were the prime contenders for mastery of the Revolution, I distinctly recall thinking to myself, I would lay solid odds on the silent one who did not dine at the stately home of Madame la Comtesse d'Eauville.

I told Jeremy about it later that night, and he said I was quite right. And Jeremy's judgment is infallible when it comes to intrigue and intriguers.

As for my horrid premonition that my own destiny was inextricably bound up with Dr. Guillotin's hideous device, that too was to prove only too accurate.

For I saw Robespierre in the Place de la Guillotine on Saturday evening, the first of September. It was three weeks to the day after the Massacre of the Swiss Guards on August 10. The next morning, after that brief hiatus, history was to begin happening again in Paris. And I, alas, was to be all too intimately involved in that new beginning.

32

In Which the Great September Massacres Almost Begin with Me

A Gibbon or a Voltaire would no doubt begin this historic chapter with signs and omens of the coming storm. "The sun rose red over Paris that Sunday morning, grim portent of the tempest that was about to break over the city." Or something of that sort, replete with rolling periods and dramatic imagery.

I must begin more modestly, with a case of dyspepsia.

My digestion had not been good for some days. "French cooking," Jeremy had snorted. "They *will* do everything to a chip!" Whatever the cause, I had suffered intermittently from abdominal pains, headaches, and a general restlessness and irritability ever since our arrival in the capital. The night before, I had been particularly uncomfortable and especially restless.

I awoke about my usual hour then—hard upon noon—and after an uncharacteristically light repast, I set out to walk off my indisposition by a Sunday stroll.

About two o'clock I found myself in the Marais quarter, only a couple of streets away from the Temple, where the King and Queen of France languished in durance vile. I loitered a moment, gazing idly at the Gothic crenellations and the cone-shaped turrets of the Temple looming above the rooftops. Then I heard the cannon.

There had been others, I realized abruptly, from other sectors of the city. Alarm guns. But there had been alarms and excursions in plenty during the preceding days. Cannon firing, National Guard drummers parading through the streets beating a call to arms. One quickly learned to pay no particular attention, to go on about one's business. This alarm gun sounded no different to me.

Then another gun went off. And another, far to the south, across the river. In the bell tower of St. Martin's, just behind me, the tocsin began to sound. A boy ran past me, shouting something, up the empty street.

I caught him by the shoulder and swung him back.

"What is happening?" I demanded in my best provincial French.

"The Austrians are coming!" the lad panted, pausing in his wild career. "And the Prussians!"

"The Army of the Rhine will stop them. Danton says so," I declared staunchly. "We must be daring and more daring!"

"Verdun has fallen!" cried a youth in a leather apron, bursting from a low shop door with a musket across his arm. "And all the prisoners in Paris are in revolt!"

"He's right!" the boy agreed excitedly. "The prisoners are in revolt at the Châtelet, at La Force, at the Conciergerie!"

"But I've just come from the river myself," I objected mildly. "I heard no sounds of firing from the Conciergerie."

"They've murdered their guards," the youth in the leather apron assured me. "It was a plot. It's the aristos, the refractory priests that the Committee of Vigilance has been rounding up. They waited until all the patriotic troops had set out for the Rhine—and now they're stabbing us in the back! They've broken out of the prisons, and freed all the common criminals too!"

"God preserve us!" cried a passing market woman. "We'll all be raped and murdered in our beds!"

"To the prisons!" the little boy shouted. "To the Conciergerie!" He set off at a dead run in the direction from which he had just come, the youth with the musket and the market woman whooping in his wake.

I shrugged and sighed and strolled on up toward the Rue du Temple. My digestion seemed much improved. I recall wondering vaguely if Verdun had really fallen this time, and if so what it might mean, if anything. My ignorance of politics is matched only by my total incomprehension of military matters.

I stepped out into the Rue du Temple a short block below the Temple itself, twirling my cane and whistling a tune—an air, I believe, from *Figaro*. I stepped into the street directly in front of a charging mob.

They jammed the street from side to side, a motley collection of *Sans-culottes* in dirty shirts and red liberty caps, shouting and waving fists, sticks, here and there a pike or a rusty musket. Just as I looked up, they burst into a rousing chorus of "Ça Ira":

> *Ah! Ça ira, ça ira, ça ira!*
> *Les aristocrates à la lanterne!*

As one of the aristocrats in question, I felt distinctly out of place, standing there in the middle of the road as the throng of indignant *citoyens* surged toward me.

"See there!" whooped a lean, lantern-jawed fellow with hollow eyes and red liberty cap, who seemed to be the leader of the mob. "Is *that* a son of the people?" He was pointing straight at me.

"*C'est un aristo!*" roared a red-faced butcher, shaking his cleaver.

"*Etranger!*" a third howled. "A foreigner—look at his boots. A foreign agent, *mon Dieu!*"

"Catch him! Seize him! To the tribunal with him! To the lamppost—"

Les aristocrates, on les pendra!

The man with the lantern jaw—a man, incidentally, whom I would see again, under even more embarrassing circumstances—led a raucous charge down the street toward me.

Not to put too fine a point on it, I bolted like a hare back up the nearest alley. I slipped and floundered over wet cobbles, leaped piles of refuse and rotting fruit. A patriotic mendicant, resplendent in a tricolor cockade and sash, started up from one such juicy pile, a long and very dirty knife blade gleaming in one hand. I slashed at him with my cane and plunged onward. Behind me the mob came on, bellowing out the "Ça Ira" like a view halloo as the hounds closed upon the hapless fox.

I burst out of my alleyway into the Rue St. Louis—and thundered headllong into a marching column of National Guards.

"*Citoyen!* Halt at once—in the name of—"

I let my momentum carry me right through the startled ranks of Guardsmen. A musket went off as I struck it aside, and the echoing report and accompanying gout of smoke scattered the citizen soldiers in all directions. I went careening on down the street, followed by shouts and imprecations. As I ducked around the next corner, I glimpsed over one shoulder the advance elements of the mob from the Temple flowing out of the alley, only to become hopelessly entangled with the milling National Guards. And another gun went off.

"*Citoyen!*" a ragged street vendor cried as I blundered into his barrow: "*Qu'est-ce qui se passe?*"

"The Guard!" I panted in my thickest provincial dialect. "The National Guards are attacking the people in the Rue St. Louis!"

"Ah, the bastards!" the citizen vendor swore. "They

have never been to be trusted. Come, my friends—*au secours!*" He and half-a-dozen of his fellow street hawkers snatched up whatever came to hand—a cutlass from under a cart, a fowling piece from a doorway—and raced off up the street.

I stepped briskly into a less frequented lane and hurried on my way.

My dyspepsia, of course, was back in full flower. I had hot flashes, quick visions of my own head perched upon a pike. The shouting and the shooting faded behind me with every twist and turn of the Paris streets. Yet I could not forbear frequent backward glances as I hastened south and east, angling toward the quais and a circuitous route home.

It was one of these nervous over-the-shoulder looks that gave me my final shock for the afternoon.

I had just crossed the Rue St. Honoré and was looking back to see if anyone was following. Someone was. He darted into an open innyard gate as my head came round. But I recognized him clearly enough. It was the diminutive hunchback figure of Captain Patch's little minion Trip.

33

Jeremy Unravels the Skein

The next twenty-four hours were not comfortable ones at the Hôtel d'Eauville.

The handful of great houses still inhabited at our end of the Rue St. Honoré stood like beleaguered castles in the midst of a medieval Jacquerie. Outside, straggling bands of insurrectionary *sans-culottes* roamed the streets, inflamed by revolutionary rhetoric and the terrors of the hour, drunk on cheap wine and the blood already shed, administering the "people's justice" to any suspected aristo, priest, or foreign agent they came across. Within the few surviving enclaves of the old order, stark terror reigned. Wild rumors flew, and wilder true stories were passed from mouth to mouth. The sound of tramping feet approaching, the raucous thunder of the various popular hymns to the Holy Guillotine froze the blue blood in aristocratic veins.

We were, in short, in a truly pitiable state.

"Goths! Vandals!" Lord Mortimer positively spluttered, dabbing at the perspiration that now gleamed perpetually on his brow and his long upper lip. "The barbarians are on the march once more! It's a second fall of the Roman Empire!"

Sometimes Lady Barbara would still lash back at him.

"Do you know what these people have lived with all their lives?" she demanded of him on one occasion. "Do you know what fate awaits them if German armies reach Paris to 'liberate' that poor wretch in the Temple? 'The most exemplary and ever-memorable avenging punishments'—were those not Brunswick's eloquent words, Durward?—'by giving up the city of Paris to military execution and exposing it to total destruction'!"

"Surely, madame," Durward answered bitterly, "surely even you cannot any longer defend this government of mountebanks and demagogues—this populace gone mad!" His hand shook so that he splashed wine upon the Turkish carpet. "Jacobins—levelers—they shall all be *leveled* before Brunswick's through with 'em. I only wish there might be some good British grenadiers among 'em, when they put this rabble to the sword!"

Most often, now, however, Lady Barbara bit her lip and did not answer him. Her face was chalky, her cheeks and eyes dark with a grief that went beyond mere terror.

The noble principles that she held most dear were steeping themselves in blood to the elbows outside our very door. The true believer bent her head and went her way in silence.

"It cannot go on much longer," the Comtesse d'Eauville reassured us, speaking with some tranquillity still. "The National Guard for the western sections of the city are bourgeois to a man. They will rally to the protection of property, never fear. And we have friends in high places, in the highest circles of the government." She smiled, her face looking oddly pinched and elfin. "Danton, Rolland, Machaud—they have wined and dined too often under my roof to let the Hôtel d'Eauville come to grief. Why, I have done such favors for all of them . . ." Yet there was a hint of doubt in the eyes of even that superbly self-assured woman of the world.

For no tricolor sashes and revolutionary uniforms came to call in the Rue St. Honoré now. And the mobs moved freely in the streets, hurling an occasional cobblestone through a parlor window and laughing brutally when no white-periwigged head dared show itself to protest.

Even I could scarce sleep past eleven in the morning that second day of the Great September Massacres.

We dined in silence at two; drifted aimlessly from room to room through the endless afternoon; tried a spiritless hand of loo or hazard; supped by candlelight at eight; summoned the Italian musicians, only to learn that they had decamped the night before, terrified that they would be hanged or guillotined for their foreign accents.

"The musicians gone!" Durward protested histrionically. "It is a rebellion against civility itself!"

It struck me as rather a revolt against clean fingernails and unsoiled linen than anything else. But my dyspepsia was fading—oddly enough—and I chose to avoid stirring it up again by futile exchanges of overheated opinion. I had never cared for the Countess's damned Italian musicians anyway.

Thus night settled with all its attendant terrors upon Paris. We gave up our feeble pretense of civilized living and wended our various ways to bed.

When I opened my own chamber door, I discovered Jeremy standing at one side of the ornate fireplace, a silver candlestick in one hand. His ratlike little face was suffused with ill-concealed triumph.

"Where the devil have you been, Jeremy?" I snapped disagreeably at him. I had not seen him since he had handed me my breakfast that morning. Under the horrendous circumstances, the game of confidential agent to which he now devoted all his days and half his nights seemed particularly silly.

"I have been about my master's business, sir," he answered me, his beady little eyes positively sparkling with glee. "If I may say so, sir."

"Yes," I sighed, reaching for the decanter and bracing myself for another round of *Mystères de Paris*. "Well. What is it this time? News of his lordship's henchmen Patch and company, perhaps? A tricolor cockade concealed in Lady Barbara's hatbox? A secret correspondence between the Countess's butler and the Commune, *in re* the wretched state of the water supply? Come, man, what is it? Don't keep me in such wicked suspense."

"It is just this, sir," said Jeremy. He reached out one scrawny yellow hand to touch a particularly extravagant shell-and-flower panel at one side of the fireplace. A door slid open in the wall behind him. A door that had not been there at all before.

"If you will step this way, your ludship?"

I discover that I have said rather little about the Hôtel d'Eauville itself. That is because there is really very little to be said about so ordinary a town house. It was not old;

it had the usual pillared terrace and pseudoclassical facade of the last years of Louis XIV's glorious reign, less than a century ago. It had been renovated at least once at the height of the rococo craze of the last generation, when seashells and floral patterns, plaster milkmaids and intimate window niches were all the fashion. It was a thoroughly modern structure, in short, pompous and overbearing on the outside, cloyingly intimate within. Not at all the sort of place for priest holes and Gothic passageways behind the walls.

Yet here, indubitably, was precisely that.

"How in the world did you ever find it, Jeremy?" I could not help but blurt in admiration.

"I have my methods, sir," he answered with hooded eyes. "If your ludship would care to explore it?"

Bemused by the novelty of it as much as anything, I stepped over the low marble threshold into cobwebby darkness. Jeremy led the way, his narrow shoulders and small head silhouetted eerily against the flickering light of the candle in his hand. I followed him, head down and shoulders hunched in the confining space.

We shuffled to the right along a head-high corridor for a dozen steps or so before we came to an even more close-pressing staircase. We ascended the rude steps slowly, reversing our direction twice at barely negotiable landings. All this within the solid stone walls of this very modern mansion! I shook my head, strove not to cough at the cloud of fine dust we stirred up as we climbed, and followed Jeremy on up the stair.

"Just here, sir," he whispered presently, "is the other door. There is a sort of peephole here. If you would care to look, your ludship?"

And I, who had sniffed self-righteously in the Prime Minister's study at Downing Street at the very suggestion of sneak thievery and spying, thrust Jeremy aside and put my eye to the tiny circle of light.

I was looking into what was clearly the master bed-room of the Hôtel d'Eauville. It was at least twice as large and vastly more splendid with gilt and carven marble than my own not inconsiderable chamber. Directly across the room, Countess Charlotte herself sat with her back to me at a low ornate vanity table, her head tilted slightly toward one half-bared shoulder, combing her long black hair. In the sizable mirror that backed the Countess's vanity, I could just descry the hazy reflection of what appeared to be a revolutionary army uniform.

The uniform moved, stepped forward into the light. The back of a head and shoulders came into view from my peephole. The face beneath the sharp cocked hat swam into focus in the Countess's mirror. It was the face of Citizen Jacques Machaud.

Countess Charlotte laughed.

"Come, Jacques," she said, "it is not the end of the world."

"It is the end of me," he answered shortly, "if I do not produce this wretched thing within the week. Citizen Robespierre grows impatient."

Machaud's swarthy cheeks were taut as usual, his dark eyes tense with that nervous urgency that I had noticed the first time my gaze met his, in the smoke and jabber of a London tavern. He paced off into the shadows to the left, momentarily out of my range of vision, only to reappear a moment later, head down, hands clasped behind his back.

"*Ah, mon pauvre chéri,*" murmured Countess Charlotte, still pulling her silver brush through her waist-length hair. "You have wagered your future upon it, ever since you went to England with Talleyrand, is it not so? And Citizen Robespierre, he has staked a good part of *his* bid for supremacy on *your* word that you could produce this precious document. Ah, *mon ami*, it is always the same. The royal court was no different in the old days. If your

Robespierre should ever succeed in establishing this Republic of Reason and Virtue he orates about so affectingly, it will be indistinguishable from Versailles."

"Citizen Danton's influence grows daily, with the people and in the government," said Machaud jerkily. "Robespierre must make his move soon." He paced back out of sight. His short-legged nervous stride carried him back and forth across the room with surprising agility. "I must have the Report now. Tonight. Tomorrow at the latest."

The Countess shrugged, still stroking her long black hair. "*Les Anglais*, you know," she said, "they are a devious race. They prate always of principles, of the higher morality. With them a simple business transaction must be a matter of balancing the future of the human race against the interest of the nation, *et cetera*." She laughed mirthlessly again. "They will never come to a simple decision, act simply and directly."

"I care nothing for the character of the English," said the Jacobin. "I care only for that which was promised me last spring in London."

"I have done my best to get your wretched paper for you, *mon cher*. It is here now, under this roof, in the heart of Paris, just as you wished. But inaccessible still, concealed behind a cloud of procrastination, vacillation, the habitual deviousness of the English. You must simply give me a little more time. In a few days, once the fury in the streets has subsided—"

"You have had time and to spare!" he fairly snarled at her. "Your best, it seems, is not good enough."

He stopped behind the low velvet-covered stool on which she sat. She put down her brush and turned to look up at him.

"Jacques," she said in a low voice, reaching out to finger the red-white-and-blue sash knotted meticulously about his waist. "You must learn patience. *L'intrigue*, it is a slow and subtle game. I have more experience in these matters, Jacques. Wait but a little longer—"

"I have told you—I cannot wait longer!" He looked down at her. I could not see his face, but there was a hard, almost hysterical tension in his voice now.

For the first time the Countess's glance fell before his.

"You think you are perfectly safe here," the Jacobin railed on. "You think you have friends in all camps, *hein?* Danton—Mme. Rolland—and Robespierre through me. You have no fear in the midst of a revolution! But I tell you, you should have fear, madame!"

His brown hand shot out, seized her by the hair. The pale oval of her face was tilted forcibly up to him once more. Her large black eyes stared up at him.

"That little patrician head of yours can fall as quick as another's into the bran, my heart!" He jerked her head still father back. "They will cut off all that beautiful hair first, you know. At the prison, before they put you in the tumbrel—into Master Sanson's most unfashionable barouche—for the long ride to the Place de la Guillotine. It is not a pleasant journey, they say, for those that sit bound hand and foot in that open cart. The crowds along the way—the vast crowds—"

"Jacques!" the woman hissed. Her lower teeth showed small and milky between her parted lips. "Do not talk that way Jacques—*mon ami, mon cher*—"

Her hand moved down from the tricolor sash. I saw him stiffen suddenly.

"*Mon chéri*—you know I will do anything for you— anything in my poor power to help, to please you . . ."

His fingers loosened in her hair. Her head bowed slowly forward till her face came silently against him.

With quick, deft fingers, she opened his breeches.

Stiff-necked Citizen Machaud, I noted with philosophical interest, was a difficult man to stimulate, let alone to satisfy. It was a full five minutes by the gilded porcelain clock on the wall behind him before the hot-eyed Jacobin responded to the Countess's most ardent ministrations. And another five at least before he shuddered to a climax. He came to his final spasm with obvious relief, and stepped back from her the moment she had closed his breeches.

"*Ah, mon gros animal*—" she began huskily. But he cut her off with a burst of short, sharp staccato phrases.

"It is enough, madame! You have had time and more than time to accomplish what I asked. Your way, the old way. The way of intrigue and calculation, as things were done in the decadence of the Old Regime. But it is a new day now, a new order in the world. It is a time for action, not intrigue!"

He stopped, still breathing stertorously, gathering his forces for a final spate of words.

"You have until tomorrow noon to fulfill your bargain, madame! If you cannot place the British Army Report in my hands by then, I shall take action in the affair myself. Direct and forceful action, in the way of the *new* regime!"

"But, Jacques"—she raised her hand as though to restrain him—"it is not possible! My servants have searched—I have done everything—"

"Until noon, madame!" Machaud inclined his head brusquely to her. "Perhaps not so long!"

He pivoted on his heel and strode out of my range of vision, across the room to the right. I heard a door open and close. There was a moment of silence, save for the ticking of the clock, the fluttering of a candle in the draft of the closing door.

The Countess d'Eauville wiped her mouth with one thin hand—a quick, savage gesture that twisted her face into momentary ugliness. Then she turned back to her mirror and picked up her silver hairbrush once again. Even from my secret point of vantage across the room, I could see that her hand was trembling.

Jeremy touched my shoulder respectfully, and we returned the way we had come.

I will grant Jeremy this. He did not gloat. In his hour of triumph, he was humility itself. Humility and, as usual, efficiency personified.

I stepped out of the dusty passageway into my own bed-chamber in a state of mind rather like that of a beef cow that has just been struck in the forehead with a hammer and is now about to have its throat cut. Confusion and disbelief mingled in my breast with an awful premonition of worse to come. Nor was my premonition disappointed.

"One more thing, sir," said Jeremy, crossing the room to unlock the tall ornamental wardrobe where he kept my clothes. "If you would look here, sir."

He fumbled under the usual pile of soiled linen and emerged with something in his hands. It was the little inlaid silver-mounted casket that Lady Barbara had transported so carefully from London to the heart of France.

"It's locked still, sir," he said, placing the little chest upon the table as carefully as though it were made of chrysolite and pearls. "But if, under the circumstances, your ludship would feel justified in—"

I took a poker to it.

In less than a minute I was holding the stolen War Office Report on the sad state of the British Army in my hands, skimming numbly over the words and numbers that I had read only once before, in Mr. Pitt's library in Downing Street.

34

Machaud Shows His Hand

From that great overturn onward, misfortune piled upon disaster until the final catastrophe swept us all away.

My first reaction to the portentous discovery was a quite irrationally exaggerated feeling of betrayal. In a literal sense, of course, I had not been betrayed at all. I had never actually *asked* Lady Barbara if her revolutionary sympathies might, under certain circumstances, outweigh her sense of Englishness. Had never, in plain English, asked her if she were a spy. But my conviction that she was not had been so massive, so overwhelming that Jeremy's demonstration to the contrary left me feeling monumentally deceived. That I had deceived myself did not mitigate my sense of the monstrousness of the deception.

I had never been a tub-thumping roast-beef-and-old-England patriot, as I am sure I have made clear in these pages. The betrayal was more personal than that. Lady Barbara MacFarlane, whom I had lusted after lo, these many weeks—toward whom I had even begun to feel those rather more complex emotions so fatuously described as "honorable"—had been lying to me all along! In deeds if not in words, she had most horrendously deceived me. I could not have been more stunned if I had come upon her in the arms of another man.

I flung the sheaf of papers down upon the table beside the shattered chest and set out at once to express my righteous indignation to her face.

"May I fetch you something, your ludship?" Jeremy

hastened to inquire when he saw my hand upon the door. "It is very late for perambulating the corridors, sir."

"I am not perambulating the corridors, Jeremy," I said. " I am going to call upon a lady."

"At this hour, sir?"

"At this precise hour."

"'Er ladyship will 'ave retired, I'm sure, sir."

"Then I shall have to disturb her ladyship's rest. She has most certainly disturbed mine!"

I marched off down the hall in vest and shirtsleeves. I was in a fine high dudgeon, with no clear notion of what I meant to say, but determined to vent the unfamiliar sense of outrage that seethed within me. Jeremy hurried along after me, protesting futilely that our discovery should surely be confidential at least for the present, that the next step in the affair must be carefully calculated, that all might be lost by precipitate action, and so forth. I believe he even cited Pitt's original letter to me, enjoining me to proceed "with discretion and dispatch." All to no avail. I was not to be dissuaded from my folly.

Jeremy was still hovering at my elbow when I halted before my lady's door. He was still murmuring urgent warnings while I rapped, vigorously, more than once. But he fell silent when the door opened perhaps a foot, and Bridget's frightened pudding face peered out at me, a terrible question in her eyes.

"Yes, sir?" she blurted, drawing a shawl more tightly about her ample shoulders. "Have they come then, those demons out of hell? O Jesus, Joseph, and Mary—"

"Who is it, Bridget?" It was Lady Barbara's voice, crisp and steady as ever.

"It is I, Lady Barbara," I said firmly. "Arundel." I thought but did not say: Arundel, whom you have deluded, misled, most cruelly betrayed. And all in the same noble name of Principle!

I thrust open the door without so much as a by-your-leave to the estimable Bridget and stepped inside.

Lady Barbara MacFarlane stood beside her high four-poster bed, on the verge apparently of climbing in. She wore a white muslin nightdress, no nightcap to contain the unbound mass of her hair. Her eyes were darker, her lips and cheeks paler than the last time I had seen her in such delightful déshabillé. But she was still what she had been since I first clapped eyes upon her, by the light of a dark lantern up an alley off the Strand: the most beautiful woman in the world. That, and the lady of the Rue St. Honoré, in whose seagreen eyes I had quite lost what remained of the tattered soul of Libertine.

"Yes, Lord Christopher?" There was the faintest of tremors in her voice. On such a night in such a time and place, it would have been incredible if there had not been.

The battle within my bosom was short and sharp and totally one-sided. When next I spoke, my voice was strangely altered too.

"It is—nothing to be alarmed about, Lady Barbara," I heard myself say.

"Nothing, Lord Christopher?" She looked gravely at me, with a faint air of puzzlement. "I am glad of that."

"I wanted to be sure that—all was well at this end of the house," I explained lamely.

She cocked an eyebrow at me then, the first gesture of normal humor I had seen in her face for days.

"Quite well, thank you," she said. "As you can see, I have had Bridget to sleep in my chamber. So I am amply protected against—night visitors."

"Indeed, it is very kind of your ladyship, I'm sure," said Bridget. "It is so fearful abovestairs, with half the servants gone, and those *people* forever marching and singing in the streets—" I noticed for the first time that the faithful maid was accoutered for sleep herself, in a nightcap and voluminous flannel nightgown under her shawl.

"Ah," I nodded, "well." And then, groping for words: "I believe the disturbances are diminishing somewhat. I have not heard a church bell rung all night, nor an alarm gun."

"We are most grateful for the news, sir," said Lady Barbara dryly. She clearly did not believe a word of my pitiful explanation. If I had a shred of self-respect about me, I told myself, I should speak up now. Challenge her at once. Tell her that her treason was known. Urge her to repent, to join me in destroying the fatal document before it could fall into the hands of our nation's enemies.

"I bid you good-night, then, ma'am," I said. And bowed. And turned upon my heel and walked away.

Bridget peered out the doorway after us, her round puffy face the picture of bewilderment. Jeremy followed close behind me, clucking pleased approval of my decision to say nothing. I blundered on down the corridor, deaf to his words, blind to all but the vision of Lady Barara's loveliness against white sheets and velvet hangings. I felt dazed and angry with myself and mortally certain that I was making a very foolish mistake.

The first thing both of us noticed when we stepped back into my own room was that the smashed casket, with its sprung hinges and broken lock, was gone from the table where I had left it. The thick packet of papers with the great red seal, which I had flung down beside the chest in my frenzy to march across the house and confront Lady Barbara, was, of course, gone too.

The silence that followed this discovery was one of the longest and least pleasant of my life.

"Perhaps," I began at last, "I did not leave it on that table at all, but elsewhere about the room. Except," I added with a sigh, "that I *did* leave it on the table, and nowhere else. And it has indubitably been taken."

Jeremy said nothing.

"No doubt the Countess has spirited it away," I proceeded on a more hopeful note, "and we shall simply have to pay a return visit to her chamber to recover it." I paused. "If we do that, of course, she will summon her footmen and her lackeys and have us both turned out into the streets. Where half the population of Paris is waiting to feed all the aristos and suspect foreigners they can find to the Guillotine."

Still nothing from my loyal valet. The woebegone look of reproach on his sallow face was comment enough.

"And then again," I babbled on, "it is quite possible that our astute friend Citizen Machaud has been doing some prowling on his own, and has had the good fortune to stumble upon his object within minutes after taking up the quest. He, or some agent of his, planted in the house. In which case, there is absolutely nothing we can do, but wait and see what *he* intends to do—if anything."

I elaborated somewhat more hopefully on this.

"It is quite possible that he will do nothing at all about us, once he has the precious Report. Of what use are we to him then, after all? It would be quite irrational of him, really, to molest us in any way, once his purpose is accomplished. And the new order in France prides itself that it is solidly founded upon Reason, you know. Reason with a capital *R*."

But even I knew better than that.

I woke up with a bayonet in my face.

It was just before dawn the next morning. I was summoned from unplumbed depths of unconsciousness by a furious pounding on the door. Before I was awake enough even to sort this out, a musket shot splintered the lock with a deafening roar, and a dozen men poured into the room. Flaring torches gleamed on long musket barrels, drawn swords, tricolor cockades. I sat up fully awake at last. A bayonet flashed redly in the torchlight inches from my eyes.

In the hall outside I caught sight of Lady Barbara's fluttered nightgown and ashen face, and heard poor Bridget's protesting wail.

Before I could muster a suitably outraged protest myself, Citizen Jacques Machaud thrust his way through the tangle of guns and uniformed men, his stocky figure looking particularly ludicrous under a huge bicorne, an awesome bandolier full of bullets slung across his pouter-pigeon chest, and informed me loudly that I was under arrest by order of the Government and the People of France.

35

The Dungeons of the Revolution: or, My Penultimate Assault on Lady Barbara's Virtue

And so, for the first time since my great-grandfather was arrested for debt on the steps of the Parliament House, an Arundel was off to prison. In the present case, however, I looked forward with rather less confidence than my inpecunious forebear to emerging from the experience unscatched.

Machaud was playing the stiff-necked Jacobin to the hilt that morning. He glowered at us, strode furiously up and down, issued terse orders. Then he stalked off to some other part of the house, announcing that every room must be thoroughly searched, no corner left unprobed. All prisoners were allowed ten minutes to dress themselves—a ridiculously inadequate amount of time, considering the complexity of that operation—and then were hurried out of the house and bundled into closed carriages. The coach to which Lady Barbara and I had been consigned set out at once, escorted by the bristling muskets of a dozen National Guardsmen. We passed quickly through empty streets and along the misty river to what was probably the strongest prison left in France since the fall of the Bastille—the Conciergerie, on the Île de la Cité, in the middle of the Seine.

There were, I realized with some surprise, only the two of us in the small closed carriage. I had heard Bridget's wail in the hall outside my room, but if she had been taken into custody, she was being brought along in some other conveyance. Perhaps she and Jeremy were being brought together, in some more plebeian vehicle—though I hated to think the great egalitarian Revolution would discriminate in such matters. And what about Lord Mortimer Durward, the only real enemy of the Revolution in our party? And the Comtesse d'Eauville herself, whose elegant head Citizen Machaud had threatened so graphically the night before?

It was all most puzzling. But the answers would surely come soon enough, and I saw no point in fretting till they did. Meantime, with my lovely fellow offender against the Government and People of France, I entered the Conciergerie at approximately five o'clock on the morning of Tuesday, the fourth of September, 1792.

The cells of the Conciergerie were located in the cellars of the Palais de Justice itself, at the western end of the Île de la Cité. This was convenient, since the Extraordinary Tribunal, which had been trying offenders against the state ever since the brouhaha of August 10, sat upstairs in the same building. And then, of course, the whole towered and turreted medieval rabbit warren of a *palais* was only a short tumbrelride from the Palace de la Révolution. The Place de la Guillotine, as we had come to call it.

Our arrival clearly did not come at a propitious time. The Conciergerie had been almost emptied of prisoners by the prison raiders the preceding Sunday, and the place was only beginning to fill up again. Regular sittings of the courts had just recommenced the preceding day. It is to this general demoralization, incidentally, that I attribute the unceremonious depositing of my lady and myself in the same cell, instead of in those separate sections of the prison normally reserved for male and female *accusés*.

So we found ourselves together in a bare stone room, perhaps twenty feet across. We didn't know it at the time, but we were in the dungeon at the bottom of the Bonbec Tower—the most dreaded cell in the Conciergerie. It was an airless, fetid hole, circular in shape, with half-a-dozen oddly coffin-shaped beds covered with straw around the curving walls. The solid oak door had only a small barred aperture for a passing guard to glance through. Otherwise, our only light and air came through a narrow window slit set well above our heads. We moved in perpetual gloom by day. Night, when it came, would be black as Tartarus.

Above our cell—again, unknown to us—was the guardroom of the prison. Above that, on the top floor of the Bonbec Tower, was what had in a less enlightened day been the torture chamber of the Conciergerie. Under the new regime, it was an antechamber to the courtroom of the Extraordinary Tribunal—the main conduit that fed the Guillotine.

"Well, madame!" I said, shrugging off my coat and flinging it upon the nearest straw-covered bunk. "We are alone at last!"

It was the perfect spot for an amorous encounter. What better place than this dim-lit chamber, securely locked and bolted, and furnished exclusively with beds? What better time than this, when we two were flung together in that peculiar intimacy that comes with shared misfortune? The dungeons of the Revolution, I realized at once, provided the ideal *ambiance* for the triumph of my passion.

The only difficulty, of course, was Lady Barbara herself.

She stood with her slender back half turned to me, gazing up at the red-orange light of dawn breaking through the narrow window slit. Her chin was raised, her cheeks pale and peaked, her lips compressed. She looked the very picture of the Tragic Muse.

"I regret, Madame," I proceeded, in what I took to be a casual, disarming tone, "that your friend Machaud's people have neglected to fetch along my razors. I shall be quite hirsute this time tomorrow." I stroked my chin, already prickly with the morning's whiskers, and offered my most engaging grin.

"Citizen Machaud," Lady Barbara responded sharply, "is no friend of mine."

Indeed he wasn't, I thought with a quick glance at our grim surroundings. I found it perversely heartening to learn that idealists, like thieves, do sometimes fall out.

"Nor is this my Revolution," she went on, her voice rising now. "This madness robed in the garments of a grand ideal! This massacre of the people in the people's own name!"

"Certainly not, ma'am," I said, placing a reassuring hand upon her shoulder. "You could not know that it would come to this!"

"I believed in it, sir!" she said with vehemence. She shrugged my hand irritably off her shoulder. "I believe in the *principles* still—in the great revolutionary ideals of liberty, equality, the brotherhood of mankind. But *this*"—

she cast a scathing look around the dark bare stone of our dungeon—"this is not the Revolution I dreamed of, spoke for, championed with all my heart and soul—"

"I assure you, madame," I hastened to interject, "that no one would hold you in the slightest degree culpable in the matter." I put my hand back upon her shoulder and gave it a reassuring squeeze.

"And yet," she continued, speaking more slowly now, "how *can* I absolve myself of all responsibility for the consequences of a revolution in society which I have supported so ardently since its bare beginnings?" She shook off my hand once again and sat down upon the nearest bunk. "I must be true to my political principles, sir. And the first of all political principles is simple honesty!"

"I could not agree more, Lady Barbara!" I sat down on the coffin-shaped bed opposite and looked straight into those beautiful gray-green eyes. "Above all, one must be honest!"

She looked right through me, her mind still a pool of platonic principles in conflict. I sighed. It was not a good beginning.

She sat there not ten feet away, trim and lovely in a fashionably close-fitting gray gown that looked quite out of place in such stark surroundings. (But then, what *does* a lady of fashion wear to a dungeon, after all?) Her dark, copper-colored hair, which she had had no time to brush and dress, fell forward over one shoulder in a lustrous cataract that flowed almost to her waist. The oval of her face, the slenderness of her bare forearms glowed palely in the obscurity. She sat there, maddeningly inviolate, close enough to touch, yet spiritually untouchable still behind her towering bulwarks of conviction, conscience, and high principle.

It was absolutely infuriating.

"At least," she said suddenly in an oddly altered voice, "we shall meet our Maker in the open, under His own sky. I do not like to be—penned up like this." She looked over at the thick oak door and positively shuddered. "I should not like to expire in a dungeon."

"Expire, madame!" I protested. I placed my hand upon her knee this time. "Do not even contemplate such folly!"

"Folly, Lord Christopher?" This time she let my hand remain. "And why do you think we have been incarcerated here, pray tell?"

"I have no idea, ma'am, I'm sure," I answered, perhaps a shade too sharply. I treasured still, I must confess, some slight resentment at the inconvenience her ladyship's political enthusiasms had put me to. "But we shall soon enough be out again, that at least is certain."

"How so, my lord?" There was a quizzical note in her voice now.

"Why, we are not French, my lady! We are not subject to their laws or their tribunals!" I spoke with an assurance that I almost felt. "We shall be back in London within the week, regaling the perfumed ladies and periwigged gentlemen at Lady Arbuthnot's with gaudy tales of our privations. We shall be the lions of the season, ma'am, depend upon it!"

"I cannot think, sir," she answered, smiling faintly for the first time, "that you quite grasp the political nuances of our situation. It is precisely *because* we are not French that we are here. We are foreign agents in their eyes, sent to Paris to organize revolt against the Republic while foreign armies menace her frontiers. We shall be tried—we may well be executed—as spies!"

"Ironical indeed, madame," I could not resist saying, "in view of your own vigorous efforts in behalf of the revolutionary cause." And it did indeed seem paradoxical that she, who had spied *for* the French, should now be arraigned on a charge of spying *against* them!

"But I must in any case apologize to you, Lord Christopher," she went on. "I have brought you into the gravest danger once more, and that through no fault of your own." She smiled ruefully and dropped her own hand upon mind, where it still rested upon her knee. "I have been no very good friend to you, I fear, in the short time we have known one another."

She gave my hand a gentle press and rose once more.

It was all too ridiculous. As tragedy it would not play a week at Covent Garden. As farce it was too humiliating to contemplate. *This must cease!* I swore suddenly. The thought was father to the deed.

I rose as she did, and for the third time in my life I caught the Lady Barbara MacFarlane in my arms and pressed her to my bosom.

"Sir!" she gasped.

"Madame!" I whispered hoarsely. "But one kiss!"

"I think, sir," she snapped, turning her face wearily away to avoid my lips, "that we have been here before."

"My lady," I groaned, raining kisses upon her exposed cheek and throat, "we may never see another dawn. Let us be good to one another!"

"For God's sake, my lord!" Her tone was more irritated than terrified.

"For your own sake, Lady Barbara—and for mine!" My words were muffled against the starched lace at her bosom.

"That is *enough*, sir!" She stepped back, straining to break away from me. Her legs came up against the bunk from which she had just risen, and we toppled over together into the straw.

She looked up at me, and I saw once more the wide, wide eyes, an ocean beating behind them, that had swept me quite away in the Rue St. Honoré. The eyes of the most beautiful woman in the world—who had turned out to be a human being too.

"Lord Christopher," she whispered, "I *am* afraid."

"Madame," I replied with equal candor, "I am terrified myself!" And I kissed her on the mouth.

Her lips moved under mine. Perhaps she murmured protests still—I could not tell, nor cared. It was enough that she responded, that her mouth was alive beneath my own. Her hands pressed against my shoulders—perhaps, again, to thrust me from her; it mattered not. Delight and desire foamed through my heated veins. I tore at the bodice of her gown, and then my kisses fell on heaving naked flesh.

It was not, evidently, the most genteel seduction of my life. There was straw across my face, and swaths of cloth between us, and the hard wood of the prison bunk beneath our thrashing bodies. But my passion would brook no denials now. In a trice I had cast up her skirts and petticoats, and my trembling fingers were sliding over her bare thighs toward the very seat of Venus. And even as I groped my hot lascivious way toward that center of all worldly joy, I felt my lady's breath against my ear, her fingertips upon my cheek.

"O my lord—O Christopher—it is too much—"

"Impossible, my lady!" I panted, as with gentle fingers I gained my end at last.

"Oh sir—it is too late!" But her eyelids were fluttering shut, her head had fallen back upon the crackling straw. "Too late for us now—"

"Never too late," I murmured, dry-throated, pressing closer still upon her undefended loveliness. "Never too late to pluck the sweetness of life . . ."

As in a dream I felt her naked breasts—stiff, proud-nippled, taut with longing—rising and falling beneath my eager kisses. Belowstairs, my fingers moved ardently, stroking, caressing, parting, and fondling those tenderest of treasures in their silken nest. And when I touched the pearl of bliss itself, the woman in my arms cried out convulsively and clutched me wildly to her.

Her hands raked my back. Her white limbs pressed fiercely around mine. She caught my face between her hands, raised it from her breast, and crushed my mouth feverishly against hers.

Her lips were hot, her tongue was wild, we were both sobbing with passion too long deferred. She who had withstood such an epic siege now welcomed her conqueror as a liberator, with cries and moans of longing for the sweet martyrdom to come. And my own throbbing weapon desired nothing more ardently than to administer that joyful *coup de grace*.

She was, in short, all that I had ever dreamed in my most flamboyant fantasies. She was a Maenad, a Bacchante, wanton beyond anything even I had ever known. And I—upon my word—I had never so desired a woman in all my life.

I had lurched to my feet and was fumbling furiously at my breeches when I heard the first footsteps on the stair. Then came the rattle of keys, the key sliding into the lock, the protesting squeal of an unoiled bolt.

Will the reader believe that by the time the heavy door swung inward, Lady Barbara and I were sitting upon opposite bunks, our clothing more or less adjusted, even my lady's tempestuous cataract of hair flung back over her shoulders in some semblance of orderly disorder? Yet it is true. My hands were shaking, my heart was pounding, and my lady was in little better case. But we were ready when the guards pushed open that door.

"O madame!" shrieked the wretched Bridget, rushing across the room to fling herself sobbing upon her mistress's breast. "Joseph, Mary, and Jesus preserve us all!"

Through clenched teeth and blood-dimmed eyes, I consigned that miserable woman to the deepest pit in the Inferno. But my fury at this first intrusion was as nothing to the sense of outrage and injustice that welled up in me when I looked up and saw, squeezed between the blue-clad gendarmes in the doorway, the pale unhappy face and dapper figure of Lord Mortimer Durward.

36

Before the Tribunal

"*S'il vous plaît, citoyens,*" intoned the shortest and burliest of the gendarmes, with a gesture toward the door. "*Le Tribunal vous attend.*"

There were four of them, all armed. I swallowed my fury and obeyed.

And so I passed in minutes from the wildest transports of love to a trial for my life. There was little time for philosophizing as Lady Barbara and I stumbled out into the low stone passageway, with Bridget blubbering on her mistress's arm. And little world left either, so it seemed, as we followed the miserable-looking Durward up a narrow, winding flight of stairs toward the courtroom and our doom.

We emerged through a low Gothic arch at the top of the steps into a sort of vestibule two floors above our cell. There was a refreshment table with a motherly old lady presiding over wine, brandy, and some plates of dry-looking cakes. A pair of legal clerks and a uniformed usher were munching cakes and joking with the woman.

The usher brushed the crumbs from his fingers and positioned himself ahead and to the right of the cortege. The woman behind the refreshment table beamed at us and busied herself with her plates and bottles. Then the chief gendarme whispered something, and the usher stepped forward into an open double doorway, banged

with his staff upon the floor, and announced the advent of
"les accusés."

At another word from the gendarme, we all marched
solemn as a parade of wooden soldiers out of the vestibule and into the courtroom itself.

That venerable chamber had an oddly raw, unfinished
look about it. The high arched windows and the pewlike
benches had no doubt graced the Palais de Justice since
Charlemagne's day, or thereabouts. But there were empty
niches and bare wood showing where statues and plaques
reminiscent of the Old Regime had been ripped down or
removed. And whatever mural pageantry had once
marched round the walls above the wainscoting was now
concealed behind tacked-up sheets of garish blue wallpa-
per.

We stood at the upper end of the courtroom looking
out upon the multitude. A barrier rail offered us some
meager protection from this motley array of *sans-culottes*,
market women, courtroom hangers-on, and nondescript
loungers generally. But their sparkling eyes and gap-
toothed grins assaulted us with secret smirking knowledge
of what was to come.

"Morti-maire Dur-var?" demanded the chief clerk of
the court, obviously struggling with the unfamiliar Anglo-
Saxon syllables.

For official purposes we were apparently to be denied
the status of *citoyens*. Not that it would affect the out-
come in the slightest, of course.

"Morti-maire Dur-var, English?"

Lord Durward sat pasty-faced and paralyzed, staring at
the clerk across the courtroom.

"Oh, do get on with it, Durward," I murmured irritably. "We'll be here all day!"

He said something. I did not catch it myself, but it apparently satisfied the clerk, who glanced at his sheet once more and went on.

"Barbara Mac-Farlane, English?"

"Here!" she answered clearly. Lady Barbara's cheeks were flaming still, her hair in some disarray. Otherwise she seemed quite recovered from our late encounter.

"Christopher A-rawn-del, English?"

"I too," I confessed lugubriously, "am here."

Bridget's name somehow did not get called at all. It was just as well, since that unhappy worthy had now lapsed into a sort of seated swoon, her mouth hanging open, her eyes as glazed as Durward's.

"Citizens of the jury," the clerk proceeded, turning to the dozen good men and true seated around the table behind him, "do you swear and promise to examine with the most scrupulous attention the charges brought against the aforesaid accused . . ."

While the jury was sworn, I stared with some curiosity at the judges. There were five of them, seated behind the long, black-draped table that served them as a tribunal. They all wore an odd costume that had been the talk of Paris ever since our arrival in the city. Each had a short black cloak and a round plumed hat of an unlikely Renaissance cut. Each displayed a tricolor ribbon stretched diagonally across his chest, and a sizable medallion inscribed in classic capitals: THE LAW. They were as grim and blue-jowled a lot of magistrates as I had ever seen.

But it was the forbidding pair who sat at a somewhat less pretentious table between the judges and the barrier rail who caught and held my uneasy attention.

The first of these was a pale-faced man with a notably low forehead and small, unpleasant eyes. He had thick black hair—though he was clearly well past middle age—and a prominent nose unattractively scarred by smallpox. He wore a modified judicial cloak and a plumed hat. The medallion on his chest bore the equally grim inscription PUBLIC SECURITY. He was one of the most notorious men in Paris in those days: Fouquier, the public prosecutor.

Beside Fouquier at the prosecutor's table sat the diminutive, swarthy figure of the Jacobin Jacques Machaud.

"The clerk will now read the indictment of the accused," intoned the chief judge. The chief judge was a gravel-voiced, red-faced man with the choleric look of a hanging magistrate. His name, as I recalled, was Dumas. I had heard that he was actually given to weeping copious tears after condemning some of the more affecting cases to the knife.

The indictment was read, in all its legalistic unintelligibility. The public prosecutor rose to address the court. "We shall prove, citizen judges," Fouquier declaimed, "that these English came to our shores with the specific intent, and for the purpose, of betraying the sacred cause of the Revolution to its enemies! We shall demonstrate that these vipers in the bosom of the Republic have associated and consorted openly with notorious aristos, refractory priests, and other counter-revolutionary elements! We shall make it incontrovertibly clear to the jury, to the citizen judges, and to the citizen spectators"—he played shamelessly to the gallery—"that these English are, all and every one of them, enemies of France and traitors to the great cause of the liberation of all mankind!"

He narrowed his little eyes and beetled his black brows fiercely. The auditory responded with scattered huzzahs and cries of *"Vive la République!"* and *"Vive la Révolution!"*

During this unseemly demonstration Fouquier consulted briefly with Machaud. Then he signaled peremptorily for the first witness of our perfidy to be summoned. I stared at a half-familiar face, spit-curled, black-moustached, double-chinned and puffy-cheeked, and obviously terrified before the Tribunal.

"You are a Venetian?"

"I am, *signori*," the fellow answered in a thick Neapolitan accent. "I am, my lords!" He bowed to each of the judges in turn, to the jury collectively, to the public prosecutor. I thought he would bow to the prisoners in the dock next, but he checked the impulse.

"You are or have been employed in the service of a former aristocrat, resident in the section St. Honoré, in whose home all four of these accused have been resident these past ten days?"

"I have been so employed, *signori*. I was so employed. Until I became aware of the treacherous intentions of these guests of the Countess—of my mistress's guests. At which time my compatriots and I, rather than associate in any way with such people, decamped at once—or attempted to—"

I recognized him now. It was one of the Countess's Italian musicians. Luigi the violinist, as I recalled. I had never cared for his cadenzas.

I saw that Lady Barbara recognized him too. She was gazing at him with a mixture of fascination and repugnance. I reached over and took her hand, cold and stiff as a corpse's. I squeezed it gently, till the fingers relaxed against mine.

Luigi spun out a remarkable tale of jeering words and conspiratorial glances observed and overheard between Italian airs at the great house in the Rue St. Honoré. Lord Durward's condemnation of the Revolution had been particularly blatant. And I did indeed recognize, with a silent curse, some of the familiar Tory clichés to which Durward had given sententious utterance on a number of occasions. But all of us, Luigi swore, had participated by dark looks and scoffing words in the general anti-Jacobin attitude of that viper's nest of counter-revolutionary sentiment. Even the *belle Anglaise*, even MacFarlane the English radical, had expressed occasional doubts about this or that policy of the Republic, had questioned the leadership of the incorruptible Citizen Robespierre. . . .

Lady Barbara's hand grew tense once more in mine. I attempted another reassuring squeeze, and ended in a nervous viselike grip that brought a gasp of protest from her ladyship.

"And these counterrevolutionary proclivities," Fouquier demanded, "became most clear to you these past few days?"

"Indeed, yes, my lord. They all of them condemned in most strong language the—summary justice which the good people of Paris have meted out to traitors and other enemies of the Republic these last days."

The scruffy *sans-culotte* audience rumbled with indignation. Fouquier smiled and cut off the testimony with a gesture. His look, his gesture plainly asked: What more need be said?

He had more witnesses, however. After Luigi came Fanchon, the jaded eighteen-year-old whore from the Palais Royal. Her orange hair was chastely coiffed, her plump cheeks scarcely touched with carmine. She wore a virginal white gown and a spanking new red-white-and-blue sash around her waist. Her eyes were moist with what she obviously intended for patriotic fervor as she rose before the court.

"Do you know this English aristo?" rasped Fouquier, with a sneering glance at me. "And can you testify to *his* opinion of our glorious Revolution?"

She did—and she could. Lady Barbara looked the witness over and took her hand from mine.

"It is all true, messieurs—pardon, *citoyens*—it is all true," Fanchon swore stoutly. "This Milord Arun-del attempted to suborn the republican virtue of a dozen of us, *filles de la Révolution*, honest working girls of Paris, from our loyalty to *la patrie*. He offered us bribes!" She rolled her eyes eloquently. "Vast quantities of English gold, if we would agree to undermine the strength and sap the vigor of the Republic—by means which I blush, which any honest girl must blush to mention—"

She was really quite convincing. She seemed, in fact, to believe every word she was saying, and soon worked herself up into a frenzy of indignation on behalf of all the honest *filles* of the Palais Royal gardens whom I had suborned to my unmentionable purposes.

"And you did not acquiesce in the evil designs of this English?"

"Never, citizen prosecutor!"

"Thank you, citizen. You are a credit to the Republic!"

Fanchon stepped down, looking more tragic and aggrieved than any nun in her crisp white gown.

I noticed two things about the interminable parade of testimony that followed. First, that no one of any social consequence, or even bourgeois independence, was summoned to give evidence against us. Only the poor and helpless appeared, those most easily bent to the public prosecutor's will. And second, that Countess Charlotte d'Eauville's name was never once mentioned, despite the fact that almost all our seditious words and deeds were alleged to have taken place beneath her roof. Madame la Comtesse, it appeared, was riding out the storm once more.

About three in the afternoon, the last of the witnesses against "the English Plot," as the prosecutor now freely described it, stepped down. Fouquier began his summation of the case at once.

It amounted to the most amazing farrago of the trivial on the one hand, and the unproven on the other, that I had ever heard in a court of law.

Most of the direct testimony was of a piece with that of

the prostitute and the Italian musician. No flippant phrase had escaped my lips, no Tory shibboleth had passed Lord Durward's, but some alert *sans-culotte* sympathizer had industriously committed the indiscretion to memory. Lady Barbara's very sighs and shakes of the head had been duly recorded. Altogether, it added up to nothing that would convince any rational human being of anything, except that the servant classes have a limitless capacity for gossip. As structured and summarized by the zealous public prosecutor, however, it clearly amounted to a hanging case—to use the technically primitive English phrase.

"Never since this Extraordinary Tribunal was convened," Fouquier thundered, "have I encountered such devious intrigue, such bold and barefaced hatred of the people, such contempt for the interest and opinions of mankind. This Republic opened its arms in fraternal embrace to these strangers. The English Mac-Farlane most especially did we welcome to our midst, offering her the freedom of *la patrie*, providing her an unparalleled opportunity to observe—nay, to share in—the most noble experiment in government ever undertaken by the human race. And the English Mac-Farlane has spat upon our hospitality, has bitten the fraternal hand extended to her . . ."

And so forth.

"I demand," the public prosecutor concluded at last, "the fullest application of the law in the case of these contemptible tools of royalist reaction, these proven enemies of humanity and the Republic!" He sat down, mopping his face with a large and rather dirty handkerchief. I had no doubt that the fullest application of the law would be forthcoming.

The jury trooped out, looking unctuously determined to do their duty.

The minutes that followed were the longest of my life.

It was late afternoon, suffocatingly warm and humid in the courtroom. I had been jarred from sleep at a barbaric hour that morning, and had had neither food nor rest since. The amazing alternations in my circumstance—from the Rue St. Honoré to a dungeon in the Conciegerie, from my lady's arms to the dock—left me totally distraught and wrung out. My skin was clammy, my breath came short. I could feel my dyspepsia surging back with a vengeance.

When the little bell rang to signal the imminent return of the jurymen, I found myself clutching Lady Barbara's hand once more in mine. I am not at all sure who reached out to whom for the futile reassurance.

The jurors had been out for exactly four minutes—a new record, I heard one habitué in the front row assure his neighbor.

Chief Justice Dumas polled each man in turn, his gravelly voice growing more savagely exultant with every response. Every juryman assented to every one of the fantastic charges laid against us. We were guilty on all counts.

The bright-eyed sea of spectators hushed and stared at us, obviously avid for any signs of weakness or repentance from the prisoners' benches. Bridget was, in fact, blubbering openly again, and I had a strong suspicion that my own attempt at a cool sardonic smile was a wretched failure. If it was half as horrible as Durward's ashen, gasping stare, I knew we must be cutting a pitiable figure indeed.

Next should come any irrelevant words we might have to offer before sentence was passed upon us. I groped for a noble sentiment, a witty quip, anything that might save the situation for our miserable group. I was pawing my way mentally through Pope in search of a suitable apothegm when the chief justice completed the polling of the jury. The public prosecutor rose at once, turned grimly to face us.

He rose from a brief, apparently rather heated consultation with Citizen Machaud. I realized then for the first time that the hot-eyed little Jacobin had given no evidence against us, had indeed not spoken a public word all day. I knew the strain upon him must have been considerable, and wondered dully why he had bothered to come at all.

I found out at once.

"The prosecution," said Fouquier, "has urged the fullest application of the law in this heinous case. The prosecution continues to believe that the most rigorous revolutionary justice must be exacted in all such cases of arrant counter-revolutionary thought and action." He paused heavily to let the point sink in, and to mop his brow. "In the present instance, however, we are persuaded that the interest of the Republic itself may militate in favor of some—mitigation of the strict punishment otherwise required." He grimaced, obviously hating the very taste of the words on his lips. "Our comrade-in-arms, Citizen Jacques Machaud, has in fact come from the Assembly with information which may make some such mitigation necessary."

The eyes of the auditory flicked down to the dark-featured little man in the green uniform. Machaud kept his own eyes focused upon the papers before him.

"It appears, citizens," Fouquier went on, "that the odious convicted criminals you see before you—or more precisely, one among them—is in possession of certain documents vital to the very survival of the *patrie*. It appears also that this despicable enemy of the Revolution has arrogantly refused to turn the aforesaid documents over to the Republic, although every opportunity has been afforded the miscreant to make such a gesture of repentence and good will. Citizen Machaud, speaking for Citizen Robespierre, Citizen Danton, and other leading spirits in the Assembly—speaking, indeed, in the name of the Revolution itself—therefore begs the court to make the following final effort to secure an honest and contrite response from the condemned."

He hesitated once more, obviously mastering with difficulty his repugnance to such perversion of revolutionary justice.

I cast a quick glance at Lady Barbara. She sat straight and aloof now, chin up, eyes flashing, magnificent despite her dishabille. I winced inwardly. It did not look as if our Lady of Principle was in any more of a mood to bargain than Fouquier was.

"The state, then, offers what clemency it can to this wretch"—Mauchaud shot a sharp look up at the public prosecutor, and he amended hastily—"to *all four* of these convicted enemies of the state, in return for the aforementioned gesture of contrition and amends. If any and all of the documents in question, first promised and then brazenly refused, are surrendered this very day to the duly appointed agents of the Republic—if this sincere and penitent gesture is forthcoming within the next twelve hours—the beneficent Republic hereby declares its willingness to conduct all four of the convicted defendants here present immediately to Le Havre, there to take a ship—at their own expense and charge—for England. They shall thus be banished from France, with the stern warning that, should they or any one of them ever set foot in any territory where the writ of this court runs, the rigorous punishment, hereby suspended in recognition of said gesture of contrition, shall be instantly and mercilessly executed."

Fouquier paused one final time for breath, his little eyes glowing, obviously considerably cheered by this sanguinary prospect for the future.

"*Morti-maire Dur-var!*" The prosecutor's voice crashed out in the stillness. "Will you now rise and tell the court your response to this most generous offer on the part of the *patrie?*"

37

An Ultimatum from Citizen Machaud

"*You* purloined a secret document from Whitehall?" demanded Lady Barbara disbelievingly, the instant the cell door clanged shut behind us. "And you offered it to the Jacobins? To the Government of Revolutionary France—on the eve of war?"

"I do not wish to discuss the subject, madame," replied Lord Mortimer stiffly, stalking away. Or as far away as any of us could stalk in the small round dungeon at the base of the Bonbec Tower.

"That appears to be exactly what he did do," said I. I was as baffled as she was, but I was certainly enjoying it more. "A report from the War Office, in fact, on the far from satisfactory condition of the British Army. And unless I am much mistaken, he concealed this illuminating information in *your* luggage, ma'am, for the journey into France."

"*My* luggage?"

"Precisely, ma'am. In a small inlaid casket with silver mountings. I myself saw it several times among your bags."

"The little silver-mounted chest—of course! But *you* told me"—she whirled accusingly back to Durward—"you told me the little chest contained old letters! Lavendered letters bound with ribbon, from your late lamented mother!"

"Letters from his *mother*?" All the calamities of the past twenty-four hours could not keep an incredulous grin from breaking over my face.

"Letters to a *chevalier* of the old school still resident in France. Letters and a fragile bit of jewelry or two, that had once come to his mamá from that anonymous French gentleman." Lady Barbara shook her head ruefully. "His lordship regaled me with the most touching account of the discovery of these souvenirs amongst the Duchess's effects, and of his determination that the *chevalier* should have them back to warm his declining years. It was affecting beyond measure, I assure you."

"And he asked your help in smuggling these *billets-doux* back into France."

"He did. His lordship expressed a fear that the officials at the frontier would be suspicious of such missives, obviously in a feminine hand, if they were found in his bags. He even worried that, if the letters should be confiscated, they might create some difficulties for the silver-haired old gentleman—though the liaison they reveal was some thirty years in the past. Far simpler, he suggested, for me to carry the letters and the rest of it, all carefully packed by him. With a letter or two of my own on top, the whole would appear as my own private effects. Not even the most diligent official would read through a lady's private letters."

"Nothing could be more ingenious," I opined.

"Or more unprincipled!" She swung round to his lordship's still unmoving back once more. "I do not know, sir, that I have ever been so miserably deceived and disappointed in one that had the reputation of a gentleman of honor!"

"His lordship's reputation," I murmured happily, "has always seemed to me somewhat inflated. But how he ever formed an acquaintance with your precious Jacobin Machaud, and why he, who has breathed fire and brimstone against the French these three years past, should suddenly agree to convey the most intimate War Office documents into their hands—"

"I made the acquaintance of the distinguished milord this past spring"—a new voice grated on my ears—"when I had the honor to serve in Monsieur Talleyrand's friendship mission to your country. Talleyrand did not succeed in negotiating a treaty of amity with your government. But I and some others, operating in a less public way, did find a few friends for France."

Jacques Machaud stood in the low doorway, hands clasped behind him, smiling mirthlessly at us.

"Some, like Lady Barbara," he continued smoothly, "were friends of our revolutionary principles, allies of the great ideals of the Republic. Others, like Lord Mortimer, were amenable to—other persuasions."

"But *what* other persuasions, in God's name?" Lady Barbara demanded. "What could persuade so hopelessly misguided, I may say so rabid and fanatical a Tory to throw in his lot with an agent of the Jacobins?"

Lord Mortimer Durward told her himself.

"Why, money, madame," he said quite calmly, turning to face her with the ghost of a smile on his thin aristocratic features. "What else?"

"Money?" she faltered, speaking as though she had never heard of the commodity in question.

"Indeed, madame. Pounds, shillings, and pence. I had none left at all. And the most scrupulous gentleman of honor can no more live without money than a blackguard can. As your friend Lord Libertine will no doubt be happy to agree."

Lady Barbara did not even look at me. Even my most notorious failings clearly paled into insignificance before this astonishing revelation.

"Money," she said again slowly. "It was for money, for my father's estates, that you so ardently pursued my hand in marriage some months ago."

"Alas, my lady, it was. Not that your ladyship lacks other charms—"

"And for this, for *money* that you consented to sell your country and your principles—that you contrived this entire base intrigue—"

"Exactly so, Citoyenne MacFarlane," interjected Machaud. "And very considerable amounts of it too. English principles come high, it seems." His teeth gleamed momentarily in the dimness, like a fox's in the dark. "Most of the funds disbursed in Lord Mortimer's case, incidentally, came from the expropriated treasuries of French churches. Monsieur Talleyrand, as you may be aware, was a bishop before the Revolution."

"I am sure the source of his lordship's profits mattered not a jot to him," snapped Lady Barbara, "so long as he profited handsomely out of the exchange."

"Ah, but that is precisely the trouble, you see." Machaud's voice lost its conversational easiness, became clipped. "No exchange has yet taken place."

"Come come, Durward!" said I. "Services for value rendered—that's the British way."

"One third of the total sum agreed upon," said the Frenchman, "was paid directly into the hands of Lord Mortimer's solicitors last spring—'on account' is, I believe, your English phrase. The balance to be paid over upon delivery of the promised merchandise—the Army Report of whose existence we knew but of whose content we were ignorant."

"Bribery, espionage, subornation to treason," I murmured. "Noble tactics for the Republic of Reason and Virtue."

"What would you, monsieur?" Machaud spread his hands. "We have a world to win!"

The gesture reminded me of nothing so much as my own solicitor Murrain, explaining that I had overspent my quarterly rents by twice, as usual, and that there were simply no more funds available—as usual. I recalled that the ardent Jacobin before me, like so many of the leaders of his faction, had been a barrister himself before the Revolution.

I noted too how the histrionic posing vanished, how easily *citoyen* gave way to *monsieur* and even to *Lord* Mortimer, here in the privacy of a dim-lit prison cell. I could not help but wonder if the brave new democratic world of tomorrow would really be so different from the world of yesterday.

"The monies to which you refer," Durward was saying querulously, "are very largely spent already. The wretched clerk in the War Office had to be compensated in advance. He was taken into custody almost at once, of course, and almost all I paid him was confiscated by the Crown. I remain, in short, almost as thoroughly out-of-pocket as before. I must have all that's due me, before I can proceed any further with this matter. I must also have proper compensation for the inconvenience of this journey, for the perils run—"

Much as I despised him, I could not help but admire his audacity, if not the occasion thereof. But there was a tremulous quality to his *m*'s that made me suspect that his breaking point was not far distant.

"The English milord is not reasonable," protested Machaud, soft and insidious once more. "I have done all in my power to accommodate you, monsieur. I met you and your charming friend at Calais, as per our agreement. At your insistence I agreed to a postponement and removal of negotiations to the secluded château of my friend, my very dear friend Madame la Comtesse d'Eauville—"

"And I in turn," snapped Durward, "accepted a further removal to Paris itself, very much against my better judgment. A judgment which, it seems," he added dryly, "has been aptly vindicated by subsequent events."

"Again, monsieur—what would you? My superiors grow impatient. War is imminent, a matter of a few days away. We *must* know the magnitude of the threat we have to face." Again his teeth showed foxlike in the gloom. "We cannot pound the podium for war with England unless we're sure that we shall beat you!"

"My terms," said Durward tersely, speaking as though the rest of us were not present at all, "can only be stiffened by this high-handed action, sir. I must have the payment we agreed upon, as well as just compensation for every inconvenience and indignity I have suffered in the carrying out of our agreement. And now, evidently, I must have my freedom too. And that *before* I divulge the whereabouts of the document in question!"

"You English," said Machaud, his voice hardening again, "are remarkably lacking in a sense of the realities of things."

"The fundamental reality," said Durward, "is that I alone possess a piece of information which your faction cannot do without."

"On the contrary," Machaud snapped back. "The fundamental reality is that you are all incarcerated in the dungeons of the Revolution! You are convicted enemies of the Government and People of France. Fouguier and Dumas have all your death sentences drawn up. They will sign them before tomorrow morning unless I can bring them word of cooperation on your part. And still you stand there and chaffer with me like any market woman in the Halles!"

His voice rose, gathered the old caustic impatience. He was every inch the hectoring, sneering radical once more.

"Now I tell you what *terms* you shall have, milord. You have until dawn to reveal the precise location of the documents you have promised us. If I have heard nothing from you by five o'clock, I shall leave you to the tender mercies of the Tribunal. You shall all see the sun rise over the Place de la Révolution, messieurs et mesdames—from the steps of the Guillotine!"

The door boomed shut behind him. His footsteps clicked rapidly off up the stone steps.

38

A Message from the Countess

"I trust sir," I said to Lord Mortimer Durward, "that you will see your way clear to modify your terms?"

"To what purpose?" He shrugged unhappily. "The man's a blackguard. He would almost surely take his prize and leave me—leave us—to his friends on the Tribunal."

"I am sure you know the character of your partner in this business, sir. And yet if you do *not* meet his demands, he will *most certainly* surrender us to the mercy of the court. A chance is better than none, I should say."

"I shall wait him out!" said Durward, his voice see-sawing upward toward hysteria. His eyes had the same foxfire phosphorescence in the darkness as Machaud's. "The damned Report is critical to him—to his personal ambitions, to the political fortunes of his faction. He'll meet my terms. He'll guarantee my freedom, anyway, far more substantially at least than he—"

"I cannot comprehend you, gentlemen!"

It was Lady Barbara, her voice crisp with disapproval.

"Ma'am?" I inquired politely—though the whole affair seemed clear enough to me.

"Can you seriously contemplate for one moment, sir," she said to me, "bartering your country's fate for the life of one"—she pointedly did not look at Durward—"one worthless poltroon?"

"But, madame," I expostulated in genuine bewilder-

ment. "This is the very British government you have condemned unreservedly these past three years for its policy
toward France! Surely you would not now lay down your
life—all of our lives—for William Pitt and King George
the Third?"

"It is not my ideals I am speaking of, sir—but yours!"
There was almost a pleading note in that voice out of the
thickening gloom. "Is there nothing, *nothing*, Lord Christopher, that you value more than another thirty years
upon this mortal coil?"

I was spared an answer by the scrape of a foot outside
the door, the rattle of a key, and the advent of another
visitor.

The door swung open. Torchlight gleamed on a grinning gendarme's face. He stepped aside, and a black-
gowned woman glided across the threshold, her face
shrouded in the hood of her traveling cloak. But there
was no mistaking that lush figure, that undulating step.

"How does it go with milord?" Marie inquired as soon
as the guard had left, muttering "Five minutes," and lock-
ing the door behind him.

"Adequately, Marie. And with you and your mistress?"

"It goes."

She held a small candle in her hand. I found a place
for it high on the wall, out of reach of the straw piled on
the coffin-shaped beds. The feeble glow made bleached
ghosts out of Lord Mortimer, Lady Barbara, and Bridget,
who by this time had all but sniveled herself to sleep on
her mistress's shoulder. But Marie, her hood now flung
back, was as warmly enticing as ever. Her lips still pouted
sensually, indiscriminately avid for bonbons or for kisses.
Her eyes were dark and mocking.

"I bring you a message from Madame la Comtesse,"
Marie said evenly. She hesitated. "I was to tell you only.
In private."

I shrugged and let her have what was left of my battered Irish grin. "As you see, we have no privacy to offer you. Even for Madame la Comtesse's message."

Orange torchlight still glimmered outside the door, and a gendarme's tufted bicorne moved beyond the bars. They were waiting for her. And the seconds were passing.

Marie lowered her voice.

"Madame sends me to say that arrangements have been made, Milord Arun-del." She paused again, flashed a liquid glance at Durward, another at Lady Barbara. In a circular chamber twenty feet across, with soldiers ten feet away outside the door, the conspiratorial tone was more than a little ludicrous.

"Arrangements, Marie?" I thought for one garish moment that she had some sort of funeral arrangements in mind. Would my head rattle loose in the coffin, I wondered, as the Countess's liveried lackeys bore it to the cemetery?

"Arrangements for your departure from this place, monsieur."

I blinked back to reality: the damp stones, the fluttering candlelight, the shadows under Marie's soft cheeks, the sudden stillness in the dimness where Lord Mortimer Durward sat.

"Our departure, Marie?" I asked. "And have you consulted the public prosecutor on the subject, or the chief justice of the Extraordinary Tribunal? Not to mention your mistress's dear friend, the ubiquitous Citizen Machaud?"

"Your departure, monsieur, has been discussed with a number of functionaries of lower rank. All the gendarmes in this part of the prison have been lavishly plied with wine and money. Madame la Comtesse values your—continuing friendship—most highly, monsieur," she added, demurely lowering her eyes.

I had a sudden glimpse of the Countess Charlotte's face upon my pillow, thin and sallow and exotically beautiful.

Her thin patrician nostrils dilated with lust, her lips parted with mingled anger and desire. And I heard her words, as I had heard them not a week since: *I shall have you for myself, Arundel! As I have my Jean-Pauls and my Jean-Louis. As Franval has his Jasmins and his Hyacinths. I shall have you for my own, so long as it shall please me. . . .*

"I see," I said. I was light-headed from hunger by this time. I simply didn't believe a word of any of it. "And when, pray tell me, are we to depart this charming place?"

"A guard will come shortly after midnight for you, monsieur. He will escort you across the prison and out through the stables to the street, where a closed carriage will be waiting."

"And where will we be off to then?"

"Madame la Comtesse has a small property just across the Swiss frontier, monsieur. Near Geneva." Marie's eyes were still cast down, her voice a husky whisper now. "She feels the two of you might enjoy a lengthy sojourn there. A good part of the winter, perhaps. And afterward, she thought that perhaps Italy—"

"Italy would be lovely in the spring," I agreed cheerfully. "But where are my fellow travelers here to while away the seasons, according to Madame's master plan?"

"It has cost a vast amount of money and all of Madame's influence in Paris to arrange your own departure, monsieur." The words were barely audible. "It would be quite impossible for more than one to go."

At which theatrically perfectly moment the bolt shot back, and Marie was gruffly informed that her five minutes were exhausted. She said not another word, but curtseyed silently, turned, and followed the gendarme from the cell.

39

In Which I Make a Ridiculous Gesture

I turned slowly from the heavy oak door through which Marie had vanished, to face my companions. The wavering wax candle had remained behind. By its fitful illumination I looked into the three faces.

Bridget's puffy, tear-ravaged countenance was as broad and open and ignorant of what was happening as ever. Her red-veined eyes drooped with weariness. She spoke no French: she clearly understood nothing of what had passed between me and that exotic messenger from the outside world.

Lady Barbara and Lord Mortimer had just as clearly understood every word.

Lady Barbara tossed her head and averted her face from me. "The Countess d'Eauville," she observed coolly, "must value your friendship very highly indeed, sir. To suborn a dozen guards, put a carriage and a château in Switzerland at your disposal—my!"

For one moment I thought I detected the faintest hint of jealousy in that toss of the head, those crisply modulated tones. But for once in my life I had other things on my mind.

"And so much," Lord Mortimer Durward was observing even more caustically, "for Lord Libertine's celebrated satiric animadversions upon others' moral principles, I should say!" He sniffed with a flicker of his old smugness. His peaked aristocratic mouth even curled in the superior little smile I so despised.

"I have never been much of a man for abstract principles of any sort, Lord Mortimer," I answered shortly.

"Not while there was concrete pleasure to be had, I'm sure," said Lady Barbara cuttingly. I was certain there was jealousy there now. I wondered fleetingly if she had really never suspected my more or less reluctant *amours* with Countess Charlotte. I remembered Lady Barbara's mouth opening under mine that very morning, the urgency of her embraces, the trembling eagerness of her limbs against mine. How cold and far away the Countess's bed seemed then.

I leaned my back against the door, crossed my arms upon my chest, and contemplated the two of them. The lady in gray sat at the head of a straw-covered bunk with her servant's head in her lap. Her shoes were dirty, her gown rumpled, her hair unkempt. She was perfectly beautiful. The periwigged gentleman stood a dozen feet away, near the flickering candle. His coat and breeches, even the lace at his throat and wrist and the white silk stockings, were immaculate still, if somewhat wrinkled. His fine-boned face was filmed with perspiration, his protuberant eyes glittering with an emotion I can only describe as supercilious terror.

"And you, my lord?" I asked him presently, lounging against the door. "Supposing it were your—friendship— that had so impressed the Countess that she was willing to spend large sums of money, strain her political connections to the breaking point, to set you free. Under such unlikely circumstances, sir, would *you* leave your fellows to their sanguinary fate—or would you stay and share it?"

"Don't talk nonsense, Arundel!" He fumbled out his silver snuffbox, inhaled a substantial pinch of the soothing powder. But he was obviously fumbling also for the proper man-of-the-world tone to control his panic. "Of course I should leave. Just as you will. Just as any human being, that had blood instead of iced water in his veins, should do." He shot a withering glance at Lady Barbara MacFarlane and put away his snuffbox. "This is not a seat in the Cabinet, a division in the House, a—a pamphlet for *hoi polloi* we are talking of, for God's sake! Those animals out there are going to cut our heads off!" His narrow shoulders hunched; he wrung his bony hands together. "They'll strap us to the board and run our heads out through the little hole and clamp us into place with our necks beneath that ax blade hanging in the sky—"

He mastered his emotions with a shudder. I was sorry to see it happen. I had never observed Lord Mortimer so poetical before.

"Of course I should go," he croaked shortly then. "Anyone would." He licked his thin lips as he had once before, at the other end of my barker in the blade below Eauville. "Here, Arundel, let's get that guard back and have some wine sent in. You know anything can be got for money in these prisons!"

I looked into his rabbity little eyes and decided it was time to get it over with.

"Life before principles, eh, Durward?" I said cheerfully. "And how about your precious bargain, then? How about this War Office document you've been at such pains to purloin and transport so far? Would you abandon that too in your flight? Would it be life before profit too?"

He actually managed a cackling laugh. "I'd throw the damned thing in the Seine, and good riddance too! This is life, sir, *life!*" He thrust a shaking hand up before my face, apparently in order that I might observe the thin blue lines of blood circulating there. "It's *that* that will gout up against the morning sky tomorrow, sir! The blood—the blood of life!"

I sighed and uncoiled from the door.

"Too true," I said, "and vividly expressed as well. But you may spare us further drama. It will not be your blood."

"Easy to say, Arundel. You do not know Machaud." He wrung his hands once more with agony. "Oh, I shall give him the damned Report. In the end, I know I shall. And once I've directed him to the papers, he will dispatch me to the tumbrel without a hesitation! I know that too—I know that too!" His voice cracked, soared into the falsetto. "The man's a devil, I tell you—cat with a mouse!

"I must—I must have wine!"

He blundered toward the door. He had raised a positively clawlike fist to pound upon the ancient oak, when I stopped him with a word:

"Don't be an ass, Durward. You'll go in my place at midnight."

I have always secretly believed that my talents were more properly suited to drama than to poetry, and perhaps more apt for life than either. Perhaps it is for this reason that I so value that instant out of time, undoubtedly the most dramatic of my life. I looked from Durward's thunderstruck face to Lady Barbara's, suffused with wonder. And I was at peace with the world.

"I shall—do what?" croaked his lordship. His craven eagerness was comical to see.

I laid a finger alongside my nose and looked him over.

"You'll have to divest yourself of that elegant periwig—you know I haven't worn one for years. You'll wear my coat, of course, and my cloak. My tricorne is considerably too large for you, I think. All the better: it will shadow your lamentably un-Irish features perfectly. It will be quite dark—the candle will be gone long before the witching hour. Keep your face down and away from the torch, try to square your shoulders and look an inch or two larger than you are, and you should do well enough."

"Marie—the servant girl!" he blurted. "She knows me! And she'll be waiting in the carriage—for you!"

"I doubt it very much. But if she should be there, I

suggest you buss her soundly the instant you enter the vehicle, and maintain the embrace till the prison and the island are behind you. That would be my strategy, at any rate!" The smile was my own again—I knew it, I could feel it—revitalized and strong. Downright jaunty even.

"After that, you may throw the poor child out and commandeer the coach. Or leap out yourself and take to your heels, whichever suits you. So long as you have no further dealings with our root-and-branch friend Machaud. So long as that blessed Army Report remains wherever it is hid from now to the crack of doom!"

After which I turned away from Lord Mortimer Durward's sweating, twitching, unbelieving face to confront Lady Barbara MacFarlane. Her eyes—I swear it—were shining like stars in her pale, drawn face.

"It is," she said, her voice quivering, "it is a noble thing you do, sir. A far nobler thing than any I have ever seen before."

"It is a far, far more ridiculous thing," I sighed, "than I have ever *done* before. And that, now that I come to think of it, is saying something!"

40

In the Tumbrel

They came for us at first light. The three of us that were left.

The gray outlines of the cell were just taking shape around us. Bridget was snoring magnificently on a nearby bunk; if the spirit was weak within her, the flesh was clearly still in excellent condition. Lady Barbara MacFarlane and I sat together, clinging to each other like lost children in the darkness.

A cheerfully intoxicated gendarme had come for me perhaps an hour after midnight. There had been no trouble at all in dispatching Durward in my stead.

"Only one, now, mind!" the guard had grinned, the torch swaying vaguely in his hand. "The one the *citoyenne* paid for! Come on, now, which is it to be?" He was a night guard and had never seen any of us before. In his present inebriated condition he was not seeing anything too clearly anyway.

Durward drew my cloak about him like a bandit in a play and scuttled through the door.

The guard bade the rest of us good-night and followed his charge on out. I could not restrain a chuckle as I turned back to Lady Barbara. Bridget, a mound of snoring gingham in the straw, slept peacefully through the brief intrusion.

For all practical purposes, then, I was finally and irrevocably alone with Lady Barbara at last.

I reached out for my lady in the darkness, and she came without a protest into my arms. And so we sat through the black hours, splintery wood and crackling straw beneath us, rough damp stone against our backs. It was not the most comfortable way in the world to spend one's last hours on earth. But I was so thoroughly besotted with love by this time that I would cheerfully have accepted the hottest seat in hell if Lady Barbara MacFarlane sat in the next pew.

And so we spent those final interminable hours clutching, sighing, breathing close in each other's arms. And doing little more than that, I must one last time confess. For hunger, thirst, and sheer exhaustion had left us incapable of more passionate exchanges. Dare I admit that nature so vanquished love in our weary bodies that both of us actually dozed through many of those last precious minutes together?

I awoke with a start to the scrape of boots and the familiar rattle of keys in the corridor. Lady Barbara raised her head from my chest with a startled gasp as the cell door swung wide.

"*Venez, mes petits!*" the gendarme called genially through the open door. "*La barouche de Maître Sanson vous attend!*" The coach of Master Charles Sanson, the public executioner.

And so we went.

We stumbled up a short flight of stairs, out through a high-arched gate, and across the exercise yard, bathed now in the blood-red light of dawn. Lady Barbara led the way, head high, clear-eyed despite her weariness. Bridget trundled along in her wake, tearfully invoking the air of an entire calendar of saints. I followed last, laboring for that insouciance which I imagined the occasion demanded.

Halfway across the enclosed quadrangle, I looked back at the gray mass of the Bonbec Tower. There at the window of the refreshment room two floors above our dungeon, a pale, dark-browed face gazed down at us—and raised a glass in ironical salute. It was Fouquier, the public prosecutor. I am happy to say that I managed a brief but genteel bow before the gendarmes hurried me on.

Then we were back in the musty interior of the prison again, moving through corridors and wardrooms to the austere, white-walled office where the executioner's assistants waited to prepare us for the tumbrel.

They took away my coat and vest, ripped open my collar. I was left in knee breeches and a loose white shirt, and that torn open halfway to the waist.

They tore open the high neck of Lady Barbara's once elegant gray gown, and loosened it about her throat and shoulders. Shears slanted up, grated through the lustrous mass of her hair. In a moment she stood before me a woman transformed—gaunt and hollow-eyed, her slender neck and shoulders bare, her coiffure scattered in ruins about her feet.

"O my lady!" wailed Bridget. Then her own gown burst open at the neck, her own curled ringlets joined her mistress's on the flagstone floor.

Then the three of us were shepherded out into the cloudless morning. The tumbrel was waiting for us: a stave-sided cart with benches along the sides, two horses champing restlessly between the shafts. We clambered up into the cart. Our hands were quickly bound behind us, and the rope run through the gap between the staves for a final knot.

Half-a-dozen soldiers formed into an escort behind the tumbrel. A black-robed priest scrambled in and inquired unhappily if anyone required "the consolations of religion." When this was translated for her, poor Bridget began at once to babble out every sin for the past twenty years, while the priest, who apparently spoke no English, murmured, "*Oui . . . oui,*" and "*Ayez de la foi.*"

One of the executioners vaulted to the box, his whip cracked authoritatively, and the tumbrel began to move.

"My greetings to Charlot!" the gendarme who had fetched us from our cell called after us. "Tell him we'll send him another batch by noon!" He gaped and stretched, spat on the cobblestones, and strolled back into the office.

The cart lurched out the courtyard gate and swung left toward the bridge.

Looking at Lady Barbara there in the tumbrel, I saw her for one moment with an odd hallucinatory double vision. I saw her momentarily as I had seen her at Lady Arbuthnot's ball, her hair a high-piled glory, her slender figure resplendent in a fashionable white ball gown *à la grecque*, with the jeweled tricolor pin at her breast. Gorgeous, gracious, smiling.

Then I blinked and saw her as she was.

Little remained of the gleaming maroon masses of hair. What there was of it clustered and curled about her ashen face. Her lips were drained of color, her nose pinched, her jade-green eyes dulled to the color of soapstone. But her throat was a swan's throat still. And the shadow of her breasts in the loosened gown could still stir my lust to life.

Which can be embarrassing when you're sitting in an open wagon with your hands tied behind you.

"My lord," said Lady Barbara, glancing down with the ghost of a smile, "you are incorrigible." It was, I realized, the first flash of that sort of wit I had ever heard upon her lips.

The bridges, the quais, the streets were already filling rapidly with people. The troops were gone from the Pont Neuf, I noticed as we clattered across it, and the city in general had a more normal air. I wondered if the authorities had finally moved to suppress the rioting and jail raiding, or if the tumults had simply subsided of themselves.

The morning crowds grew thicker as we progressed. But the mood was far different from that of the preceding weekend. Jovial *sans-culottes* even waved and jested at us as we passed. "Enjoy the carriage ride, citizen!" we were admonished an unconscionable number of times. "The coachman's fee is paid by the Republic!" Or again: "I hope the view through the Little Window pleases you, citizen. You'll never see such a view of Paris again!" I could not help but wonder what it was about public occasions that stimulates such wretched attempts at humor in otherwise harmless citizens.

The tall narrow houses of the Rue St. Honoré frowned down upon us. Sunlight glimmered on weathervanes and upstairs windows. A maid in a mobcap looked down from a balcony, turned to call her sisters to come and see. A tavern wench pointed up at us from an open window. "*Mon Dieu*," I heard her cry shrilly, with her eyes fixed on my bristling chin, "look at the whiskers on that one!" "*Oui, c'est un milord*," another responded. "The English never make love, so their whiskers grow!" I bowed gravely, and they withdrew behind the shutters, giggling.

I felt like nothing so much as Dick Turpin on the way to Tyburn Hill.

Then we came in sight of the Guillotine.

Tall and gaunt and gray, it loomed against the bright blue sky beyond the trees of the Tuileries Gardens. There were people under the trees, and a flicker of movement from the Place de la Révolution, where a vast crowd had gathered. I wondered if Fanchon would be there, promenading with a soldier on her arm.

At the top of the two high vertical posts, I caught a flash of sun upon the blade.

The mobs were pressing closer now, as we neared the place of execution. The tumbrel was slowed almost to a halt. I felt the new rope gnawing at my wrists, the warmth of midmorning plastering my grimy shirt to my back.

Then I realized that the cart was no longer moving at all.

"*Où est-ce qu'on va, citoyen?*" a derisive voice boomed over the jabber and laughter and catcalls of the mob. "Where are you off to—St. Denis or Versailles?"

"St. Denis?" the driver called back. "Why, to the Place de la Révolution. Just yonder, beyond the trees. Don't you know Master Sanson's cart?"

A lean, lantern-jawed man in *sans-culotte* pantaloons and a red liberty cap—a man whom I had seen before— stood in front of our horses, barring the way. He had a battered cavalry pistol in one hand. Most of the men around us now, I realized suddenly, were also armed.

"The prison wagons have been used to move prisoners out of the city before," the lantern-jawed man replied, "to escape the people's justice." His voice was thick with wine, his eyes bleary with sleeplessness. He was obviously very drunk, and he looked half mad.

"Aye, justice!" called another voice, hoarse with shouting. "We've been giving 'em justice all this week, citizen!"

"Justice! People's justice on the people's enemies!"

"*À la lanterne!*"

The sweating driver was getting irritated. "Out of the way, citizen," he shouted. "Can't you see the Guillotine? We're heading straight there. Come along and watch the people's justice!"

"You're heading for the Pont Royal," the drunken man in the red cap insisted doggedly, "and the road to Versailles. We know your tricks."

"*À la lanterne! À la lanterne!*"

The crowd surged restlessly around us, buffeted the cart. Muskets and rusty sabers waved and glittered.

"*Les aristocrates,*" someone began to sing, "*on les pendra . . .*"

Suddenly I knew the ravaged features of the long-jawed man in the liberty cap who still held our horses' heads. *See there!* his voice echoed in my head as it had a week before in the thick of another mob—charging down upon me in the Rue du Temple. *See there! Is that a son of the people . . . ?*

My luck had held to the end. We had been caught by the last of the jail raiders—within sight of the Guillotine.

41

Ça Ira!

The horses were backing and neighing shrilly in the press. The crowd also was milling about in excited confusion. Some assured the citizen jail raiders that they were in error, that this was in fact Master Sanson's celebrated barouche, the open cart that normally carried a batch or two of public enemies to the Guillotine each day. Others sided with the exponents of vigorous popular justice, declaring that we were no doubt important prisoners being smuggled out of the city for safekeeping and protection from the people's vengeance. It seemed for the moment to be something of an impasse.

Then the long-jawed man in the liberty cap took matters into his own hands. Pushing his way up to the tumbrel itself, he reached up and hauled the driver, still shouting, off the box.

A soldier, one of our obviously all too meager escort, lunged forward, swinging an awkward musket at the chief of the prison raiders. A red-faced man in a butcher's apron knocked the soldier sprawling for his trouble. In an instant each of our half-dozen troopers was the center of a wild melee. The street crowd and the jail raiders also began to shout at each other, and some to make their points with kicks and blows. In a matter of seconds there were fights everywhere, and a sizable battle, growing rapidly toward a full-sized riot, on the broad steps of the Tuileries. A ragged chorus of "*Ah! Ça ira, ça ira . . .*" rose briefly and vanished in the howling of the mob.

Bridget left off her confessing and stared about her in

round-eyed astonishment. The priest looked round in terror.

"My God," Lady Barbara MacFarlane murmured. "Has the world finally all gone totally mad at once?"

The tumbrel rocked violently as she spoke. I came within an ace of sliding forward off the bench onto my knees. But this, I realized instantly, was impossible, since my wrists were securely lashed to the staves behind me. I tugged, and discovered that this was no longer so.

"If you'll just shove your 'ands back 'ere again, your ludship, we'll 'ave 'em loose in a jiffy!"

The words came in a hoarse whisper from behind me. I turned my head and beheld the sallow ratlike face of my man Jeremy smiling reassuringly up at me out of the howling mob. In one narrow hand a knifeblade flashed.

I scarcely need say that I instantly did as I was bade.

I felt a sawing at my bonds, a brief stab of pain where a clumsy stroke went awry, and then my hands were free. A gasp of surprise from Lady Barbara told me that the cords that bound her too were falling away.

"Christopher!" she hissed in my ear. "What's happening? Someone is—"

"It seems to be my valet, Jeremy, madame," I whispered back. "He appears to have found his genuine *métier* at last."

"I do not"—she winced—"I do not follow you, sir!"

"He was never much use as a gentleman's gentleman," I explained quite candidly. "The mysteries of statecraft, and the fine art of espionage in particular, seem to provide him with a much more natural outlet for his peculiar talents."

"Mary and Joseph!" cried Bridget, sitting across from us, in dismay. "Somebody's grabbed my hands!"

The crash of a soldier's musket close at hand, followed by still louder howls and shrieks from all around us, made a verbal response impossible. I gave her a comical wink instead, hoping she would have the sense to keep her freed hands where they were and await developments.

At that instant the cart jerked violently again, and the long-jawed, hollow-eyed leader of the prison raiders heaved himself up upon the recently vacated box. He held his pistol in one hand and the former driver's saber in the other. He fixed a maniacal stare upon us and stepped slowly down into the bed of the cart itself.

Then Bridget slowly drew her pudgy hands from behind her back and stared at them in dull astonishment.

The jail raider's face lit up.

"*Citoyens!*" he shouted into the uproar, pointing wildly with his saber at the unbound hands. "*Citoyens! Voilà ce que—*"

At which point the tumbrel tilted violently away from me, and just as violently back. We were all catapulted off our seats, and the wild-eyed lunatic with the liberty cap went down like a tenpin.

His pistol skidded down the tumbrel, fetching up within inches of my hand. I scooped the heavy weapon up, lunged forward, and broke the fanatic's head with his own gun barrel. It was the most satisfying feeling I had had in days.

"This way, your ludship, if you please!" Jeremy's voice urged through the hullaballoo. I seized Lady Barbara's hand, swung round in the general direction of the voice, and precipitated us both over the side of the still wildly agitated cart into the seething mob.

"Bridget!" cried Barbara. "Christopher—we must get Bridget—"

A moment later that worthy followed us, skirts plucked up around her knees, burying several startled *sans-culottes* in her fall. I saw the black-robed priest disappear over the rear of the tumbrel.

" 'Ere sir, and as rapidly as you can, if you please. We 'ave the rout of the retreat all calculated, sir."

There was Jeremy, unrecognizable in a street hawker's outfit, complete with a wicker hamper of fish upon his bowed back. His beady little eyes glowed with excitement. He had indeed found his *métier*.

"We, Jeremy?"

"Yes, sir. Meself and this gentleman 'ere, sir."

The blue-jowled, one-eyed face of Captain Patch grinned at me almost jovially out of the press. His bulky figure was swathed in beggar's rags. A huge tricolor cockade festooned his barrel chest. But I recognized the British naval short sword stuck in his belt, the wide, hairy face—and the beefy arm in a sling, shattered by Master Fag's pistol ball at our last encounter.

"Captain Ulysses S. Patch, sir," the big man grunted, breathing his familiar mix of mackerel and garlic into my face, "of 'is Majesty's sloop of war *Cyclops* at your service!" He tipped me a wink and a furtive approximation of a salute, and then turned to snap a quick order into the crowd. Fag, disguised as a scissors grinder, took his beefy shoulder from the side of the tumbrel, and Figgis scuttled out from under it, putting away his knife.

"And now, sir, if you *please*—"

There was no arguing with Jeremy's urgency. I caught my lady round her slender waist and plowed off through the oblivious crowd in the wake of Captain Patch and Jeremy. The little Cockney used his fish hamper as a battering ram, and Patch flung his sheer massive bulk into it. The rest of us made shift with shoulders, elbows, and knees to force our way through that sea of sweating, struggling bodies. We encountered no deliberate effort to impede our progress at all. The excited citizenry were far too busy pummeling each other to pay us any mind.

We were not, however, to escape so easily.

We were knifing our way through the gawkers on the far fringes of the mob when a familiar strident voice rose above the tumult, shouting exhortations and instructions, striving to bring order out of the swirling chaos. It was the harsh, unmusical voice of Citizen Machaud.

I turned my head and saw him. He had clambered up into the tumbrel itself. The people close in recognized him, were beginning to listen, some shouting for silence that they might hear more clearly. I saw him waving toward the Place de la Révolution, making clear no doubt that our ultimate destination had in fact been as fatal as any *lanterne*.

"He's a leader, sir," rumbled Captain Patch. "He'll 'ave 'em straightened out soon enough. 'Op it, lads, or we're for it now!"

I saw Machaud's head swivel slowly, surveying the sea of faces, looking for us. And I realized suddenly that I still held the jail raider's pistol in my right hand.

"Give us a shield then, Patch," I said briskly, pausing to examine the weapon. "Mustn't have the neighbors noticing!"

"No, indeed, sir!" Captain Patch caught my drift at once. He shifted his massive bulk to shield my operations from any milling citizen's gaze. "You too, Figgis—there's a lad!" The rail-thin Scotsman drew himself up and planted himself between me and nobody in particular.

I cocked my weapon and drew a bead over Captain Patch's shoulder.

Machaud's dark face lit up as his eyes found us at last. I saw his lips part, his arm come up to point. I squeezed the trigger almost tenderly.

The flat bang, the flash and belch of smoke made no great display in that heaving mob. But Machaud clutched at his shoulder and went over backward, out of sight into the tumbrel.

"Well shot, sir!" said Fag admiringly. "Lieutenant Clarence Fagotson, of his Majesty's Navy, sir," he added, his heels clicking inaudibly in the whoop and hullaballoo.

"Yes, indeed, sir," Patch's little hunchback Trip chimed in, appearing suddenly under my left elbow. "Beautiful, sir! And at this range!" And who might you be, I wondered dazedly: Nelson, or perhaps Sir Francis Drake?

But any further discussion was washed away in a new burst of noise from the mob. They had got the prison cart to moving again, it appeared. Some enterprising *citoyen* had taken the reins, others were clearing the way, and Master Sanson's barouche was once more in motion toward its inexorable destination in the Place de la Révolution. I glimpsed the long-jawed villain's red cap through the staves: he still lay stunned where I had dropped him. And now Citizen Machaud was showing signs of life once more. I saw the swarthy little Jacobin draw himself painfully up to the driver's box, expostulating with the driver, then with the crowd. The driver tilted back his head and laughed—and drove on. The crowd responded by bursting into song:

> *Ah! Ça ira, ça ira, ça ira!*
> *Les aristocrates à la lanterne!*
> *Ah! Ça ira, ça ira, ça ira!*
> *Les aristocrates, on les pendra!*

The last I saw of Machaud, he stood swaying in the rear of the tumbrel as it trundled off through the screaming multitude toward the Guillotine. He was still gesticulating feebly, waving his one good arm into a veritable gale of song:

> *Aristos to the lamppost!*
> *Aristos, hang 'em all!*
> *Ah, ça ira, ça ira, ça ira!*
> *Ah, ça ira, ça ira . . .*

BOOK IV

Afterward

I sit at the Captain's desk under the stern windows with these last few sheets before me. Beyond the little panes, the wake froths and fades into the undifferentiated surge. Sea gulls wheel and dive for supper scraps. The sunset sky is a brilliant orange, the heaving swells slate-green, darkening in the onrush of evening over the ocean.

There is nothing else. France has long since vanished over the horizon. We are two days at sea.

"Must you finish it now, Lord Christopher?" says Lady Barbara, behind me.

"Indeed I must, madame. Honor demands a full accounting. And my time is almost run."

"Ah. And what is so precious as Lord Libertine's honor?"

"It is Lady Barbara MacFarlane's honor, madame, that I am vindicating!"

I swivel about in the low-backed captain's chair to grin at her. She sits propped up on the chastely made-up bunk, well recovered now from our ordeal. Her ravaged gray gown has been somewhat repaired, and the salt sea air has brought a touch of color back to her cheeks. Her clipped, auburn hair curls charmingly about her neck and face. She is altogether a lovely sight, and my grin broadens into a smile of sheer aesthetic appreciation.

Partly aesthetic, at any rate.

"Will there be anything left of my reputation in England

now?" She smiles back, with her eyes as well as her lips. "The Judith of the Jacobins has had little enough of honor in her own country these last years. And now—"

"This memoir of our late adventures," I cheerfully advise her, patting the massive pile of manuscript at the back of the little desk, "will vindicate you utterly. As well as settling an—ah—business affair or two of my own."

She cocks a doubting eyebrow, but says nothing more. Only the smile lingers in her eyes. The smile that has been mine ever since I turned that rogue Durward out of our prison cell in the exalted name of principle—in order that I might spend my last night on earth, at long and glorious last, alone with Lady Barbara.

It is with a distinct effort that I take up my pen once more. What, after all, really remains to be said?

The matter of Captain Patch, perhaps.

I got the perspicacious Jeremy to explain that worthy's role to me in some detail while we drifted down the Seine in the bottom of a barge. Patch and his fellows were forward, supervising the terrified French bargemen who had been prevailed upon to ferry us downriver to Le Havre and the sea. Lady Barbara and the faithful Bridget both slept the sleep of utter exhaustion under a stiff tarpaulin at my side. It was a starry night, a dozen hours after our escape from the howling mob in the Rue St. Honoré. Jeremy took his time, and answered all questions with precision and dispatch.

The key to it all, of course—so Jeremy patiently explained it—lay in the devious Machiavellian mind of William Pitt. His Majesty's First Minister of State, it seemed, must always have two strings to his bow. In the matter of Lady Barbara MacFarlane, I was one of these. Captain Patch was the other.

The Prime Minister had responded to the shocking news of the theft of the Army Report with the diplomatic

sophistication that was the hallmark of the true statesman: he had ordered two or three rough-and-ready naval
crews onto detached service to steal the document back
again. Most of these agents—like Patch and his scruffy
crew—had risen through the ranks and had had considerable experience in press-gangs. Their methods were
simple and direct, and they had soon narrowed the circle
of suspects down (quite erroneously) to Lady Barbara
MacFarlane. They had been half sure of her guilt that
first night in Hog Lane; quite sure of it within a week.
And so all our troubles had begun.

Patch, in sum, had never been in Lord Mortimer's em-
ploy at all. Nor had his object been to carry the lady off;
he and his mates had simply sought to conduct a thor-
ough search of her property and person for the missing
papers. Lady Barbara had of course resisted their assaults,
and I had seconded her. Pitt's Machiavellian instincts
had compounded the confusion when he commissioned
me also to seek the stolen document—without informing
either me or Captain Patch of the other's involvement
in the affair. And so the two of us had labored at cross-
purposes from start to finish. Might still be doing so, in
fact, if the excellent Jeremy had not fallen in with Patch
and explained my mission to him.

"How did you ever come upon them, Jeremy?" I asked
him, peering over the low gunwale at the black silhouette
of the shore moving past. It was close on midnight, and
we were within half an hour of the coast and H.M.S. *Cyclops*, anchored offshore in the darkness.

"I didn't, your ludship. More properly speaking, they
came upon me." His sallow face looked positively corpse-
like in the starlight, but his eyes were lively as a hedge-
hog's. "You see, sir, when that Jacobin chap Machaud
dragged you all off, and the Countess and 'er servants cut
and run, why, I told myself that prudence was the only
course for me. So I 'id myself in that passage in the wall,

sir, that you're aware of. I'd be more 'elp to you, sir, and more service to my country if I was free than not—that's 'ow I reasoned it. So I 'id myself away and waited for things to quiet down.

"As it 'appened, I was just come out of my little priest hole and was collecting a few neccessaries about the empty 'ouse, when Captain Patch and 'is lads came charging in. They 'ad decided to put all at 'azard in a direct attack upon 'er ladyship's bags and baggage, sir. And upon 'er—ah—person. They were 'eavily armed for the purpose.

"So there I was, all alone with three pistols at my 'ead, sir. And once again, I chose the prudent course. I put myself at their disposal, in 'opes of a little 'elp from them later on. I 'elped 'em search 'er ladyship's things most thoroughly, and the rest of the 'ouse as well. The document was not to be found. Which was not surprising, since I 'ad it 'id away very carefully myself at the time."

"*You* had it?"

"Of course, your ludship. The first thing I did when the Frenchies came pounding at the door was snatch the rutting chest back from Lord Mortimer's rooms, and stow it away with me!"

"You knew, then"—I groped for comprehension—"that his lordship had the inlaid casket all the time?"

"Not all along, sir, no. But most of the time, certainly. You see, sir—"

"Never mind," I said wearily, passing a hand across my brow. "Just tell me what you've done with the bloody thing now."

"It's right beside you, sir."

There was nothing beside me but the wicker hamper full of fish that had bounced halfway across Paris on Jeremy's obstinate back. Under the anchovies and herring, of course, the Army Report lay still snugly concealed in its broken casket.

The shoreline was breaking up now into dim steeples and gabled roofs. A merchant vessel, anchored in midstream, floated into view. It was Le Havre, the harbor opening up around us. I closed the hamper and informed Jeremy that he had been wise to keep the document's whereabouts secret from Patch and Company.

"Yes, sir. But that was the point, you see. If these bully-boys could not find what they were after in 'er ladyship's effects, I knew they'd 'ave to go looking for 'er ladyship 'erself again. And the only way to get at 'er would be to take 'er back from the Frenchies. And *that* would mean a chance for yourself, sir, too, since you were sure to be in 'er ladyship's vicinity. If you take my meaning, sir."

"Jeremy, your ingenuity takes my breath away."

"Thank you, sir. There was only one problem, sir."

"And that was?"

I was less concerned than I might have been with the intricacies of the problems Jeremy had so magnificently surmounted. The shipping was growing thicker about us in the midnight channel now, and I was preoccupied with the dangers of the moment. We had only to foul the anchor chain of one of these sleeping Leviathans, and it would be all up with us yet.

Jeremy looked toward the bow, where Patch's bulky silhouette was clearly visible beside the steersman.

"Well, sir," he said, "it seems that Captain Patch's final instructions were that, failing all else, and the purloined papers eluding 'im still, 'e was to take 'er ladyship of 'Olyrood 'Ouse into custody, and bring 'er 'ome in irons."

It was at that point that I decided we must find ourselves some more congenial means of leaving France than His Majesty's sloop of war *Cyclops*, Ulysses S. Patch, commander.

"My lord," Lady Barbara calls again. "You are an

unconscionable time about your memoirs. Does honor really require such prolixity?"

She has ensconced herself more comfortably underneath the covers now, I see. And the battered gown that she had worn these three days past now hangs upon a hook beside the door.

I must indeed hasten to my close.

The *Tristan da Cunha*, in whose after cabin I am now writing, was simply the next shadowy shape to drift past following Jeremy's final revelation. Patch and his colleagues were still keeping vigilant watch over the bargemen in the bow when Jeremy, Bridget, Lady Barbara, and I climbed quietly into a trailing dingy, severed the hawser, and pulled silently but vigorously for the nearest merchantman that did not display either the tricolor or a French name under the poop.

She was a Portuguese vessel, outward bound in the morning. And since money was among the "necessaries" Jeremy had brought with him from the Hôtel d'Eauville, we had no difficulty in striking a bargain with Senhor Coelho, chief officer of the *Tristan*.

I sit in the creaking cabin of that admirable vessel at this moment, completing this faithful record of our exploits and misfortunes. Captain Coelho touches at La Coruña in the morning, then sets sail for the Azores, Brazil, the West Indies, and America. Jeremy Twill will debark at Coruña and make his best speed back to Britain. He will carry this manuscript to my sole surviving respectable friend left in England: that pillar of the English Church and center of every drawing room where wit is honored still, the Reverend Dr. Throgmorton (who will, I hope, ignore any facile animadversions on his character which may have slipped into these pages). I hope the reverend doctor will find some delectation in this narrative, and that it will enable him to counter any slanderous rumors that may circulate in society concerning any of the matters discussed in these pages.

Jeremy will also bear with him the purloined Army Report, somewhat damp and strongly redolent of French herring, but otherwise complete. He will present this document at Number 10 Downing Street, with my compliments, to Mr. Pitt. His Majesty's Government, I need scarcely add, could certainly not do better than engage the bearer on the spot for any sort of espionage, intrigue, or similar chicanery said government may deem necessary to safeguard the subjects of the Crown on every land and sea.

"Christopher," says my Lady Barbara from the swaying bed. "It is too dark now to see the paper. Have you not writ enough?"

That haunting smile—the smile of a lady of passion for one who has proved himself at last a gentleman of principle—plays still about her lips. Her arms lie slender and white upon the counterpane, which sculptures the body beneath it to perfection. Between the sheets, I see her limbs move restlessly.

I have indeed writ enough. Yet there is one thing more.

I shall, finally, entrust my man Jeremy with the following message, dated this present instant and addressed to Lord Mortimer Durward, to be held for him at White's Club, St. James's, London:

> Aboard the *Tristan de Cunha*
> Off Cape Ortegal
> 7 September 1792

My dear Durward,

    It is now precisely one month since the wager to which we both engaged ourselves in the clubrooms at

White's, on 7 August of this present year. At that time, I pledged myself to perform a specified task by a specified time, or to pay the forfeit agreed upon. The details of this engagement are fully known to you, and to the witnesses there present. I need not rehearse the particulars here.

The object of this present communication is simply to confess that I have in fact *failed to accomplish* the task set by the date prescribed. I therefore have the honor to inform you of my immediate departure from Europe, never to return, as per the terms agreed upon.

> Your most obed't servant,
> Arundel

I hope, my dear Throgmorton, that you will see to it that this missive is sufficiently circulated to curb any slanderous aspersions on the honor of Lady Barbara MacFarlane (of Holyrood House, Berks), who, for reasons of politics, is also seeking refuge in America at this time. It is Lady Barbara's belief—and I quite share it—that she will find more scope for her *strong democratical principles* in the New World than in the Old.

And so farewell to Pall Mall and Vauxhall, to Child's and White's and Covent Garden, to the Cheshire Cheese and the Blue Periwig, beefsteaks at the Beefsteak Club and fried sole in butter sauce at Mr. Hayward's in Water Lane. Farewell to Betsy Murrain and Sally Love, to Marie and Countess Charlotte and dear Caroline, Lady Arbuthnot. A fond adieu at last to all my follies and philanderings—

"Christopher!"

To all, dear Lord, but one.

FAWCETT CREST BESTSELLERS